VULGAR THINGS

LEE ROURKE

Vulgar Things

FOURTH ESTATE • *London*

First published in Great Britain by
Fourth Estate
An imprint of HarperCollins*Publishers*
77–85 Fulham Palace Road
London W6 8JB

Typeset in Minion by Palimpsest Book Production Ltd, Falkirk, Stirlingshire
Printed and bound in Great Britain by Clays Ltd, St Ives plc

MIX
Paper from
responsible sources
FSC   FSC™ C007454

For Wilko Johnson

My mind shudders recounting.

Virgil: *The Aeneid*

MAYBE SOMEONE IS WONDERING JUST WHAT I'M DOING HERE

an office

Look at them both sitting at their desks, feigning important business. What do they think they're doing with their lives? What are they hoping to achieve, acting the way they do, alienating everyone else in the office? I've asked myself many, many times: *What am I doing here?* I'm pretty much resigned to the fact that I've more or less chosen the wrong path in life. Not that I have any idea what the correct path might be. I look at what my life, until now, has amounted to: a boring job, a failed marriage, a small flat I can barely afford, and each working day the same agonising prospect of these two loathsome cretins, sitting at their desks, constantly talking to one another. It sickens me. To be honest, I don't think I have the strength for it any more.

lunch hour

Jessica, the younger of the two and my line manager, had taken me to one side in the company kitchen earlier that week. Her words had been rattling around my head ever since, delivered, as they

1

were, in her usual pseudo-flirtatious manner: 'What's wrong with you these days? Have you been having trouble at home again?'

'I beg your pardon?'

'Have you been having trouble at home, you poor dear? I know things didn't work out for you last year . . . *your marriage* . . . I'm genuinely worried for you. Is that why you've been letting things slip here?'

'*Slip?*'

'Your journals, some haven't met cover month, when you said they would. Editors have been complaining, plus those suppliers' invoices haven't been sent that I asked you to send last week.'

'Oh, those . . . I'll send them today . . .'

'Are your journals even on schedule?'

'Yes, of course they are. I might not have hit cover month on a couple, but everything else I publish is published on schedule, on time and to budget, you know that.'

'Jon, you know . . . I only ask you this because I actually *care* . . . It's just that, things are slipping, people's confidence in you has started to drop . . . We're thinking of taking some journals from your list . . .'

'What!?'

'Just a couple . . . Maybe *IBD* and *VVA* . . . Nothing's concrete yet, just to ease the pressure you must be feeling, you know . . . It'll help ease your schedule . . . and if, you know, if there are *problems* outside here, this should ease the stress levels, too . . .'

'Jessica, there are no *problems* outside here . . . and I'm not stressed . . .'

'Well, you sound stressed . . .'

'You've just told me you're taking journals away from me, depleting my list . . . of course I'm going to sound concerned . . .'

'Jon, I know you can pull through all this, it's just a phase . . . a bad patch. I know you can get through this.'

'Jessica . . . there's no . . .'

'Oh, I didn't say . . . You're still on for my engagement drinkies this weekend, yes? Blacks of course . . .'

My time is up. Publishing is nothing to me. To be honest, I don't even remember how I fell into this profession in the first place. I'm a good editor, I think, but the job bores me to tears. It must have been some kind of accident, some heinous sleight of hand – something that happened when I was looking the other way.

I've had a sense something has been wrong for some time. Jane, Jessica's boss and the head of production, has been in a strange mood for a number of days, singing loudly and quite inappropriately to Jessica across the office, annoying the editorial team to her immediate right, who suffer on a daily basis at the hands of this bizarre office friendship, which I and a few others have always thought unprofessional at the best of times and verging on surreal the rest. Today, each time I look up from my proofs Jane is staring at me, and then I'll notice her glance over to Jessica when she thinks I'm not looking, who in turn pulls some sort of face back at her, as if to say: '*I know, I know, I'll sort him out.*' I try to ignore this behaviour as best I can, but it's no good. I bury my head in the proofs I'm working on, hoping this phase will pass – but it doesn't.

As usual I go for my lunch alone. I sit on a bench in St James's Park across the way from the ICA in some sort of stupor. I don't think, or look at much in particular. I can sense people all around me, office workers and tourists going about their business. Everything in front of me – people, birds in trees, dogs and squirrels in the park, cars and cyclists on the Mall – I can't reach, whatever it is that is happening, because I'm stuck in it. I feel helpless. There's nothing I can do – and the way I'm feeling, even if there were I probably wouldn't bother to do it. This sense of helplessness stays with me all through my lunch hour, like a bad smell.

I walk back into the office and immediately notice Jessica staring at me. I ignore her and walk over to my desk to check my emails. There are thirty-seven unopened emails in my inbox, all of them from this morning. I sit there looking at them, pretending to be busy. I can feel Jessica's eyes on the side of my face, my cheeks reddening. I try my best to ignore what is happening. Then, just as I let out an exasperated 'What!?' in Jessica's direction, I notice the email from Jane. It had been sent exactly one minute after I had left for lunch, as I was walking out of the building. I don't bother reading all of it. I know immediately what it is.

everything looks as it should

I knock on the door to Meeting Room 4 as requested. Jane is sitting at the table. She doesn't smile. I sit opposite her.

'Jon, there've been some serious complaints made by editors . . . about your productivity and capability . . . The editors of *IBD*, for example, they didn't see the final set of proofs before issue 5 went to press . . . and . . .'

'It's okay, I know.'

'We just don't think it's working, Jon.'

'Really.'

'Jessica thinks you're unsuitable for this role, she's been keeping me posted for the past few weeks . . . She feels . . .'

'Jane, I'm not interested in how Jessica *feels* . . . Just give me the letter.'

I walk out of the office without clearing my desk. At the door I look back – everything looks just as it should: people are at their desks, oblivious, heads down correcting proofs, or up staring at their monitors, working. Only one thing looks out of place: Jessica's empty desk. She hasn't even bothered waiting until I've left the building before scurrying over to her pal in Meeting Room 4. I exhale and walk out of the door.

into a room

I walk into Soho. I need a drink and something to eat. I take a seat in Spuntino's on Rupert Street and order a bottle of red wine and some *truffled egg toast*. Two portions for myself. I immediately feel calmer, but it doesn't last all that long. Two men sit down beside me and ruin my thoughts. They are loud. Media types. They work in the film industry and want everyone to know. I can't hear myself think, so I just sip my wine and listen to them instead, staring down at my food.

'When are they shooting?'

'June.'

'Where?'

'Dunno. Somewhere near Kingsland Road. They've found some old buildings.'

'Who's shooting?'

'Stevens.'

'From United Agents?'

'Yes. He's shooting that before he heads out to LA for the location meetings on Rob's project.'

'Really.'

'Yeah.'

'Never really liked his stuff . . .'

'Really?'

'He holds back. Tries to fuck the lens. In fucking love with the lens. Spends too much time finding the right shot and then when he's found it he spends too much time wanking all over it. He should just fucking shoot . . . He's not an artist, say, like Dom is; now Dom's a true artist, he finds the right shot without thinking, bam, bam, bam . . .'

'Bish bash bosh . . .'

'Ha, yeah, right . . . but seriously, he doesn't fuck about. His art just happens; do you know what I mean?'

'Yeah.'

'And then there's all the fucking gak . . .'

'Yeah, that.'

'He puts too much up his nose, thinks it's the fucking eighties . . . He can't see for gak sometimes . . . I saw him last week. He was with some office temp from his production company, giving it the large with her; she's all wide-eyed around him like he's some fucking god. He's got his fat married hands all over her skinny arse. Fucking sad to witness . . . He bought me drinks, though, so what can you say? I don't care if it was just to impress the slag, I'll fucking drink them. I spent the afternoon in the French with him, before he fucked off to the Groucho with her. He told me about the shoot, he told everyone about it . . . Everyone in Soho knows how much his fucking budget is . . .'

'Really.'

'Just go and fucking shoot, that's what I say, stop fucking talking about it and go and fucking shoot the fucker.'

'Yeah.'

The two men continue in this manner for the rest of their meal, fiddling with their phones all the while. I listen to every word and finish my food. It's a cyclical, looped conversation: a spiral of 'shoots', 'budgets', 'gak' and 'locations'. It's pointless and completely fascinating. Just as they are leaving, I look up at the taller of the two, intent on gaining eye contact.

'What's the name of the film?'

He looks at me quizzically when I ask him this, and then looks at his colleague as if to say: '*Why don't these people just leave us the fuck alone?*'

'Pardon?'

'The film you were just talking about . . . What's it called?'

'It's an ad, not a film . . . for Nike.'

I don't know why I ask him this. I feel compelled to ask. I'm not remotely interested in what it is they do for a living. I just feel they need to know I've been listening. I'd tuned into their frequency by accident. I can re-tune, should I wish, to something far more interesting. They walk out of the door, heading up through the alleyway that leads to Old Compton Street, both still embroiled in the same conversation. I watch them until they vanish out of view. I even lean forward on my stool to see if I can catch a final glimpse, but it's no good, they've gone. I finish the rest of my wine, settle the bill, and walk out onto the street.

I head in the same direction: out through the alleyway, past the clip joints and porn shops, and out onto Old Compton Street. I am buzzing, distinctly aware of each and every person sweeping around me, each sight and sound on the busy Soho streets. I'm not really sure where I'm going, or why. It doesn't matter. I bathe in the dislocation from my usual routine, allowing the *nowness* of my predicament to cover me. I trust it completely. So I follow it without thought or question.

petty dramas

Rather predictably I find myself in another bar, the Montagu Pike, a horrible, cavernous wreck of a place stuffed with chrome furniture and blatherskites. I sit upstairs on the balcony, looking down at the swathes of daytime drinkers. It feels good up here, drinking beer after beer, looking down on them. It feels like I belong on some separate level, something higher: a plateau designed only for people like me – whatever I am. Sometimes I catch people looking up at me between sips and conversation, flashes of face and eye, vacant features pointing upwards, like you see in old religious paintings. I feel like the icon, the subject of their gaze. It's a good feeling, no matter how fleeting and inconsequential. So I stay here all afternoon, until the streets of Soho darken – drinking, watching, being watched.

As I am about to leave I strike up a conversation with a member of the bar staff as she wipes down the tables around me. She is young and looks bored. I feel a bit sorry for her, stuck in such an awful pub at this hour.

'Not long to go, eh?'
'Pardon?'
'Not long until closing . . .'
'Oh, yeah, closing . . .'
'You must hate it here?'
'It's okay . . .'

'People like me bothering you all the time; it must bore you to tears?'

'Not really.'

'Oh, why?'

'I like being around people . . . What about you?'

'Me?'

'Why are you here? I've been watching you all day sitting up here, looking down on everyone, drinking cheap beer; surely it's you that's bored?'

'I was sacked from my job today . . .'

'Really? What do . . . *did* you do?'

'I was a production editor, at a small academic publisher. They sacked me because I wasn't . . . *productive* enough.'

'Silly billy.'

'Yeah. I guess I am.'

'Maybe this is the start of something new? . . . a new adventure for you.'

'Another petty drama? . . . I doubt it.'

She continues to wipe down the tables, long after our conversation has run its rudimentary course. I like her. She seems to bounce from table to table, the same bored look on her face. I want to be just like her, I want to look and feel just like her. But I know this isn't the case – should a mirror be at hand, I'd see a look of abject terror on my face. A deep fixed terror. I stumble up from my chair and walk somewhat clumsily back down the stairs towards the front door. I feel the cold night air as I step onto Charing Cross Road. I have two options: a) go home to my poky flat, or b) carry on drinking. It doesn't take much thought to go with the latter.

some sort of theatre

I stumble into the Griffin on Clerkenwell Road. What I can only describe as some kind of miasma, a fug of sorts, has blurred my vision, in fact my perception. I feel behind-time, having no idea

8

at this moment what time it is or what I am really doing. I stand at the end of the bar, near the stage, sipping a whiskey, watching a girl dance around a pole. She is no more than twenty years of age, bored, filled with contempt for the assorted men salivating over her in the room. She is wonderful. I didn't expect to think like this about her, having never ventured into a strip club before. I expected to hate everything and everyone in here, but something else has happened: some form of rapture.

I am soon interrupted by a small lady, maybe in her thirties, dressed in nothing but a red thong, heels and a latex tube around her chest. It looks crude. I suppose that's the point. She thrusts a pint pot towards me.

'Quids in . . . I'm on next, darling.'

She doesn't really look at me when she says this. I don't mind, it all feels right somehow. I rummage through my pockets and drop a pound coin into her pot.

'Come and see me for a private dance later.'

She walks away, swinging her hips, towards a group of men dressed in expensive-looking suits. Married men out for a drink after work. Probably lawyers and solicitors with too much spare change in their pockets, their wives and children tucked up in bed at home. But who am I to judge? They huddle around her, cracking jokes – crude gags – with a familiarity that suggests to me they're regulars. I decide that I might as well see her later on for a private dance, even though I don't really like the look of her.

I wait for her at the other end of the bar, near the curtain into the private room. She takes her time getting from the stage and over to where I'm standing. While watching her dance I'd been listening to a conversation between two of the bouncers standing just inside the door. Big, hefty men, who look like they enjoy the constant threat of violence that comes with their job.

'Listen, I don't care how much money I owe him. He's not coming through that door. And if he does, the cunt's going straight back out through it . . .'

'He's going to be angry with you . . .'

'Fuck him.'

'He could bring trouble . . .'

'Fuck him.'

'Real trouble . . . *gun* trouble.'

'Let him, I'll fucking eat him alive . . .'

'You've got to calm down . . .'

'Fuck him.'

'Just calm down. We've got a job to do.'

'I don't care. It's his own fault . . . the fucking lag. Flashing his fucking cash. If he's so fucking flash and he gives me his money when I want it, then he brings it on himself . . .'

'Just pay the man his money back . . .'

'Fuck him.'

As she walks through the bar a thought comes to me: this primordial scene is fuelled by absence: wives, children, work, daily lives. It's a detachment, an easy step aside from the general order of things. It makes perfect sense to me. I smile to myself and order another whiskey from the short, stocky barmaid.

Before I know it the dancer is standing next to me. She acts like I don't really exist, looking back up to the stage.

'Will you dance for me?'

'Of course, darling.'

'How much?'

'Fifteen.'

'Good.'

'Come with me.'

I follow her through the curtains into a room that I immediately find disappointing. It isn't 'private' for a start: various dancers are dotted about on low platforms, dancing for other men. She leads me to an empty platform in the corner of the room.

'You can put your drink on there . . . sit down. What's your name?'

'Jon . . . What's yours?'

'Paris.'

10

She dances for me, taking off what little she is wearing. Having never experienced such a thing before, I enjoy it, at first. Then something terrible begins to happen: her skin starts to peel away, quickly, revealing her red, blood-sodden muscle and sinew – decaying, bubbling and oozing stuff. It feels like I'm watching speeded-up footage of a rotting corpse, the flesh putrefying, turning to liquid, finally foul gas. I try to rub my eyes to shift the terror from them, hoping it's just the drink fooling me, but it's no good, the more I try to shift these rotten images the more intense they become. Her flesh falls from her bones, like slow-cooked shanks, onto my lap, my shoes, smearing down my shins, collecting in a purplish, stinking gloop by my feet. I want to be sick. I want to run away, to run out of the bar, but I can't move. I want to scream at anyone who'll listen: 'She's dead! She's dead!' But I can't make the words in my mouth. The whole room seems to collapse in on me, I whirl within it, spinning.

'Hey . . . hey . . . what's wrong? Are you okay?'

I look up at her. She's standing over me, her performance over, trying to feign a smile, but clearly worried.

'Are you drunk?'

'No . . . no . . . I've made a mistake. I shouldn't have come here . . . I'm not supposed to be here . . . that's all . . . I really shouldn't be here . . .'

'Fifteen pounds, then . . .'

'No . . . no . . . I can't pay. If I pay then it's real . . . I'll just go . . . I'll just get out of here and go home.'

'You've got to pay . . .'

'No . . .'

She signals to someone near the curtain who I hadn't noticed was there when we walked in. Other dancers have stopped now and people are looking over at me. She puts her thong and stockings back on, nearly tripping up as she steps back away from me, just as the hefty bouncer I was listening to moments before walks over to us.

'He refuses to pay.'

11

'Really.'

It happens quickly. I am on my back, chair legs interrupting my vision. He stands over me and demands my wallet. I give it to him. He passes the fifteen pounds to the girl and then throws the wallet back at me. Something hits me in the ribs and the air disappears from my lungs. I am gasping for breath. Suddenly I'm being dragged across the stinking carpet; I can feel it burn my knuckles. The door swings open. Cold air. I swallow it. I can see blackness and orange, headlamps and paving stones. The whiff of petrol fumes. I come to my senses on the pavement; I scramble to my feet, clutching my wallet. He's standing by the door, looking down at me.

'Now, fuck off!'

I walk away. My ribs hurt, but it's manageable. The traffic beside me is waiting at a red light at the junction of Rosebery Avenue. I can sense passengers on buses looking at me. I continue to walk, in a strange myopia; just the pavement ahead to lead me away from what has just happened.

the phone call

I can't remember my journey home. I figure I must have used the usual route. I just remember opening the door to my flat and the smell of something stale irritating my nostrils. I think I must have fallen asleep on the sofa, after making myself some food, as I have a vague recollection of being in my kitchen for a short time, standing over a hob, eating something from the pan before it was even cooked properly. Then blackness.

I'm interrupted by a persistent ringing, which becomes louder and louder in the blackness until I realise it's my phone. Before I know it my eyes are open and I'm fumbling for it. I stare at it as it rings. I answer just in time. It's my brother.

'Where've you been?'

'Something bad happened . . .'

'I've been phoning all day . . .'

'I've been asleep . . .'

'All day?'

'. . .'

'Listen, I need to talk to you . . .'

'I'm all ears . . .'

'It's Uncle Rey . . .'

'What's he done now?'

'He's dead . . . Suicide . . . Hanged himself.'

'. . .'

'It happened the other week, but no one knew. He's been in that caravan all week . . . dead . . . I was . . .'

'No one knew?'

'No, no one . . . I was supposed to be travelling to the island today to clear things up. They asked me to come down, to clear his stuff, but I have to go to France to meet our new clients. I can't get out of it . . .'

'And . . .'

'You need to go to the island . . . to clear Rey's caravan, to go through his belongings and pack them all away . . . sort it all out before it's removed.'

'Jesus . . . Uncle Rey . . .'

'It has to be done . . .'

'Jesus, Cal . . . I don't need this right now . . .'

'Jon, please, it needs to be done . . . since Dad died there're only us two, we have to take care of shit like this now.'

'Fuck, Cal . . . Okay . . . I'll go . . . I'll go . . . I'll do it.'

'You need to go there first thing . . . You need to go to the Lobster Smack pub near the sea wall at the jetty and ask for the landlord, Mr Buchanan, he's the owner of the caravan site, too . . . he has the keys . . .'

'Right, right . . . Fuck, Cal, you owe me . . .'

'I know . . . Like I say, I can't get out of the France trip.'

'Bye.'

'Bye.'

13

I roll off the sofa and fall into a dirty heap on the floor. My ribcage is seized in a paroxysm of pain. The previous night comes flooding back. I groan and think about what I should eat for breakfast.

FRIDAY

recollections

The train journey from Fenchurch Street Station to Benfleet passes
without incident, apart from a couple of trips to the toilet in the
next carriage to vomit – something that repels the other passengers
unfortunate enough to be able to hear my retching. As I walk back
to my carriage the second time I hear two women talking about
me, and I purposely slow my steps so I can hear each word.

'Probably on drugs . . .'

'It's disgusting . . .'

'Really . . . on a train?'

'It's disgusting . . .'

'Other people around, too . . .'

'Horrid.'

'Some people have no manners.'

'It's disgusting . . .'

'I hope he cleaned it up . . .'

'Stop it!'

'What?'

'I can't think about it . . .'

I walk down the aisle, back to my seat in the next carriage. I
don't care. It doesn't matter to me. I've packed a bag with enough
clothes to last a week. I figure that's how long it should take me
to clear up Uncle Rey's caravan. I'm not sure what to expect. I try
to remember when it was I last saw him, but I can't pin down any

single encounter. He comes to me in a blur of phrases, the most prominent being: 'I like it here, below the sea . . .'

He would always talk about the sea: how the island lay below it, everything in his life existing below sea level. It seemed to suit him, out there, all alone. Other phrases, other words appear in fits, as do events, songs and smells. I have vivid recollections of his stinking caravan from when I visited the couple of times to smoke weed with him, when I was a teenager. I liked him back then, even though my father distrusted him. Whenever I returned, my father would be there waiting for me. He would always say the same thing: 'We lost him to wacky baccy and strange ways. He's better out there on the island. It suits him out there below the sea.'

This was before my dad died. I can't remember Dad ever visiting Uncle Rey. I just thought they didn't get on. I never gave it much thought really. I always liked Uncle Rey, the few times I met him. His gnarled face cheered me up, his rasping cigarette/marijuana-burned voice, the songs he'd sing, his dreadful ukulele playing. Everything about him intrigued me: the fact that he'd never worked, had opted out. He seemed real in ways my father never could. Uncle Rey was lost; he made perfect sense to me.

I look out of the window. Green trees merging with the dark mud of the estuary, turning to a constant brown, a slutch that seems to stretch all the way to the horizon. It's an unforgiving, blank landscape that exposes any irregularities: a church, a tractor, horses, a boat in a yard – before they too become dirt blots, blurs, interrupting the flatness of things.

the island

I stand on the platform at Benfleet with my rucksack. At first I'm unable to move, so I just stand there and watch the train crawl away towards the wilds of Essex: Southend and Shoeburyness. I watch it until it slips out of sight, around a curve in the track. No one else has alighted from the train with me. I stand on the platform alone.

Once the train can't be heard I am immediately struck by the silence, the slight whiff of iodine and a sense of déjà vu. I head towards the exit. I'd decided on the train that I'd walk onto the island. Some seagulls are swirling above me, a sonorous spectacle, their vibrant and beautiful sound all around me.

It strikes me that I'm not really sure of the way. I know the general direction, I can see the oil refinery in the distance, but I'm not sure where the bridge is that takes visitors over the creek and onto the island itself. I know it's next to some yacht club by the muddy creek, but I'm not sure which road to take from the station. Just as I step out onto the road, outside the station, I notice a man on a mobility scooter. I decide to ask for directions.

'Which way is it to Canvey?'

'Follow this road. It'll take you across the creek. Good luck.'

'Thanks.'

Good luck? I'm only walking to Canvey, to clear my dead uncle's caravan. I shrug my shoulders and continue to walk in the direction he'd advised. After about one hundred yards I come to the creek. The yacht club is on the other bank to my left, on Canvey, close enough that I can lean over and touch it, it seems. That's the extent of the island's distance from the 'mainland' yards away. I realise at this moment just why I used to laugh when Uncle Rey referred to Canvey as 'the island', as most people on Canvey do – it hardly looks like one. But it is, and as soon as I cross the bridge things feel different: the whole landmass of the UK is behind me, stretching towards some other horizon. My understanding of its separateness must have been born within me the very first time I stepped onto the island. I'm sure of that. I've always understood, deep down, beneath the laughter, why the locals refer to it as the island, deep down it's always made perfect sense to me: to feel dislocated, to feel lost and forgotten.

The streets are empty. I remember a man I used to see walking the streets when I once visited Uncle Rey in the summer holidays. He was an old man, the locals used to call him Captain Birdseye, or Barnacle Bill. He would walk the streets all day long in his fisherman's yellow boots and sou'westers. All day long. I would see him everywhere I went, from the jetty to the High Street. Years ago I asked Uncle Rey whatever happened to him.

'He moved away . . . to a mobile home site like this one, over near Stock in Chelmsford. Once, I hadn't seen him for years, I was over in Stock for some reason, some woman I think, and I saw him. He looked frail, like death was close. He was waiting at a bus stop, still wearing the same yellow boots and sou'wester . . . It was all very sad. He'll be dead now, I guess.'

I half expect to be greeted by an array of old characters but, after the seagulls and the old man on the mobility scooter, I am met with silence again, maybe the sound of the odd car or two passing me on the road. The houses to my immediate left, tucked away just behind the yacht club, look not just empty, but a strange kind of empty, like their inhabitants have all suddenly upped and left the island, leaving all their personal belongings behind, just as they were. I can even see that some of the houses have left their plasma TV screens on, yet there's still no sign of life inside, or children playing on their bikes outside, or the odd family pet. I ignore this; I don't want to feel any more spooked than I am at this moment. I know I have saddening work to do and I want it done quickly and without interruption.

I've forgotten just how flat and eerie the island is: the idea that the land beneath my feet actually lies below sea level – the estuary looming, high up behind the sea walls – becomes more worrying with every step. The sky above me, massive and grey, stretched to its limits, bears down on the island. I look over to the large oil refinery that dominates the immediate horizon to my right. There are people in hard hats over there, bobbing about, doing stuff with pipes and machinery. Maybe that's where everybody is? Working hard at the refinery. It is 'Oil City', after all.

I can hear something, off in the distance. It comes to me suddenly. There it is, the rumble of an oil tanker's engines ahead of me out on the Thames, a constant baritone, its vibrations felt from the tip of my toes to the hair on my head, all around me, quivering on my tongue and through the fine hairs in my nostrils. There it is again, a slow, aching, constant rumbling, from somewhere within the water above, making slow progress towards Tilbury. I stop dead and listen to it pass, until it fades from my range and the tingling subsides within me.

It shakes me: an image of the sea wall cracking appears in my head. The dark sea reclaiming the land that was taken from it, rushing through the streets, into homes, factories and ancient lanes. The sea wall crumbling away at the eastern edge of the island, giving way to the tide, a black wall of water. The last time this island flooded was 1953. Fifty-eight people died. Uncle Rey was a young lad then. I don't know if he was aware it had happened until he moved here. If it was ever mentioned, he'd go quiet.

being here makes perfect sense

I walk along Haven Road, leaving the houses behind. I know the Lobster Smack pub is somewhere at the end of it. I'm starting to recognise the place. It's up at the far end, just below the sea wall at Hole Haven Point. I try to think back to when I last saw Uncle Rey, but I can't remember. It was a long time ago, probably longer than I think. It strikes me that I've been in my flat, the same dreary Islington flat, for over a decade now, and that I've been working – without promotion – as a production editor, for the same lousy publisher, for all but three of those years. It certainly doesn't feel like a decade has passed.

Time is a funny thing like that. It seems to me that we're made by time, at least it feels like I am. Over the years it is time that has forced me to look at myself the way I do. I've often sat alone in the dark, able to feel time physically rushing through me, pounding me into submission. Late at night in the darkness it is time who speaks to me, not the ghosts, it is time who tells me I am alive. I don't know how I came to think like this, I'm not a philosophical person. I feel I may have read it, or heard someone else say it. I'm not quite sure of its origins. It's important for me to see things this way – especially in the light of Uncle Rey's suicide. Time will make sense of these events, change them into a shape I can cling on to. That's how I see things. It makes it easier for me to exist here.

This is how it all feels to me: Uncle Rey's suicide is just another strand, part of the braid, something that has frayed over time. It's up to me to rebind things, tightly, I guess. At least that's how it feels walking along the road, the sea and sky above me, everything else behind me. It makes immediate sense, my *being* here, to help decipher things, to tie up all the loose ends of Uncle Rey's life. I phone Cal. It takes me a long while to reach him because I don't get much of a signal out here. Cal doesn't answer anyway and my call goes straight through to his voicemail. I leave him a message, telling him everything is okay, that it will be good for me to take this break and that I'm happy to sort through Uncle Rey's belongings. Before I say goodbye I suddenly become aware of my own voice. It sounds incongruous, an impostor's. It booms all around me, startling pigeons and other birds. I quickly say goodbye to Cal in a whisper and put the phone back into my pocket. I am not alone either: I turn around to see a man walking behind me, about twenty metres away, walking quickly, it seems, with purpose. My skin begins to prickle. I wonder whether I should quicken my pace also, so that he can't catch up, but I figure this might look too obvious, so I decide to walk even slower than I am, to stop and look at things at the side of the road, so that he can pass me by and I'll look natural, like I should be here. Locals can probably sniff out a stranger on this island and I don't want him to think that I might be up to no good.

After about five minutes of this I look back, and he's about ten metres away: a big, stocky man, tattooed arms, thick with muscle. He looks odd, out of place too, but I know he's not, I know he's local. He's wearing a pair of tracksuit bottoms and a Dr Feelgood T-shirt, but he's not a jogger. I figure he's just left one of the houses I passed earlier and, like me, he's on his way to the Lobster Smack. He catches up with me, just as we reach the first of the giant oil storage containers to my left, on the peripheries of the refinery. Huge round things, all full of oil, gallons upon gallons of the stuff.

'You heading up to Hole Haven Point?'

'Pardon?'

'The point . . . are you heading that way?'

'Well, yes, I am . . .'

'Me, too . . . Long walk, eh?'

'Yes.'

'You in from London?'

'Er . . . Yes . . . How do you know?'

'I saw you get off the train at Benfleet, plus . . . you look like a London type, asking for directions, looking at the map on your phone . . . I could just tell.'

'Oh.'

We walk together, side by side, for two to three minutes. He doesn't look at me, not in the eye, at least, fixing his on the road ahead. Then he begins to pick up pace.

'No doubt I'll see you in the Smack?'

'Yes, that's where I'm headed . . .'

'Enjoy the walk.'

'Yes, thanks.'

He walks away from me at great speed, heading up Haven Road towards the Lobster Smack. Either there, or the sea wall, as there isn't much else at the end of this road. Along the way I count twenty-seven oil storage containers, big round domes, each of them easily as big as a small office block. I feel minute beside them; the island has a way about it, it's all coming back to me: it seems as if it's stuck out on a ledge, too far into the great expanse of things. It feels like it's clinging on, and at any given moment each of the twenty-seven containers will slip off with me into the abyss. I look around, goose pimples covering my arms; there are only trees around me to cling on to should this happen, but it feels like we are so far out, even the trees would be uprooted. Walking along, the strange man up ahead, heading towards Hole Haven Point, the jetty, the sea wall, the Lobster Smack, I am certain of this catastrophe.

I look up. The sky is beginning to blacken, bad weather from the hills of Kent across the estuary. I quicken my step, pulling the straps down on my rucksack to tighten things up. The rain comes quicker than I expect, and it falls heavily. It's cold and sharp, driving into the earth beside the road.

because there's nothing else to do

It hasn't changed since I was last here. Why should it? There's nothing to dictate that sort of thing out here. I'm sure the two men sitting at the bar are the same two men who were sitting at the bar when I was last in here. I look at them again: one of them is, but now he's with a new companion, he's sipping his stout slower now. He's still repeating the same conversations throughout the day. His new drinking buddy nods away like his predecessor once did, though. I've often thought that the clientele of such establishments are like the wondrous mechanism of the great white's mouth: as soon as one tooth is lost another one flips into its place. Pubs like the Lobster Smack are always the same: you can see the younger generation of drinkers growing in the shade of the towering men at the bar, readying themselves for the next old-timer to fall, eager to pick up their stool and take their place.

I stand at the bar and order a pint of cider with ice. I'm aware people are staring at me. I take a sip of my drink, take my change and walk over to a table by the window. The bar itself is quiet, except for the man in the Dr Feelgood T-shirt who I'd met in the road. He lifts up his drink to greet me when I look over to him, before resuming his loud conversation with a woman. The rain is hitting the window beside me; it rattles the Essex weatherboard that forms each exterior wall of the pub. I stare into my pint of cider, feeling snug and warm. I figure that I'll have a couple more, and something to eat, before I speak with the landlord, Mr Buchanan. The cider is cold. I watch as the ice cracks. I can't imagine Uncle Rey sitting in this pub, it doesn't seem quite right somehow. I never thought of him as the sort of man who would see out the rest of his days sitting at the bar of his local pub, although he must have frequented it at some point. I mooch about the place, looking for what might have been his favourite table or something, but they all look the same. Then I glance out of the window, through the rain, towards the roofs of some caravans in the distance. Uncle Rey's caravan isn't that far from the pub, just a short walk along the sea wall if I remember correctly, towards Thorney Bay, or 'Dead Man's Cove' as he called it. I remember him telling me about the numerous things that would be washed up on the beach there in the bay: unwanted hospital waste, like needles and prosthetic limbs; the odd dead animal; dead swimmers of all ages; plastic from far-off lands. Whatever got lost out at sea would eventually be washed up there.

I'm sitting with my back to the sea wall, which stretches out behind me to my right, just outside the window. It isn't far to walk from here. I watch people in the bar; they hardly notice my presence now. They've forgotten about me, I've already settled into the background. It's the perfect place to sit, somewhere cosy to settle in for the evening. Apart from the rain lashing down, rattling the weatherboard behind me, all I can hear are the clientele's murmurs and the odd cackle from the man in the Dr Feelgood T-shirt. If I concentrate, between the rain hitting the window and their voices disappearing, I can just about decipher what he's saying to the woman: he's explaining something to her, something about Southend. Then the sound goes again as the rain hits the window and I concentrate on the movement of his mouth instead, his scabby lips filling in the blanks for me.

'It's changing over there. It used to be different, Southend . . . Remember when . . . No one really went out . . . The pubs used to be full of National Front, some of them still fucking are . . . I hated it, you couldn't move for fear of bumping into some fucking knuckle-scraper, the sights I've seen by the Kursaal at kicking-out time, the detritus of human existence, fucking real scum, drunk and angry, sexually frustrated . . . fucking soulless . . . Those flats . . . Houses . . . All gone now, they took them down in the seventies, I think. But

23

let me tell you, go down Southend now and it's all cappuccinos and students, even the old Irish pub by the station has changed, it's a really nice place now, does good food . . . All gone, they must drink elsewhere, not as bad as the East End though, fucking Dalston's full of boarding-school dropouts spending Daddy's cash thinking they're all new, they're all individuals when they're really a bunch of deluded, privileged scumbags dressed up in sequined rags . . . there's that bit though, in Southend, there's always that bit, down by the seafront, you know the bit, where the arcades are, those filthy pubs, at night they're such seedy little places, the ones with the saggy dancers, fucking filthy pubs they are, all run by London and Eastern European gangsters, they're always there, hanging around on the doors, looking for trouble, watching the tills . . . Always that bit, you know the bit? That little bit that spoils everything for everyone else, gives the rest of the town a bad name, some of the characters who drink in, what's that place? . . . The Cornucopia, what a fucking shithole, some of the characters in there, the small place, what a wretched excuse of a pub, a wretched, wretched place . . . Their girls are all on smack . . . needle marks in their arms as they're stripping off their Primark best . . . Who'd go and watch that? Filthy little place, the Cornucopia, and the Forrester's, when are they going to knock that place down? It needs knocking down that place. But, you know, you don't have to drink down there, there's always the nice Irish place by the station, they do well, take care of their beers . . . and their customers. I was only in there the other day, lovely staff . . . but fuck . . . this fucking estuary . . .'

More people enter the pub, workers from the refinery and a couple of regulars. I order another cider and ask for the menu. I'm hungry now. The Lobster Smack has become a gastropub since I was last here, it seems. I order the steak, rare, and a bottle of red wine to go with it. I sit back down by the window, trancelike, sipping my drink, watching the group of workers and then looking out of the window from time to time. I finish my drink just as the barmaid arrives with my steak and bottle of house red. I pour myself a glass and tuck into my steak like I haven't eaten for a week. The steak is cooked just how I like it, tender, oozing natural juices. Halfway through my meal a group of old ladies sit down at the next table. They're locals, probably in their seventies, maybe older. I wonder why they are here, considering the weather has taken a turn for the worse. I didn't see or hear a car drop them off, yet they couldn't have all walked here. It doesn't take them long to settle and order their drinks and food. They all order steak and gin and tonics. One of the ladies, grey hair all sprayed up, dripping in gold, asks for her steak to be cooked 'well-done'. She repeats this several times to the barmaid taking the order. As the barmaid walks away from the group, the old lady calls after her: 'I won't eat this thing if it's still alive!' Her companions laugh in a way that suggests they are all accustomed to her behaviour in public, accepting it as banter. I look at her: she's showy-Essex, bold as brass, tough-skinned and lippy. I reckon she's never had a steak cooked any other way.

I drink my house red, which is surprisingly pleasant, and listen to the ladies. They're mostly discussing things they've read in the tabloids and stuff they've seen on TV the previous night. The chatter is led by the lady who insisted that her steak be well-done. It ends abruptly as soon as their food arrives. I watch as the salt is passed around, liberally shaken over their meals. They slowly begin to eat, struggling to cut the meat and to chew, some of them struggling with their knives, holding them incorrectly, others moving the food around on their plates with their forks, before they even start. Suddenly, the lady who wanted her steak well-done shouts out to the barmaid.

'Excuse me! Excuse me!'

The barmaid dashes over immediately, smiling, although it's obvious she's been expecting something like this to happen, as if it's happened on numerous occasions.

'Yes, my love.'

'This steak is well-done, I can't cut through it, it's too tough, and I can't chew it.'

'You asked for it well-done . . .'

'But I wanted it tender as well . . .'

'Have it rare next time, then it'll be as tender as you like . . .'

'I don't want my steak like the bloomin' French have it.'

'A well-done steak, a really well-done one, like you asked, won't be tender. You say this to me every time you come in here . . .'

'Yes, because you always cook my steak too tough . . .'

'And you always ask for it well-done . . . Every time, and you always come back at me with the same complaint . . . I've told you about this so many times . . .'

'It's too tough . . .'

'Okay, do you want your money back?'

'No, I want some food I can chew . . .'

'You say this every time . . . Every time you come in here.'

'Okay, I'll eat it. It's too tough, but I'll eat it.'

such a long time

After the old ladies have gone and I've finished my wine I grab my rucksack and walk up to the bar.

'Same again?'

'No, thanks . . . May I speak to Mr Buchanan, please?'

'He's over there . . .'

'Where?'

'There, talking to that man . . .'

'Oh yes, I see him. Thanks.'

Mr Buchanan is speaking to the man in the Dr Feelgood T-shirt. The woman is with them too, but she's drifted off and is staring out of the window as they talk. Mr Buchanan's a large man, with a thick beard and small-rimmed, round glasses. I walk over to them. The man in the Dr Feelgood T-shirt stops their conversation as if some dignitary had just arrived.

'Ah, come and join us. Although I must warn you, we're as boring as two old fuck-ups can be . . .'

'I'm sorry, I'm looking for Mr Buchanan . . .'

'I know who you are . . .'

'Really?'

'You're Rey Michaels' lad . . .'

'I'm his nephew, yes . . .'

'Well, of course . . .'

'Yes, well . . .'

'Excuse me . . .'

He takes me to the other side of the bar and through a door into the back office. We sit down at his desk. He offers me a whisky, good Scottish stuff, cool as you like. I want to tell him that his actions are just like actions in films I've seen – the way he slouches in his chair and pulls the bottle of whisky from a drawer underneath his desk – but I don't, instead I nod and watch him pour my drink. He hands it to me and I slouch back in my own chair just like him. The whisky burns the back of my throat, it starts a beautiful fire inside me.

'It was sad . . . What Rey did . . . I liked him. He was a private man, kept himself to himself . . . You know, not that many people came to visit. I knew nothing about him, really, only the things he wanted me to know . . . I liked that about him, I even admired him for it. There's so much space in this world, yet most of us feel restricted, like there's no scope for another perspective, trapped in the moment, one to the next . . . With Rey, it didn't seem like that, not to me, it seemed like he had all the space he wanted . . . then, you know, all this . . . He was a good man, I think, underneath it all . . .'

'I never really . . . We didn't see much of him, I guess . . .'

'Whatever his problems, you know . . . Whatever was going on inside his head, in his life for him to do that, you know . . .'

'I know . . . It's hard to imagine . . .'

'He would come here . . . He'd sit in the corner, reading a book, something about the stars and the planets, he was into all that . . . Sometimes he'd talk into his phone, but not like a conversation with someone, just into his phone, like he was recording his own voice . . . He had all the new gadgets . . . I don't know what he was saying, he'd just speak into it, you know, discreetly. Some people thought it was odd behaviour, but I didn't. I liked it, it kept people in here on their toes, they thought he was talking about them, keeping an eye on them or something, but he wasn't . . . but what were they to know, eh? If he wasn't doing that, he would sit there reading his books, he was always doing that, obsessed with the stars, he was. He has a huge telescope at his caravan they say, did you ever see it?'

'I can't remember ever having . . . maybe this is a new thing . . . I haven't seen him in such a long time.'

'. . .'

'. . .'

'Here . . . These are the keys . . . I own the site he lived on, so I have spares.'

'Oh, thanks . . .'

'Do you know where it is?'

'I'll find it.'

'Number 27 . . . The address is on the key ring. It's not far . . . Give me a call if you have any problems.'

'Okay, thanks.'

'Right, I'll get back to that lot outside.'

'Yes.'

I walk back into the bar after Mr Buchanan, leaving him to serve the man in the Dr Feelgood T-shirt another drink. Before I leave I buy four bottles of strong cider. I figure I'll need more to drink once I'm inside Uncle Rey's caravan. The barmaid looks at me pitifully as I hand her the money. I shake my head when she offers me the change. I thank her and walk to the door; just as I step out into the cold air, the smell of iodine and salt in my face, I hear Mr Buchanan wish me luck from behind the bar. I turn round to thank him, but it's too late, the door has already shut behind me.

caravan 27

At least it's stopped raining now. I walk up the grass verge and along the sea wall, with the jetty on my right, in the direction of

Thorney Bay. The wind seems warmer walking this way, blowing in from the estuary along the water, up past me, following the oil tankers and container ships as they plod towards Tilbury in the opposite direction. I stop just before I reach the caravan site to watch a large container ship pass by. It takes about ten minutes. The whole of the estuary and its immediate surroundings must be reverberating with me. I wonder what all the fish must make of it? It must affect them, such a tremendous force echoing through the water and the earth below it, all the way down, shaking everything in its wake: my feet, the sea wall, the Lobster Smack, Mr Buchanan, the caravans, the entire island.

The caravan site is surrounded by a perimeter fence topped with huge, ugly rolls of barbed wire, running its entire length. It looks like a prison yard. The early evening light doesn't help, and the lack of sufficient street lamps only heightens the all-round miserable mood of the place. I walk down from the sea wall and all the way around it to the main entrance. At first I want to turn back, but then I think of Uncle Rey: what he did, what I have come here to do. So I continue towards the main gate where I can see a small wooden hut with a light on. There's a shoddy-looking sign on its door: 'SITE OFFICE'. A man is sitting inside reading a crinkled copy of the *Sun*. He's young, younger than me by a mile, but his face seems old: his eyes look like two oyster shells, and his skin is tough-looking, battered and bruised, weathered in all seasons like a fisherman's. He looks up at me. His face is expressionless; all manner of emotions could be pouring through him for all I know.

'Mr Buchanan's just phoned. Number 27 is just over there, back towards the sea wall. It faces the wall. The generator is on, you'll be pleased to know, but you'll have to pay the ten-pound fee, of course. We're running it, you see, so that you can use the caravan in comfort.'

'Thanks, here.'

I pay him the money and leave him to his newspaper, walking out of his office without saying anything else. I can hear him shout something to me, something about 'contacting' him 'should there be any problems'. I shake my head. Why do people always say these things? I make a decision not to use the main gate, if I don't have to, again. I wave my hand, hoping that he might see this and read it as some kind of acknowledgement. I leave it at that.

It takes me longer to find Uncle Rey's caravan than I expected it to. They all look the same, for a start. This, coupled with the fact that many of them aren't actually numbered, making it difficult to determine the layout of the site. In fact, I stumble on Uncle Rey's caravan by accident, just as I'm about to break my word and walk back to the small hut at the main entrance. It's a sorry-looking thing and I half wonder how Uncle Rey managed to live in it for so long, pretty much the majority of his adult life. But he had, seemingly choosing this God-awful place deliberately, as if to ridicule himself, or persecute himself, even: a constant reminder to him that his life was meaningless.

Looking at caravan 27, it makes perfect sense to me: just the way it looks, the way it feels, how it sits there, all dishevelled and broken-looking. Though I didn't expect it to have been painted dark green, thick with brushstrokes like an oil-painting. Nor did I expect it to have its own fenced-off, scruffy garden area, complete with garden shed. A big shed, too, like a workshop: the sort of shed media types have built in their gardens. It looks incongruous next to the brutal barbed wire on the perimeter fence and sea wall: a proper den of solitude and tranquillity, a man's castle, where he can retire, sheltered away from the world in peace. I can see Uncle Rey right here, before I even open the door. I can see him pottering about, sitting in his shed, watching the sun set behind the sea wall, looking out through the barbed wire. It feels really odd.

The door has seen better days. I could force it open without the key if I want to, but I don't. The first thing that hits me is the stench: a musty, earthy smell that seems alive, like something is growing inside. Which is odd, as it's a place of death: Uncle Rey's suicide. I run inside holding my nose and open all the windows, leaving the door open, too, hoping the cold sea air will start to clear through it all, eventually expelling whatever it is that's causing the smell. I stand in the middle of the room, holding my breath, taking it all in: the complete and utter mess. Ordered chaos reigns supreme: tapes, records, books, newspapers, videos, DVDs, radio equipment, magazines, stacked in every available space, huge towers of information, which look like they might topple over if I move. My first thought is: *I'm going to fucking kill Cal.* Followed by: *It's much bigger than I thought.* And it is; it's a huge caravan. I exhale slowly. The living area is huge; offset from it is a kitchenette; and beyond that there is the bathroom and master bedroom. I'm surprised, I thought it was going to be dingy, way too small for me, but it's actually big, bigger than my poky flat in Islington even. At least it seems like it is. The living space and the bedroom certainly are.

The stench continues to make me gag. The whole caravan is thick with it and the more I move, the more I seem to interfere with it, as if my contact with it helps each particle to multiply. It moves around me in great thick swirls, slowly. I wade through it to sit down on the sofa. I sink into it and wait for the cold sea air to begin its work. The thought that this is where he was found, hanging from a rope he'd attached to a support in the caravan's roof. I'm thinking of it as an actuality now. It happened in this room, just by the side of this sofa. His body found in a crumpled heap, after the rope had eventually worked itself free from the support. His body lay here for a whole week before it was found festering among all his stuff, his body fluid in a pool beneath his feet, the pile of newspapers his body had knocked over still strewn across the floor. I look at the pile of newspapers; there they are, all over the floor, next to a box of CDs. I start to shiver as the cold sea air begins to fill the caravan, through the windows and open door. Soon the musty, dead odour is replaced by that familiar smell of the sea around here: iodine, salt and seaweed mixed with something industrial, something from the oil refinery.

I look around the room. Somehow I have to make sense of all this: his belongings, his life. I have to work out what can be thrown away and what should stay, and the more I think about it, the more

I don't want to throw anything away. It doesn't seem right just now. It all belongs to Uncle Rey, none of it is mine, I don't have the right to any of it, and besides, I hardly knew the man. It's his detritus, not mine. It's the aftermath of an event I had no part in. His event, his aftermath. It doesn't seem right just to discard it all.

I stretch out on the sofa, resting my tired arms and legs. To my right is a huge record collection, all of it vinyl. I look down to find an old record player on a shelf, speakers on either side of it. I switch it on. There's a record already on it, an album by Dr Feelgood. I've never heard of them before today. Then I realise that it must have been what Uncle Rey was listening to the night he took his own life. It was the last thing he'd listened to. It must have meant something to him. I put the needle onto the record and wait for the first track to fill the room, and I smile as I hear the distinctive vinyl crackle before the opening track, 'She Does it Right', begins. At first I think it's just some ordinary, bluesy pub track. But I sit there and listen to the whole album, enthralled. When it ends I look through Uncle Rey's collection, where there's more of the same: about thirty Dr Feelgood albums in total, some of them live recordings from the BBC. Before I put on the next record, I phone Cal. I open a bottle of cider and pick up my phone. He answers immediately.

'Jon, where've you been?'

'I phoned you earlier . . .'

'I must have missed it. Are you there?'

'Yes, I'm here.'

'I've been travelling to France today, been a fucking right 'mare . . . What state is the place in?'

'It's as I imagined it to be, how it's always been, I guess. Stuff everywhere, I mean loads of stuff . . . gadgets, records, books, piles of newspapers and magazines, paper all over the floor. I don't really know where to start.'

'Just clear some space and try to locate anything that might look important. We can sell all his shit. Just look for his legal papers and all that crap, letters, bank stuff. I'm sure there's money tied up somewhere, that's the main thing . . .'

'Right . . . There's lots to go through . . .'

'And family stuff, don't throw any of that away . . .'

'I don't want to throw any of it away . . . It's quite sad, Uncle Rey living here all alone . . . It's such a sad, depressing place, Cal. Like a prison camp. Was it always like this?'

'Listen, you know I never liked him, the creepy fucker. And Dad hated him. Just strip the place and then get the fuck out as fast as you can . . .'

'Okay.'

'Keep me posted, Jon. I have to shoot now, need some shuteye, meetings all day tomorrow, on a fucking Saturday, what sort of life is this . . . keep me posted.'

'Sure, Cal.'

'Bye.'

'Bye.'

SATURDAY

along the sea wall

It was an uneasy night's sleep. I dreamed that the sea was pouring in through the windows of the caravan and I couldn't get out. When I awoke in sweat-drenched fits, taking sips from the dregs of my cider, the tankers' engines and the low, intermittent foghorn blasts kept me awake. I mostly just lay there on the sofa, looking out of the window into the night. I listened to more Dr Feelgood in the early hours, just before sunrise. I became lost, listening to each track while trying to map the whole of Canvey in my mind. I had a vision of Two Tree Island in the moonlight, just away from the creeks; the muddy shallows of Heron Island and Puffin Island; the warm, thick mud along the banks of Benfleet Creek, a barren inlet, crafted in time. Images of Curlew Island and Sandpiper Creek, which I explored in my youth when the tide was out, came back to me, memories I hadn't realised I owned, reappearing at first in shards.

Here it comes now, the sun, slowly up over the sea wall. I get up off the sofa and open the door to the caravan; the cold air rushes in. I decide that I will explore the island, putting off the job at hand. I have more than enough time. I'm suddenly hungry, but there's nothing to eat. I find a pot of coffee in the fridge and make some of that, drinking it out of a bowl the way French people do in films. The odour that had first greeted me has shifted, it seems. Although I'm not sure if it's simply because I've become accustomed to it overnight. I give the room a couple of deep sniffs: nothing, not a trace. I potter about for a bit with my coffee, finish it by gulping it down like a meal, and then walk into the bathroom. It's small, as in an aircraft: everything fitting together, usable in that coolly cramped way designers go for. I take off my clothes and step into the shower. The water is cold, despite paying my ten pounds for the heating. I let the freezing water wash all over me, but it's not long until I have to get out. It's too cold. Rummaging through my rucksack, I realise that I've forgotten my toiletries. I have no towel. The tube of toothpaste that I find on the shelf above the small sink has a thumb-sized indentation at the bottom of it: Uncle Rey's no doubt. I gently rub my own thumb over it. At first I want to keep it intact, squeezing the paste from the top of the tube, but this pushes some of the tube's contents down as well as up, and Uncle Rey's thumb mark is altered as paste fills the indentation, so I begin to squeeze out the paste from anywhere I please, obliterating any trace of the thumb mark. I figure, during my clearance, that I'll have to take extra care. I don't want to obliterate any other marks or traces, no matter how small, Uncle Rey had inadvertently left behind. I brush my teeth with my finger.

I am suddenly startled by the smell of sea-grass and weeds. The odour begins to fill the caravan. The tide is on the rise. I put the same clothes back on and walk out of the caravan and up to the fence and the barbed wire. There's a gate to my right, which is unlocked. I walk up the grass verge to the sea wall and then manage to clamber up that, so that I'm standing on it. I stand there, like I've accomplished something, my back to the sea, gazing out across the caravan site and the entire island, over to the creeks in the distance. I spot little yawls, floating and swinging at anchor. I can hear the familiar sound of curlews in the distance, over to my left beyond Canvey Heights, gathering on the marshes, feeding from the fruits of the sea washed up on the thick mud.

I'm still hungry, too. I decide to walk along the sea wall, around Thorney Bay, to the Labworth, a café on the south shore, built in the thirties and a place I know will serve me a decent breakfast. I run back to Uncle Rey's caravan to grab my wallet and lock up. Just as I walk back through the unlocked gate I notice the shed. I hesitate for a moment, the urge to look inside rising in me, but my hunger prevails and I decide to look in the shed on my return.

eating in silence

The walk takes longer than I expected. When I eventually reach the Labworth I notice Mr Buchanan sitting at a table by the window. He greets me with a broad smile and gesticulates for me to come and join him.

'Mr Buchanan, it's a lovely morning . . .'

'Yes, I like it at this hour, the freshness of the air, the smell of sea lavender . . . And Jon, it's Robbie, you can call me Robbie, everyone else does . . .'

'Yes . . . Okay, thanks . . . Robbie.'

'How was it?'

'What?'

'The caravan?'

'Oh . . . It's weird being there, knowing . . . but I knew the first night would be like that . . .'

'It must be difficult . . . Listen, there's something else . . .'

'Oh . . .'

'Rey left me another key . . . with an address . . . I think it's for a safety deposit box in Southend. I forgot to give it to you yesterday. It didn't click. I was expecting Cal, your brother, that's who I'd been speaking to . . . That's who I spoke to when Rey was . . . found. I didn't expect you to be here. But, a few weeks ago now, before . . . you know . . . Rey came into the Smack and gave me this key. He said that it "shouldn't be given to Cal, and only given to Jon". That's what he said to me. It didn't click yesterday, I was too busy thinking about that key, and who *not* to give it to, that I totally forgot to pass it on to you, I do hope you forgive me . . . Come to the Smack later and I'll give it to you . . .'

'A key . . . Right. Okay.'

'Sorry about this.'

'I wonder what it's for?'

'Like I say, it seems to be for a safety deposit box in Southend.'

I eat my full English breakfast sitting opposite Mr Buchanan while he picks out horses in the paper, taking notes in his notepad, muttering to himself about this jockey and that trainer. We don't really speak much after our initial exchange. I don't mind eating in silence. After I clear my plate, mopping up the egg yolk with thick-cut buttered toast, I stare out of the window, thinking about the safety deposit box. The sea is flat, mirroring the fattening vapour trails criss-crossing the sky above.

into the depths

I spend the morning wandering around the island in some kind of hushed daze. I venture up to Canvey Heights, which used to be the local dumping ground, its height the result of the island's accumulated detritus. The views over to Leigh-on-Sea are extraordinary; to my right my eyes trace the built-up sprawl of Westcliff and then finally, in the real distance, the high-rises of Southend, and the pier, jutting out into the estuary. The sky above me is grey now; the vapour trails have all been covered up for the day. I look directly upwards, craning my neck, my head falling back. It's immense and it frightens me a little, pressing down on me. I feel like I'm an ant or some other insect scurrying about in the dirt. It's best to keep moving, to keep walking along so that I don't notice it as much. I remember that I had decided to look in Uncle Rey's shed after my breakfast so I head back to his caravan. I know the sky is above me all the way back, and it's a struggle not to look upwards again, but I somehow manage it.

It takes me an age to find the key to the shed. I find it on Uncle Rey's bedside table, which I think is an odd place to keep a key; he must have been in the shed each night, walking straight to bed with the key. The shed is much bigger than the other sheds scattered around the site. It's set away from the caravan, a little further back from the perimeter fence. I open the door: the walls have been painted black so there's not much light. I notice astronomical charts pinned to each wall. In the centre, before me, is the biggest telescope I've ever seen, easily bigger than me, set up on a tripod fixed to a round base that swivels. Next to the telescope, on the wall to the left, is a pulley-lever, a crude thing that Uncle Rey had obviously made himself. I naturally begin to pull it. A slanting shard of light bursts into the shed from the roof, which when I look up I notice is peeling back the more I pull. It's made from thick, rubbery tarpaulin, and the more I pull the further it folds back, and the brighter the shed becomes. The light reveals a table behind the telescope that is stacked with more charts, books, notepads and coffee cups. I tie the pulley to a hook, leaving the roof open, and pick up one of Uncle Rey's notepads. He's listed everything he'd observed in the night sky: times, positions, durations and distances. I flick through pages and pages of the stuff. Underneath the table I spot two or three boxes, each filled with more notepads he'd used to record his stargazing over the years.

If only night would come now, for me to gaze into its depths, to see what Uncle Rey had seen, to reach into those ever-expanding depths. I want to study constellations, to try to work out their movements, just like he had done. I sit down and read through more of his notebooks. I spend about an hour or so doing this, before closing the roof and locking the shed back up. I put the key back where I found it. I feel excited, I've never really gazed at the night sky through a powerful telescope before and I can't wait for night to fall. I sit on the bed thinking about this for some time before I notice the huge row of bookshelves on the opposite wall. I notice that it's not filled with books, but with video tapes – old ones, some of them Betamax – DVDs, CD-ROMs and cassette tapes. At the foot of the bed are two video recorders, a DVD player, an armchair identical to the one in the other room, and a large TV. Next to the TV are four cine-cameras of varying ages, from an old VHS thing to some compact digital gadget. The TV is on a table, under which I spot a couple of old boxes filled with more CDs and DVDs, all of them, just like those up on the bookshelves, labelled by hand. I crouch down and run my fingers across them, stopping to read random titles. A number of them catch my eye.

Rewriting Aeneid #34 1988
Rewriting Aeneid #48 1991
Rewriting Aeneid #101 1999
Rewriting Aeneid #120 2002

I count well over two hundred of these recordings – or whatever it is they are – all of them with the same title: 'Rewriting Aeneid . . .'. I know the book but I've not read it. At least I don't think I have – I remember Uncle Rey being into stuff like that. I pick up one of the tapes from the shelf and switch on the TV and VHS recorder. I feed the tape into the machine and press play, sitting on the end of the bed to face the TV. Uncle Rey's face suddenly appears on the screen. It makes me jump. The tape is from 1982 and he looks how I remember him: kind of old before his time, greying and wrinkled, his large oyster-shell eyes staring right back at me. He's smoking a hand-rolled cigarette, sitting in his armchair, the one that's still in the other room. He's oblivious to the ash falling from his cigarette onto his T-shirt as he fidgets and positions himself before the camera. He starts to talk, at me, he's talking at me, his voice hits me, it's his voice, it's unmistakably his voice. He stares into the lens, into me.

Rewriting Aeneid #8 1982

. . . I always wanted to achieve . . . a new understanding of Virgil regarding Western morality . . . These writings . . .

[He takes a long drag from his cigarette.]

. . . have impressed themselves, not merely upon my memory, but . . . on the very marrow of my being . . . They have rooted themselves deeply in the innermost recesses of my mind, my addled brain, the grey matter of my being . . . so much so that I have forgotten who wrote them in the first place, it seems . . . which rings true, I didn't write that, you see, I wish I did, he did . . . all of this, everything I am trying to do, is a mere appropriation of it, nothing is original. It can't be . . . He wrote the words for me, old Petrarch, who himself rewrote Virgil and Homer. Old Petrarch, king of the poets, lover . . . not *lover*, ha! . . . of Laura . . . Heavenly Laura . . . He wrote that, not me . . .

> [He shuffles from his seat. He leans forward to adjust the focus on the camera, the screen blurs for a second before correcting itself. He glances at the TV to his right, smiles, stubs out his cigarette, wipes himself down and resumes his conversation.]

It's like I have taken possession of them . . . Petrarch and Virgil . . . like them, my work is left open-ended. This book I cannot write, this book I try to finish, to construct each day, this fucking book which is killing me because I can't reach the truth . . . I can't write it without their words . . . it haunts me each day . . . I am ill-equipped to deal with this sorry situation without them by my side . . . And even then, it's too much for me . . .

I hit the pause button. His large face is frozen, flickering a little, contorted on the screen mid-sentence, his mouth ajar like he is about to scream. His voice, his voice is so real, like sitting beside me, talking to me. Only he isn't, he's dead and these words are from 1982, another time, another existence. It's a strange feeling, one that sends prickles of electricity through my skin. I take a deep breath, trying to calm myself, I look around the caravan, at his things, his voice has brought life to them. I'm surrounded by his stuff, by him. His words have brought everything to life.

How long have I been planning this book, this work of beautiful fiction that will reach closer to the truth than any work of autobiography? Good question . . . to appropriate Virgil's words, to bring them back into the light of day, to revalue them in my own formation, just to give them a crumbling sense of my own being, from the depth, from deep within, shedding light onto the blackness . . . bringing the mystery back into the light of day, each ink mark on the white page my struggle . . .

[He lights another cigarette.]

This book will be the death of me, that's for sure. That's all I know, the rest is for you to fathom. All I know is that it won't be a beautiful book, it'll be ugly, it'll cut the heart wide open . . . that will be its beauty . . . How many words have I written? How many hours have I slaved away over each page? The rest I've burned, the stuff I hate, all of it . . . I start all over, again and again and again . . . I will start again at a later date, after I've lived, when I have absorbed more anguish, when the time is right.

[He gets up out of his armchair and roots about for things in the room off-camera. His voice fades, but is still just about audible.]

Where is it? Where is it? I put it here. I put it here fucking yesterday. Where the fuck is it? Fuck. Where the fuck . . . Ah . . . Fuck, here it is. Fuck . . . Fuck it . . .

[He reappears in front of the camera, sitting back down in his armchair.]

So . . . this is all I retrieved, what a fucking mess, saved from the flames. What did I burn it for, a good two hundred pages of this shit? This is all I have left . . .

[He waves a manuscript at the camera.]

I don't need it. I'm going to tear it all up now for you and start all over again . . . Every word will be different from this, this attempt is useless, nothing will be the same . . .

[He tears up as many of the pages as he can in front of the camera, throwing it over his head like confetti.]

See! See! . . . See! . . . The nuclear fallout . . . a nuclear fallout of my own creation . . . destroyer of worlds . . . I am become death, destroyer of words hahah! Ha! . . . My wishes fluctuate, and my desires conflict, they tear me apart . . . The outer man struggles with the inner . . . There he is again, old Petrarch talking for me, I can't help myself . . . maybe he's my inner man? It's definitely not

Virgil, as much as I love him, I just cannot get to grips with him
... he wrote for an audience ... I don't know who mine is ...
Who are you? Who the fuck are you? Ah, the watchful eye of the
moralist watching his own, his every move ... move ... move ...
fucking flies, fucking things ... get to fuck ...

[He tries to swat a fly.]

One side of Petrarch, it seems to me, which found classical culture
more engaging than that of ... the age, yes *the* age ... in which
he was born, was as we have seen, articulated in his first eclogue
where ... what's his fucking name? ... Fuck, yes, Silvis, he declares
the poetry of Homer and Virgil superior to that of the psalms ...
that'd be a serious thing to say back in his day ... a new morality
drawn up in these men. Who wrote these words? ... I didn't ... I
sure as fuck didn't. I'm just a riff man, like Wilko Johnson ... I'm
the conduit ... I move shapes in time, I create the vibrations, I
alter them, to make sounds ... I repeat, repeat, repeat ... Ha! ...

[He cracks up into laughter.]

I stop the tape right there. It's too much to take, he'd obviously
been drinking and it's difficult to watch. All I know is that, before
I do anything with his belongings, I will have to watch more of
these recordings.

vulgar things

I walk across to the Lobster Smack to see Mr Buchanan about the
key he mentioned over breakfast at the Labworth. I feel quite appre-
hensive, like he'd made some kind of mistake and the keys were
meant for someone else and not me. Maybe Cal? I put this down
to having just viewed the tape. I'm rattled by it, that's for sure, Uncle
Rey's words, and his face, younger but still ravaged. His piercing
eyes, grey, like the sky, and that strong, forceful voice of his. It rattles
through me in bursts and fragments: '*I can't write it without their
words*'. It strikes me as odd that he was trying to write a book, he'd

never mentioned it, and I don't think of him as a literary man. It must have been his secret, one of his many secrets, something he battled with all his life, something personal to him and no one else. '*My desires conflict, they tear me apart . . .*'. What on earth does he mean? Desires? The night sky? The island? Sitting alone in the Lobster Smack? Living in that wretched caravan for the majority of his life? It doesn't make sense to me, he didn't seem like the type of man who might have battled with his own desires. He just seemed like a man who endured life alone, and all that it threw his way. Then I remember how he ended it, his life. Some form of desire must have caused him to do that. I can't explain it to myself any other way. There's no other way around it.

Mr Buchanan is standing behind the bar when I enter the pub. He greets me, like it's the first time he's set eyes on me today, with a broad smile. I walk over to him.

'The key, young Jon . . .'

'Yes, Mr Buchanan, the key . . . Is that all right?'

'Only if you call me by my name like everyone else does . . .'

'Oh, yes . . . *Robbie* . . . Sorry Robbie . . .'

'Come with me . . .'

I follow him into his office again. He opens the drawer in his desk and hands me an envelope.

'I remember the day he gave me this, he said: "*It goes to Jon. No one else. Not Cal, or any of the others. I don't care how long you have to wait until Jon turns up, just make sure he receives this.*" You know, I'd never heard him speak in such a tone before, all sombre, stern, even authoritative, like his life depended on it . . . Of course, I had no idea that . . . you know . . . That he was ill, or . . . you know, what he did . . .'

'Thanks.'

'That's okay. Just take the envelope.'

'Thanks, Robbie.'

'Seems good that I played some part in his final wishes . . .'

'Yes . . . wishes, yes.'

I walk out of his office after shaking Mr Buchanan's hand and booking a table for dinner that evening in the restaurant section of the pub.

'It's on me, young Jon . . . The meal's on me.'

I put the envelope in my pocket and walk back to Uncle Rey's caravan. I sit myself down in his armchair, the same one I'd just watched him in, and open the envelope. There's a key inside, just like Mr Buchanan said there was, and a small note:

Jon, maybe you've found out already and all this makes sense to you? I don't know. Well, my finger points down from the sky at you nevertheless: Big Yellow Storage, Airborne Close, SS9 4EN. Rey.

Why had he chosen me? *Found out* what? In my perplexity I drop the key. It falls to the left of the armchair. I reach down blindly to see if I can feel it, but I can't. I lean over, spotting it immediately. It has landed on what looks like a manuscript. I pick up the key and then the manuscript. I thumb through its typed-up pages, maybe about 300–350 of them, double spaced, about 90,000 words or so. I put the key back in the envelope and into my pocket. I hold the manuscript up. There's a title on the front page:

VULGAR THINGS

By

Rey Michaels

I read through bits at random. I'm shaking a little. I'm not sure what it is I'm reading. I'm not sure if it's a novel, a memoir, or some form of literary criticism about Virgil's *Aeneid*. I settle on a rewriting of it, just like he says in his tapes, or some form of appropriation; great swathes of *Aeneid* have been retyped, it seems, retyped verbatim, interspersed with commentary and fictionalised fragments, photographs, charts and drawings. It's littered with solecisms and cliché, and seems slapdash. I fall back into his armchair. I decide that I will attempt to edit it, to see if it can be deciphered. I set it down on the coffee table, clearing the bottles of cider I'd drunk last night. I sit back in the armchair and stare at it: it makes no sense to me. I'm even doubtful it made sense to Uncle Rey.

feel like walking

I drag myself up and walk back into the bedroom. There's only one way to try to make sense of it. I select another of his tapes and slot it into the machine after taking the other out and putting it back in its proper place.

Rewriting Aeneid #64 1994

Through savage woods I walk without demur . . . why would I have that in my head all day stopping me, halting me in my tracks, unable to write a word without thinking of these other words, words already spoken. Petrarch owned them before me, as much as I own them now . . . Like him, I'm charged with oblivion and my ship careers through stormy . . . what's the rest? . . . yes . . . through stormy combers in the depth of night . . . Who steers me? My enemies . . . Who? . . . Why do I even bother? What is there for me to gain here, out here? Nothing . . . Nothing . . . Nothing but oblivion . . .

[He gets up out of his armchair and can be heard off-camera.]
Where's my fucking baccy? Bastards . . . I fucking own it . . . There, come here, you bastard . . . Baccy . . .

[He reappears suddenly.]
Fucking things . . .

Again I stop the tape. His gnarled face frozen on the screen, fuller, fatter around the cheeks, his piercing eyes staring at me. I'm not in the mood for this. Too much is happening, too quickly. All I can think about is the key in my pocket. I decide to get off the island for the day, to venture into Southend and see what's in the safety deposit box. I check my pocket for the envelope; it's still there. I switch off the TV, leaving the tape where it is. I get up off the bed and grab my coat and some money. I make sure to bring enough. I'll spend some time there and arrive back here for dinner later tonight. I feel like walking, and decide to walk the whole way into Southend. I'll start at Benfleet and follow the seafront in, past Leigh-on-Sea and down into Southend. It should be a leisurely walk, if I pace myself correctly. It should only take a couple of hours to get there; if it gets late, I'll take a cab back here for dinner. Maybe I'll be able to watch more of the recordings then, after dinner, when things are more settled.

the stick

I get waylaid right from the outset. I walk along the High Street, past the old Canvey Club and am immediately drawn into a ramshackle old shop called 2nd Hand Rose, a strange little place that seems to sell pretty much all the tat in the world. Rubbish, mostly. Inside the shop is an old man. He introduces himself to me as 'Tony'.

'Do you want to see some models?'

'Pardon?'

'My collection of model boats and cars made out of everyday rubbish?'

'All right.'

I follow Tony into the back of the shop. Out on display is his collection: cars, boats, Ferris wheels, all with moving parts, all made from scraps of metal he'd found: tin cans, bits of machinery, household products.

'I make them every day.'

'They're . . . great.'

'They take me a long time to make.'

'They're really great, honest.'

'I scour the island, especially the old dump, Canvey Heights, for rubbish, every day.'

'You're really talented . . .'

'What's everyone else going to do with the unwanted scrap of their lives, eh?'

'Yes . . . Yes . . . Well, I'd better be going.'

'I bring life back to the dead . . .'

As I'm about to leave I notice a big walking stick, carved out of a branch from some tree. It's gnarled and twisted, perfect for my walk along the sea wall at Benfleet.

'How much for the stick?'

'It's 50p.'

'Here's two quid . . .'

'Thanks, son.'

'No worries . . .'

I take the stick and walk on to Long Road. It's a perfect fit: neither too long nor too short for my arms and legs. It feels normal, right; like it's an extension of some part of me. I actually forget its presence within half a mile or so. Halfway along Long Road I spot a 'Heritage Centre' in an old church. It's open. I don't feel like I've much else to do so I walk inside, dropping a couple of pound coins into the visitors' box. A man rises from a chair in the corner of the room to greet me – it's obvious that he's been sleeping and I'm the first visitor of the day. The church – including the old altar and confessional – is filled with all manner of strange and wonderful stuff; all of which, it seems, has had some historical connection to the island. I'm drawn to an old wooden axle and half a wheel, up on the altar. It's part of an old horse-drawn carriage, I think.

'Ah, you've found the wheel, then . . .'

'Yes . . . it looks old, what's it from?'

'A sad story that one . . .'

'Really.'

'Yes.'

'What happened?'

'The horse was pulling a carriage with a boy travelling to the island from London. It got stuck out in one of the creeks . . . before we had bridges. The whole thing stuck in the mud, the bog, the horse, the boy, his mother, the driver, the whole thing got sucked down into the creek in the night. They died there. People from the island couldn't find them for years, they'd been sucked down so far . . . until it was eventually found, they recovered the bodies, the boy, the driver, but not the mother . . . I don't think they ever found her. She was taken by the sea . . . the boy had been preserved in the mud. Do you want to see something?'

'Sure . . . What is it?'

'Over here . . . follow me . . .'

'What is it?'

'We've got the head . . .'

'The head?'

'Yes, the horse . . . We've got its head . . .'

'Really.'

'Yes, come with me.'

He ushers me into the next room, to the left of the altar – in what must have been a confessional, an extra prayer room, or the chapel to Our Lady. Then he shows it to me: it's behind a glass cabinet: a horse's skull.

'There she is . . . a real beauty . . .'

'Yes, she's certainly something . . .'

'She's a specimen all right, our pride and joy . . .'

It looks like an alien being; I've never seen a horse's skull before.

'We've had it for years . . . they gave it to us, some farmer had kept it in his hay shed for years, God knows what happened to the rest of her . . . At least we have something, something here of importance, historical importance, the actual horse's head, here in the centre . . . to remember them by . . . They say the mother . . . the mother of the boy . . . they say she haunts the creeks . . . The "lady of the lake" they call her . . . There's an old book, a novel, I forget its name, in which she makes an appearance . . .'

'I think I'd better get going now . . . I'm walking into Southend today.'

'I did wonder about your stick . . .'

'This thing . . . I just bought it from 2nd Hand Rose . . .'

'Good old Tony . . . I'm hoping to have him in here one day . . . Ha ha! I'm only joking.'

'Okay. Bye.'

49

'Bye.'

Long Road is so named for obvious reasons and it takes me quite a while to reach the end of it. Once I cross the creek, back onto the mainland, I find it easy along the sea wall from Benfleet and before I know it I've reached Leigh-on-Sea. I take a rest at the Crooked Billet pub, feeling quite at ease with my stick. I order a pint of beer and sit outside at one of the many tables overlooking the estuary and fishing boats. I order a seafood platter from Osborne's Cockle Shed to accompany my beer. The sky's beginning to open out into a vast blue, which seems to fade to milky white the closer it gets to the horizon. I drink and eat and think of nothing.

towards the sea

Here I am now, and Southend is busy. I'm not ready for it. The streets are teeming with all sorts of people: mostly gaggles of teenagers on skateboards in low-cut jeans with their arses hanging out. The place feels alive, buzzing. People are going this way and that, groups of scruffy men with bulldogs shouting at each other, smoking weed and drinking Tennent's Super. Old ladies jostle for position through the general brouhaha of mothers and their assorted children hanging around the High Street on their way to M&S. I notice a crowd of people gathering around Waterstones; at first I think there's a celebrity in town, but on closer inspection I realise what's attracting the crowd: it's the local 'owl man'. The same one I remember seeing in my youth, when I came here on holiday. I hated him back then, too. He's standing there with his pet owls, showing them off in broad daylight, allowing all manner of people to have their photo taken with these two magnificent creatures. The owls – both tethered at the leg by a rope – are passed from child to teenager, to mother to random man, eager parents snapping away with their phones. It's a terrible sight. Those poor things. Those beautiful creatures. I walk over to the 'owl man'.

'Are you aware these are nocturnal creatures?'

'I have authenticated approval from the council . . . I'm doing them no harm. They're well looked after . . .'

'It's wrong.'

'I don't care what you think, mister . . . I have the papers to prove it.'

'I don't care about your fucking papers, you're holding these beautiful creatures captive . . . it's wrong. It will always be wrong. You cruel little man.'

I walk away in disgust, children looking at me, shielding themselves behind their mothers' legs.

'DO-GOODER!'

I turn to look at the woman who shouts this at me. Her sour face is contorted in a tight fist of hate, her fingers pointing at me. I smile after a moment or two when I realise that her face is stuck like that and is not a result of my actions. She moves forward from her pram to give me the Vs. I smile again, knowing this will aggravate her more than her own tired old gesture aggravates me. I turn and carry on walking down the High Street towards the seafront. At Royal Terrace I find a bench to sit on, overlooking the pier and the estuary. Uncle Rey loved Southend Pier. He loved its history. He used to bring me here to see it when I was young, I don't remember when, or how many times to be exact, maybe only the once, I don't know. We'd walk all the way together to the very end – the longest pleasure pier in the world – to see the bell. We'd never get the train to the end, we'd always walk there and back. I loved it out there on the pier, above the sea and the mud. I decide that after I've been to the safety deposit box I'll walk along the pier to see the bell, in memory of Uncle Rey if nothing else.

box 27

The safety deposit box is on the other side of town. It takes me a while to find it, even with directions on my phone. The man behind the desk looks at me disapprovingly, so I have to explain to him that I have a key. I hand it over. I tell him that I'm here to pick up something. He stares at me for a while, then leans back in his chair after handing me back my key.

'Ah, number 27 . . . Yes, we were told about this one . . . It's held under Mr Rey Michaels . . .'

'Yes, that's right . . . My uncle.'

'Can you give me your name please?'

'Jon Michaels.'

'Jon, right, that's the ticket . . . You were here earlier, right?'

'Pardon . . .?'

'You came by earlier . . . Without the key?'

'Er . . no . . . I don't know what . . .'

'I have some instructions for you . . . I'll need to check with the manager first . . . Can you just hang on?'

'Sure, I'm not going anywhere.'

'Ah, sorry, may I . . .'

I hand him back my key. He walks off. I feel a little panicked; tiptoeing from one foot to the other, like I need the toilet. What does he mean I 'came by earlier'? Without the key. I begin to shiver. I look around, out through the window. I see someone sitting on the wall outside, but it's hard to make out who they are. At first it looks like they're looking back at me, but they turn away. I turn back to the desk, hoping they'll let me through. I'm desperate to find out what's in the box. I can hear the man talking with his manager. I listen to them.

'You know . . .'

'Which box?'

'Key 27 . . .'

'Eh?'

'You know, that man . . . He came in . . .'

'What man?'

'Mr Michaels.'

'Oh, him . . . a tricky one, that.'

A tall man appears who I presume is the manager. He looks me up and down, as if scrutinising something just washed up on the beach. He makes me feel uncomfortable, but I manage not to show it. I hold on to my stick like it's the most natural thing in the world.

'Right . . . Hello . . . Box 27 . . .'

'Yes.'

'Can you just fill this out?'

'Sure.'

'And do you have ID?'

'Yes.'

'I ask this . . . I would ask it anyway . . . I ask this because I am under instruction only to open the box for a Mr Jon Michaels.'

'Yes, that's me . . . Here . . .'

'Right, great . . . Yes, come with me . . . Jon.'

I follow him upstairs to Box 27. It's a huge room and not some little box as I'd imagined, the type of storage room an entire household would use. I look around. It seems empty at first, but then I spot the envelope in the middle of the room on the smooth concrete floor. A small, brown, flimsy envelope. I must look embarrassed; I feel embarrassed if I'm honest, I was expecting a lot more than a little envelope in here.

'Is that it? Is that all there is?'

'Yes. Mr Michaels instructed me that he'd keep paying by direct debit, until you arrived to pick this up. He stressed that no one else should be allowed in here under any circumstances. Even if they said they had a key . . .'

'Oh, right . . .'

I walk over to the envelope and pick it up, the bones cracking in my knees, each pop amplified by the size of the empty room. The envelope feels empty, but it's sealed and my name is on the front, so there must be something in it. I look at my name, printed in his handwriting – my full name, including my two middle names.

'Right . . . Thanks.'

'Whatever it is, good luck . . . He went to all this trouble, so it must be something important.'

'Yes, I hope so.'

I sense he wants me to open the envelope but I walk out of the room, forcing him to lock up behind me and follow me down to the main desk. I sign some further papers and then bid farewell. I hold the envelope close to my chest; I don't want the wind to steal it from me. I hold it tightly, walking back to Royal Terrace, which overlooks the estuary. I get the feeling I'm being watched all the way back.

I sit at the same bench, the pier below me, the vast blue sky stretching from left to right, and out over to the docks in Kent. Vapour trails cross it, creating a canvas, a unique piece of art-in-progress. There's a container ship just behind the pier; I can't hear its engines as I'm too far away, but I know they're there nonetheless. I mark its journey, millimetre by millimetre, the envelope in my hands, eager to open it but putting it off. It feels strange sitting here again, on the bench, overlooking the daily progress of the estuary, the island to my right, just hidden by the trees on the cliff gardens in the distance. Ordinarily I'd be at my desk in London listening to Jane and Jessica's prattle, editing the proofs of some journal or other. It feels funny: the strange feeling when life suddenly takes an unexpected turn.

The envelope is in my hands; the container ship is now parallel with me, it feels like it's taken an age to get here; up above an airliner cuts a diagonal streak of vapour thirty-seven thousand feet up. I look at the envelope and carefully begin to open it. I look at the cheque in my hands. It's made payable to me, Jonathan Michaels. I look at the amount a couple of times before it registers with me. It's a cheque for one hundred thousand pounds. From Uncle Rey to me. I sit here on the bench unable to move, for a good hour or so, I think, the cheque in my hands, before I get up and make my way down the cliff footpath, past those thronging around the hotel and towards the esplanade and the entrance to the pier.

a kind of shuffle

From where I'm standing, up above the pier entrance, by the Palace Hotel, the entire pier looks empty. I lean on my stick, looking out along its full length. I take this as a good sign: the empty walkway, the lack of people. It seems right that I should venture it alone, the whole pier, the mile or so of it stretching out into the estuary. As I'm considering I notice a girl walk up to the ticket office at the main entrance to the pier. She pays her fee and walks out onto the planks of wood. I rush forward, down Pier Hill towards the ticket office at the main gate. It takes me some time to cross the road, as the traffic is bad and no one seems capable of slowing down enough to allow me to walk over to the other side, so I wait for the lights to change and then dash over to the main entrance. I look up along the pier. I can see her, she's about two hundred yards ahead of me now, walking up to the end of the pier.

I hand the man in the ticket office some money after explaining to him that I just want to walk to the end and back again, and not catch the small train. He looks at me without smiling and hands me my change.

'Through the gate.'

'Thanks.'

I step onto the pier. I can see her up ahead; I follow discreetly, looking back from time to time at the widening landscape, Southend in all its ragged finery. The sky also widens out here, in all directions, and I begin to feel minute beneath it. She's walking much slower than I am, so I slow down, I don't want to catch her up. It's best I keep a safe distance, so that I can observe her, so that I don't seem a threat to her. There's no one else on the pier, so I don't want to frighten her, or for her to think I'm some kind of predator, out looking for lone women.

I remember Uncle Rey telling me all about Southend Pier. He loved it out here, when the 'sky was grey' and the 'wind was up' – when everyone else was 'tucked-up inside' away from the elements. He always said something like: 'A man could get lost out here. You walk all this way out here, beneath the sky, and there's nothing to do at the end of it. Sums this place up.' He was right, too. At least that's how it seems to me now.

Apparently, the cottages scattered along the shoreline were mainly occupied by fishermen and farmers. I look back at the same shoreline and it kind of sickens me, not that I'm in any way nostalgic for a past I've never known. But I feel like I need to accelerate away from it, Southend, the past, the present, a possible future. I just want to keep walking away from it all, following this girl for as long as I can. I check my pocket for the cheque. It's still there: I push it deeper into my pocket. I'm still dazed by the amount. I'm effectively rich; I can pretty much do what I want – within reason. I look up at the sky, at the seagulls gathering above the pier, hanging in the air above me. Further out, towards the horizon, the oil tankers and container ships are motionless, it seems, the murky Thames holding them there. I follow the sky down towards them, the power stations of Kent in the distance. They're moving, I can see that now. There it is, wait – yes, there it is. I can hear them, that familiar rumble, their engines pushing them ahead, forward.

The pier was initially built by three men, Uncle Rey used to say, which is hard for me to imagine standing on it today, looking at the immensity of it all. A carpenter, an engineer, and a labourer, each of them working where and when they could, going on pure instinct, with no real 'plans' to speak of, just a desire to build, outwards, away from the land. Work began later on the 'new' iron pier, the one I'm standing on, designed by James Brunlees. It was built, Rey said, alongside its wooden predecessor, as if out of respect. It's a magnificent structure, supported by a series of cast-iron screw piles, each extending 12 feet into the foreshore, each column spaced 30 feet longitudinally and 9 feet laterally. The thought makes me smile. The sky widens around me with each of my steps, as though infinite space is revealing itself to me; it feels like I can see and feel everything hurtling through space and time, the feeling broken only when my eyes return to the girl in front of me, the elongated

56

sway of her arse leading me on. I feel like she's hypnotising me with each step. I keep a good distance still, enough to go on observing her, a good 10 to 15 metres now, just close enough to see what she's wearing, the colour of her hair, what she's doing. She's looking down into her phone, ignoring the view, completely oblivious to her surroundings. It looks like she's texting someone, though she could be on Twitter, or Facebook. In any case, she doesn't look up to see where she is going. It's as if she is on some form of monorail, part of the structure of the pier, just moving along effortlessly, part of the mechanism. She relaxes me, so I carry on walking behind her as if it's the most natural thing to do, like she's the furthest thing from my mind, like all of this isn't really happening. Every so often a seagull will swoop down and hover alongside me, just out of reach, one of its beady eyes on me, in the hope that I might throw it some food, like the tourists do. But I don't have anything to give, I just feel like holding out my stick for it, like a perch, to see if it will land, but I don't do it. I don't want to draw attention to myself. I don't want to startle her, so I allow the seagulls to go about their business, ignoring them as much as I can. I concentrate on the girl. I like the way she walks. It's the first thing that strikes me about her: a kind of shuffle, her feet barely lifting up off the planks, head down, hands up, holding on to her phone. The sway of her hips and arse, gentle and soothing, side to side.

Soon we both reach the end of the pier, on the landing, past the 'station' where the *Sir John Betjeman* train waits for those who want to take the train back along the pier to the shore. I look back once more at the shoreline, the whole of Southend, Thorpe Bay and Shoeburyness to my right and Westcliff, Leigh-on-Sea and Canvey Island to my left, all of it spread out, flattened into two dimensions. The island looks especially flat, only really notice-able because of the towers and chimneys of the oil refinery sticking out of it; the rest of it sunk below the water, out of view. The whole landmass is morphed into a creamy brown and green gloop before me. I turn back to the sky ahead of me, stretching out over to Kent and beyond, above the tankers and container ships. Then I see her again, she's heading up the steps, onto the viewing platform above the RNLI station, where the pigeons hang out and rarely anyone else goes because of the years of pigeon shit on the boards. I follow her up the steps and onto the viewing platform. Below my feet I can hear the pigeons, and to my right I can see men fishing on the platform below us; they must have been here all morning, lots of them, patiently waiting in silence. She walks over to the large bell at the end of the platform, standing there, looking out towards Shoeburyness in the distance. I walk up behind her casually so as not to alarm her. I stand at the rail beside her, looking out across the estuary in the same direction. Suddenly she turns to me, the sadness in her eyes momentarily reaching out to me. I freeze, and my lungs seize up. Then she looks down at her feet and through the gap in the boards, at the pigeons beneath us.

'Can you hear them?'

'Who?'

'The pigeons, just under our feet, a whole colony, maybe about one hundred or so I think . . . I have no idea . . .'

'Yes, I can . . . What a racket . . .'

'I don't blame them . . .'

'For making a racket?'

'For being out here . . . I don't blame them, living out here, away from everyone back there . . . You know, people, that lot . . .'

Her voice is Eastern European, harsh but fluent in English. She nods back over at Southend.

'Yes, that lot . . . I know what you mean.'

'I like them living here . . . they fly over to the land, taking scraps of food from it, and then return here with them . . . away from all the hassle, all the people, the nasty ones . . . I sometimes wish I could do that.'

'Really . . .'

'I'd be happy living out here all alone, away from them, just the birds and the sea and the sky to keep me company . . .'

'I like the sound of that . . .'

'Yes.'

'I'm living over on Canvey . . .'

'Canvey?'

'The island, just behind us . . . Over there . . .'

'Island?'

'Look . . . see it?'

'Oh, yes, there . . . That over there . . . Yes, I see it.'

'The island is like being out here, at the end of this pier, the furthest point away from civilisation, as far as possible, without even having to travel that far, it seems. Does that make sense? I mean . . . there are places to hide all around us . . .'

'I suppose it does . . . If only something like that was possible . . .'

'Yes.'

' . . . '

' . . . '

'Look, I shouldn't be talking to you . . . To you . . . Anyone . . .'

'What do you mean?'

'It's . . . well . . . I could be seen. I shouldn't really be here, if they see me talking . . . to you . . . They could be watching me, they're always watching me . . .'

'Watching? . . . Who?'

'I've said too much . . .'

'Wait . . .'

'I've got to go . . .'

'Wait . . .'

It's too late, she runs down the steps and onto the landing, towards the train. She runs along until she reaches the front carriage. The train starts to take her back to the shore. I'm sure she's the only passenger; it's like the driver was waiting for her. I stand by the bell. I put my hands on the rail, just where hers had been, trying to detect some trace of her. I smell my hands. Nothing. I turn away and walk down the same steps and back along the pier, the train slowly rumbling ahead. I walk behind it, and as soon as it reaches the main gate I begin to run after her, my stick in my hand, along the pier. I know I can't reach her, that I wouldn't know what to say, but I continue to run. I brush past some tourists who are heading towards me. I think about asking her for a coffee, or something like that – any excuse to spend some time with her. She looked so lonely back there by the bell, she looked like she needed a friendly face, someone to listen to her.

When I reach the train she is nowhere to be seen. I look for her all along Royal Terrace, the esplanade up to the Kursaal and back again, in the arcades and the funfair at the foot of the pier, but it's like she's vanished. I walk up and down the High Street to try to find her, but it's no good. She's gone. I just want to see her again, that's all. I sit on a bench outside H&M, watching the college kids and a gang of lads on mountain bikes smoking weed on the corner next to Caffè Nero. Then I remember the cheque in my pocket. I get up, my knees cracking, and walk to the nearest bank to pay Uncle Rey's money into the automated machine.

floating in space

I'm strangely not in the mood to eat, so I phone the Lobster Smack and cancel dinner. I spend the evening back at Uncle Rey's caravan attempting to edit *Vulgar Things* but my mind is elsewhere. I'm haunted by her, and as much as I try to banish her from my thoughts I can't. I stare at each page, blankly, page after page after page, making the odd correction here and there, but nothing like the line edit I should be doing. Soon enough, I find myself staring at the same page, then the same paragraph, then line, then word:

shudder

I know it's surrounded by all the others, but I can't stop staring at this one word: *shudder*. I say it aloud, *shudd-er*, spitting each syllable out of my mouth. Something has happened to me, *is* happening to me. It's growing from within me and it makes me tremble, shake and stutter trying to look at it. *Shudd-er. Shudd-er.* I keep spitting it out, an *S* then an *H,* then a *U,* the *Ds* stuttering onto my lap, followed by an *E* and finally the *R.* All of it falling into a mess. All over me. I'm mesmerised by it.

When I eventually look away I notice it has gone 11 p.m. and it's pitch black outside the caravan. I put the manuscript aside and decide to walk to the shed. The night sky is full of stars, constellations upon constellations. I suddenly feel frightened by the immensity of it all and dash over to the shed, where I fumble with the lock. I close the door behind me, as if the stars were chasing me. I stand in the darkness to compose myself, take a few deep breaths and then pull back the roof with the pulley-lever. The sky falls into the shed. I feel safer, tucked away next to the telescope. I look for the familiar constellations with my naked eye: Orion's belt, Scorpio, et cetera, but most of them look like nothing else I have ever set eyes on before. It's astonishing. I swivel the telescope and point it at a cluster of stars that look interesting to me. I put my eye to the lens and the shock of what I'm greeted with forces me into the chair in the corner of the shed. I begin to breathe heavily, my legs are shaking and my heart feels like it is about to escape from my chest. I regain some of my composure and look through the lens again. I'm right, it is what I think it is: dead centre, in the middle of the viewfinder, is Saturn. It's Saturn. There are its rings. I'm looking directly at Saturn, by complete chance. It's Saturn. I look at it there, floating in space, everything around it disappearing into inky blackness. I marvel until a strange kind of vertigo envelops me. I feel like the earth beneath my feet is about to freefall at any second, down through the abyss. I can't stand it any longer. I sit down in the chair for a while before regaining some more of my composure. I wind the roof back with the pulley-lever and lock up the shed behind me. I walk into the caravan and take out a torch from a drawer in the kitchenette and pick up my stick from the front room. I decide to go for a walk along the creek to clear my head. My mind is swirling, I feel dizzy. I need to bathe myself, by moonlight.

The island is quiet. The tankers and container ships out in the estuary are quiet, too – invisible in the darkness. The whole island feels like it's sleeping. It's just me and Saturn, the stars, the moon. Behind me, although I can't see further than a few metres without my torch, I can sense the ruins of Hadleigh Castle, up on the hills past Benfleet, and the spire of Leigh Church, Southend beyond that. I walk around the sea wall, eastwards from Uncle Rey's caravan, but then for some reason or other, I wander inland, down towards the creeks.

The tide is high; I can see it sparkling in the moonlight ahead of me, in the distance, like a carpet of jewels. The marshland seems plump, full, flooded with sea water. The stench of iodine mixed with lavender is in the air around me. I follow the darker patches of dry land, using my torch and stick to guide me through it, cutting in diagonally across the island. The moon is directly above me now, and seems to be moving about, trying to get a better look in or something. Its silvery-blue light comforts me. It's fantastically bright now, so I switch off my torch and allow the moonlight to show me the way. I slip my torch into my pocket, digging the stick into the marshland for support. Over the sea wall, to my right, I can just about hear the sea, lapping rhythmically against the small shore before the wall. Then if I listen again I can hear a deep, low murmur out in its depths, in the shipping lanes and rays. It calls me onwards. I look ahead through the shadows. I can see a multitude of street lights in the distance, further out to my right: Southend. Then a wide strip of complete and utter darkness, the mouth of the estuary opening like the gateway to an abyss, a line of dense ink-black, blacker than anything I've seen before: a maddening, pitch nothingness separating Shoeburyness and Sheerness, Essex and Kent its pillars.

With each step I feel more alone and the silence of the sleeping island grows deeper all around me. I continue like this, sheltered by the moonlight from the gaping abyss to my right, for ten minutes or so, maybe more. I find an old disused garage on what must be an old disused plot, where people used to live in train carriages and trucks, dumped on the land. I climb up onto the roof, using the smashed-in window frame as a step up. I sit down staring at the moon, wishing for it, wanting to own it and all the stars that surround it. It's a beautiful sight and I can understand why books and films have been filled with similar thoughts and scenes. I look inland, towards the creeks. About twenty metres or so from me is the first of these creeks; it's the brightest and looks bigger, deeper. Beyond it I can just make out the marshy, grass-covered slope that is obscuring my view of anything else around it. I see it immediately. I'm not quite sure what it is, but it's moving eastwards along the creek, in the water, like a black jewel, switching to white, then black, then white again, shimmering itself in the moonlight, surrounded by diamonds on the water. It's alive, I'm sure of that. I can see arms moving, swimming, the whole thing submerging itself momentarily, just for a second or two, before bobbing back up again just a little further ahead. Then I see her face – a woman's face, her wet hair plastered across it. She's swimming in the creek. I can't believe what I'm seeing. There she is, swimming completely naked, her skin like marble, white then black, changing with each movement. I throw my stick down from the garage and jump down after it. Picking it up as I land, I head towards the creek, through the marshes, towards her. I have to rub my eyes, hiding, crouching behind some shrubs, just by the bank. It's her, I'm sure it's her: the girl from the pier, the girl I spoke to on the pier. It's her, I'm sure it is. The lady in the lake. She turns around, full-circle, and heads back along the creek, past me and towards the grassy slope, diagonally now, slowly away from me, a little turn here and there, adjusting her direction to a patch of dry land. I want to call out to her, but I know this is a risky business. She's a ghost; a perfect ghost. She steps out of the water, her figure illuminated in the moonlight, and wraps a towel around herself. She looks like some beautiful sea goddess, my beautiful goddess from the pier, an entity from the deep. Suddenly, taking me by surprise, she looks over in my direction – I bob down, I can sense her looking over me, towards the blackness, the abyss. I can see her through the shrubs; she flicks her hair back over her shoulders and walks away from the creek, carrying her clothes in her hands, walking slowly, heading back to some low houses in the distance.

I feel strange: half paralysed with fear, half frantic with joy. I'm convinced it was her, the girl from the pier. She must live on the island? She didn't mention that she did. Maybe it was a ruse? Maybe she just didn't want me to know? And who in their right mind would swim naked in the creeks at this hour? Only the mad, surely? My mind is fizzing with possibilities, my heart is pumping uncontrollably. I can hardly breathe. Suddenly the moon is obscured by a passing belt of cloud and everything falls into complete and utter blackness. I fumble for my torch, but then think better of it: she might turn around and see me. I don't want to alarm her; if she sees me she'll probably phone the police and I can't have anything like that happening to me this week. I open my eyes as wide as I possibly can, turn back to her but she's vanished into the night. All I'm left with is an image of her standing there on the dry land by the grassy slope, the sea water dripping down her pale skin, statuesque, the moonlight on her. And then: the way she flicked her hair back, the droplets of sea water falling from her. The way she slowly bent over to pick up her clothes, the shape of her thighs through the wet towel, the way she seemed to glide away from me into the night.

There it is again: that familiar rumble, breaking my thoughts, trembling through the depths, underneath my toes, that beautiful, baritone growl: a container ship's engines shaking the island, much louder in the dead of night. I listen to it, making my way to Uncle Rey's caravan. It's travelling in the same direction, just up ahead of me. It doesn't take long for the fear to grip hold of me again; something tells me that I shouldn't be out here. I make my way up to the sea wall and walk back along it, a good vantage point. Every so often I gaze inland to my right, just to see if I can catch another glimpse of her. But it's no good. It's no good.

black screen

When I reach Uncle Rey's caravan I lock the door behind me and put some Dr Feelgood on the record player. I need something other than myself to fill the space between each wall. I sit down in the armchair and contemplate picking up *Vulgar Things* again, but I'm not in the mood for editing. I'm still shaking and I can't rid myself of the image of her bathing in the creek, or her on the pier today. I'm trying to match each image, but it's not clear enough, even though my instinct tells me they're the same. I stare straight ahead, at Uncle Rey's collection of CDs, DVDs and videos. I want to see him now, I want to hear him speak. I want to feel his presence with me, to obliterate everything else. I want to know why he chose to live here, away from everyone, keeping himself to himself, creating his recordings, writing his unending book, listening to the sea outside his window, gazing at the stars from his shed, lost in time, forgotten. It all seems so sad and miserable. I wonder why he'd just sat back and allowed this to happen to his life. I want to know why we weren't there for him, why my father ignored his plight? Why weren't we there at the end? When everything had become too much for him? What had happened to us to make us forget about him? It's too much to think about, time does funny things to us. I get up and walk over to his collection of recordings, picking up one at random. I turn the record player down, leaving it playing, and put a DVD into the machine this time.

Rewriting Aeneid #68 1996

We take things and make them our own. That's how we do things, right? Nothing is pretty and polished, nothing happens like that . . . not to me it doesn't, no, it's all gone, all happened before, all gone in the blink of an eye . . . Woosh, there it goes, there it goes . . . Woooosh . . . Wooooooooooosh . . . I'll take from it what I can, like a sneak thief in the night, I'll take it and make it my own, my only truth . . . like everything else, for the taking . . .

[He lights a cigarette.]

I'm another man from what I now appear to be . . . I want to keep order. Things to be secure, as they should be, you know. But they're not . . . things are vulgar. I see them every day . . . So in my heart I feel ashamed, alas . . . Nothing . . . Nothing . . . Nothing but shame, the cause of my vanities . . . My vanities have caused me my shame. Like everyone else – you, me, everyone – I have lost all order.

[He stares at the camera for about six or seven minutes without speaking.]

Sloth . . . Gluttony . . . These vulgar things have stolen virtue away. Hah, hah, hahah . . . Who gives a fuck anyway? Eh? What's the fucking point . . . in writing this book?

[He lifts up some pages of his manuscript and waves them at the camera.]

It's all a sham . . . writing truth . . . it's impossible . . . It's fucking broken, and no one sees it, and if they do they turn away. Liars! Liars! Liars! . . . Can I get this right, my old friend Petrarch . . . Backward at every step and slow . . . These limbs I turn which great pain I bear . . . Then take I comfort from fragrant air . . . That breathes from thee, and singing onward go . . .

[He gets up from his armchair and puts on a record. He turns it up loud.]

Stand and watch the towers burning at the break of day . . . Steadily slowing down, been on my feet since yesterday . . . Gotta get a move on tryin' to find a man I know . . . Money in my pocket, looking for a place to go . . .

[He is singing along, shouting at times, moving closer to the camera with every line.]

I've been searching all through the city . . . see you in the morning down by the jetty . . .

[With this he begins to jump around the room to the music. Laughing. Falling over. Dropping his cigarette, still singing along, picking up Dr Feelgood albums and looking at them, lining up more records.]

Streets are full of signs, arrows pointing everywhere . . . Parks are full of people trying to get a breath of air . . . Listen to the weatherman praying for a drop of rain, ah, ah love this bit . . . Look into the sky, the sky is full of aeroplanes . . .

[He crashes towards the camera. Knocking it over. He stumbles towards it and switches it off. Blackness.]

I stare into the black screen for what seems like hours. I've never seen Uncle Rey in such a state before. Drunk and stupid, yes, but not manic like that. I look around the caravan; it's strange to think that what I've just witnessed on the screen took place in this same room in 1996. I walk over to the record player and turn up the volume. To my complete and utter amazement the same track is playing, the same track he was just stumbling around to in here, on the screen.

> I've been searching all through the city,
> See you in the morning down by the jetty.
> I've been searching, I've been searching for you.

SUNDAY

the same girl

I wake up in the armchair with only one thing on my mind: the girl. I need to find her, that's all I know. I decide that I'll search the housing estates near the creeks, where I saw her last night, then I'll go to Southend, to see if I can find her there. I'm sure I'll find her in Southend, if not the island. It's not a big place; you see the same people again and again on a given day. It can't be that hard to find her.

After a cold shower and a cup of coffee, slipping back into the same clothes, I open the door to let in some fresh air. I'm immediately greeted with a vast blue sky, stretching out towards Kent, above the barbed-wire fence and the sea wall. I spot Mr Buchanan. He's walking along the sea wall, with his dog. I call out to him. He stops and waves me over.

'Good morning, Jon . . . We missed you at dinner last night.'

'Good morning, Mr Buchanan . . . Oh, yes, I was tired . . . Long day . . . Sorry.'

'Robbie . . . *please* . . .'

'Sorry, Robbie, yes . . . out for a walk?'

'Yes, she takes me every morning . . . All good with . . .'

'Yes, that's all been taken care of . . . Thanks for your help with that . . . Listen, I wanted . . .'

'Yes . . . What?'

'The creeks . . . Do people swim in them?'

'Not if they don't want to risk death . . . The mud, you see, the tides . . . It's not the safest thing to do . . . I'm sure there're some idiots after one too many, or bored teenagers in the summer holidays . . . But no one in their right mind would think of it.'

'Oh.'

'Why? Are we thinking of taking a morning dip?'

'. . .'

'You'd be lucky, tide's hiding at the moment . . .'

'What? . . . Oh, no, no . . . I was just wondering . . . Something I saw, that's all . . . Last night . . . It got me thinking . . .'

'Well don't think about doing that . . .'

'I won't. Don't you worry.'

'Shall I book you a place for dinner tonight, Jon? It would be lovely to see you in the pub . . . You missed some good specials last night.'

'Yes, please, yes . . . That would be great . . .'

'How about 8 p.m.?'

'Yes, 8 p.m.'

'See you then, Jon.'

'Yes, see you later, Robbie.'

suburban drabness

It was definitely somebody swimming, and I'm sure it was her. I'm sure I didn't imagine it. It's not like I was drunk last night, maybe over-tired, that's about it. It was the way she just casually walked away that bothered me, into the darkness. I wanted to reach out to her, to help her, to save her from the blackness. I shake my head, annoyed with myself for thinking like this. I know it's claptrap, but I can't help it. I can't help myself. I want to find her with every atom of my being. I can sense she's in danger, in some sort of trouble that's beyond her control. If that was her swimming, the same girl from the pier, and those things she said to me were true, then last night was a cry for help, a sign, and I need to respond to it.

I walk back to Uncle Rey's caravan. I lock the door and head inland, towards the housing estates of Small Gains Corner and Kings Park. It doesn't take me long to reach the High Street. It's surprisingly busy for a Sunday. I walk along it, passing families and shoppers, onto May Avenue, where I decide to stop and walk up and down each of the roads that run parallel with it, back along to Small Gains Corner. Off the High Street the roads are eerily quiet: suburban drabness, parked cars, the rustle of leaves in the trees and the odd teenager on a BMX, nothing much to look at, and certainly no sight of her. It's no use. I need sustenance. I need to formulate some form of plan, something to stick to. All this aimless wandering is getting me nowhere.

falling

I take a seat by the window at Rossi's Café on the seafront at Southend. I sit and wait for someone to take my order, but it's a self-service café so I get up to join the queue at the long counter. I order a sausage sandwich on granary bread and a huge mug of black coffee. When I ask for the coffee black the woman behind the counter frowns at me. It makes me smile at her; as I do this she passes me my change and frowns again, her eyes narrowing, tightening into an angry 'V'. It doesn't make sense; I'm polite, I smile, and yet she's clearly disappointed in me. Maybe it's my stick, or my muddy shoes? I don't know. I walk back over to my table by the window. Almost immediately a woman approaches me to ask if the chair opposite me is free.

'Sure. Feel free . . .'

'Thanks, love.'

With this she sits down opposite me, putting her iced bun and milky tea down. I'm a little perturbed as I just thought she needed the chair; there are other tables she could sit at. I'm in no mood for talking if I'm honest. I just want to sit here, looking out of the window at the sea and trying to think of some sort of plan.

71

'You've got an injured leg, then?'

'Pardon?'

'An injured leg . . .'

'What?'

'The walking stick . . .'

'Oh . . . that . . . No . . . I just like it. There's nothing wrong with me.'

'Don't see many young'uns with sticks . . .'

'I'm not that young.'

'You look it.'

'Thanks.'

'You here on holiday?'

'No.'

'Live here?'

'No.'

'I do.'

' . . '

'Up in Westcliff, above here, with a view of the sky and the sea . . .'

'Look, I'm . . . I really have to be . . .'

'Which do you prefer?'

'I'm sorry, what?'

'The sky or the sea . . . Which do you prefer?'

'Dunno.'

'Dunno, he says, dunno . . . You must prefer one over the other?'

'The sky then.'

'Me too, day or night?'

'Listen, I'm sorry, but . . .'

'Do you prefer the sky during the day, or the sky during the night?'

'Up until this week, the day . . . But now it's the night.'

'Me too . . . It's much more detailed and beautiful at night, isn't it? The day sky gets peeled back . . .'

'Where I'm staying I have a telescope to look at the stars.'

'What type?'

'I don't know.'

'A reflector?'

'I don't know.'

'Well, do you look through the end, straight through it, at the bottom? Or is there a lens sticking out of the side, near the top?'

'There's a lens, with different lenses that fit in it . . .'

'A reflector . . . They're the best . . .'

'Oh.'

'The best for constellations and deeper ventures into the solar system . . .'

'Really . . . Well, I'd better be . . .'

'What have you seen through it?'

'I just look through it . . . I don't really know what I'm looking at, I don't know much about the stars. I just like looking at them, the way they fill the blackness, the way they hang there. It amazes me that they're there, just hanging in the blackness, it scares me and fascinates me and I don't understand any of it. It doesn't make sense. Them just being there, all the time, always there . . .'

'There's nothing better to put things into perspective.'

'I saw Saturn last night.'

'Beautiful, isn't it?'

'Yes.'

'It's low in our sky at this time of the year. The lowest it's been in a long time. That's probably how you found it so easily.'

'Like I said . . . I just point the thing at things I like the look of, things that look like they might be something, and hope for the best . . .'

'Funny . . .'

'What is?'

'How random that is. It matches how random everything else is.'

'. . .'

'. . .'

We both drift off into silence. I drink my coffee and finish my sandwich, looking out of the window at nothing in particular. I

73

think about Saturn, the way it looked like it was just hanging there all alone, motionless in space. I think about the strange sense of vertigo I felt, the way it rushed through me. I wonder where something like that might come from; that feeling, why it might happen. Falling: the sense that everything is about to drop. I think about the earth hanging in space, too: motionless to look at, but spinning on its axis, hurtling through space. I begin to feel dizzy again, the same vertigo pouring into me. I manage to gulp down the last of my coffee, but I can't finish my sandwich. I grab my stick and rucksack, and say goodbye to the strange lady. She's lost in some reverie and doesn't look up, just kind of nods her head a little. I stumble out of the café. Once outside, taking in as much of the air as possible, I cross the road, over the cycle lane and the esplanade and down onto the beach to the water's edge. The tide is in, a series of small waves, no more than little ripples. I gulp down more of the sea air and stay there until I begin to feel better. I'm not that bothered how long this might take. I just want this feeling of sheer terror to pass. I want it to go away.

afternoon drinking

The sun is high in the sky. Southend High Street below is busy. I keep to the shade, away from the brightness and the heat. The first stage in my plan of action is to search the arcades on the esplanade, the ones just below the Palace Hotel. My idea is that she looked bored when we spoke on the pier and that she might be filling her day with time at the arcades, gambling on the machines, mundane activities in order to pass the time. For some reason I envisage that whatever it is she does for money she does at night, enveloped in blackness. Not that I think she's a prostitute, or anything like that, even though she could have been. It's because she seemed detached, like she'd switched herself off when I spoke to her on the pier. That's how it seemed to me. And then: that strange image of her, of the ghostly woman, last night in the creek. The more I think about her the more beautiful she becomes – like how people become beautiful when captured on film when in real life they are humdrum and nondescript. I could see each curve of her body, the sea water dripping from her back into the creek, the angular sharpness of her cheekbones. Then her eyes are on me, like I'm there with her in the creek again. Or like I'm watching her through a lens, in real time, a more lucid real time – recorded that way. The way she brushed her hand across her face – I see it more clearly now – removing her blonde hair from it, over and over again as the breeze took hold. These repeating images, forcing the original image to change from a murky, faint one of her swimming in the creek to something clearer, bits taken from bits, repixellated and reassembled, images I knew I'd never forget – simple everyday images that are driving me to distraction.

I need to find her. The arcades are bustling with activity, with boys and girls, rushing this way and that, huddling around machines. The schools must be out, it's pandemonium. They can't be all playing truant. Then I remember what day it is. This is what the children of Southend do on a Sunday: they escape reality in the arcades. It all makes sense: boredom. But it's a mess, like the world has short-circuited and there's not much time left, so everything is accelerated: everything is happening too quickly for me to assimilate what is actually taking place. It's all out of control. Older lads sporting tattoos and bulldogs try desperately to impress younger girls, who giggle and text each other, updating Facebook statuses and Twitter accounts, taking photos of boys they like, as the boys blow the shit out of enemy lines, or charge along, racing each other in exotic locations without a care in the world. Other boys eye them up menacingly, thinking they own this room; that it's theirs to do what they like with. But it's not the case and they don't see it. The threat of violence is palpable, like it's part of the decor. My feet stick to the carpets; cigarettes and weed are smoked casually here, with aplomb. It's a practised art, of course: kids huddle in doorways just outside, along the esplanade, blue smoke rising from their cheap cigarettes, onlookers are milling around in gaggles, doing nothing, or waiting to do nothing with other people. Each large, maddening room is a cacophony of sounds: each machine competing with the next. Everything programmed that way: to seduce the money from our pockets with electronic music and voices, snippets of familiar hits, explosions, cheers, whoops, crashes and bangs. The flash of bare skin, of eyes across the room, threatening looks, winks, kisses blown, gropes. It's no good, I can't see through it all, I can't make out one person from the next. Everything is one spectacular mess. I have to get out. I walk back up to the High Street, up Pier Hill and away from it all.

I find the Irish pub by Southend Central Station that the man in the Dr Feelgood T-shirt was talking about to the woman the other night in the Lobster Smack. I'm happy to be away from it all. It's a popular chain bar, Irish-themed in the way Irish bars are everywhere except in Ireland: where the only Irish people you meet are working behind the bar. It's a busy, friendly place. I order a pint of Guinness. The Irish barmaid smiles. She has striking red hair, dyed that way: bright, burning, metallic red. I like her, I guess. The pub doesn't feel like the usual type of place you'd get next to a railway station in a small town: those watering holes for the lost, the innocent types simply bored, waiting for a train, and, of course, for the criminally insane. I look around the bar as I wait for my Guinness to settle; everyone looks relatively normal. I begin to relax.

I spend most of the afternoon drinking Guinness and whiskey and watching the barmaid with the red hair. She doesn't seem to mind. Barmaids have a sixth sense for this sort of boorish behaviour; they know when they're being watched. So I make no real effort to hide what I'm doing. The bar is beginning to fill up around me, and it takes me a while to notice the man and the woman sitting beside me at the bar. They are talking loudly. I turn to my right slightly, so that I can hear them. The woman is younger, much younger, and she looks Thai. They're eating food and drinking beer, talking talking talking, much of it nonsense. They're the sort of couple who are together but not really there, their minds elsewhere. Every so often the man points at something on her plate.

She's eating scampi and chips; something beige, in any case. She looks back at him in disbelief each time.

'What!'

'What!'

'What!'

'What!'

'What!'

'What!'

It's clear to me and everyone else hanging around the bar that she hates this man with an intense passion. This strange display continues for about ten or fifteen minutes. The only time she addresses him at all politely is when he becomes too tired to finish his own meal: a well-done burger. She takes his plate with a smile and scrapes his leftovers onto hers. As she does this he swivels around on his stool to watch a group of teenage girls through the window as they congregate on the steps up to the station, his Thai wife chomping away on his food, oblivious. I turn away and leave them to it.

When I look back up the red-headed barmaid is standing in front of me behind the bar, smiling awkwardly.

'Would you like another?'

'Do you have champagne?'

'Er . . . Yes . . . I think we do, let me just check . . .'

She bends down to look in the fridges behind the bar.

'What do you have?'

'We've got Moët . . . That's it.'

'. . .'

'Do you want a glass?'

'No, the bottle.'

'Right . . .'

'Do you want to share it with me?'

'I'm at work.'

'Well, after work?'

'I don't think so . . .'

'It's okay . . . I can afford it, I'm rich, you see . . .'

'That's very nice for you, but I'll be going straight home from here.'

'Where do you live?'

'I'm here to serve drinks, not to give strangers my address . . .'

'Okay . . . A bottle of Moët, please . . . One glass.'

She brings the bottle over to me in a cheap plastic cooler with so much ice in it that the bottle is sitting on rather than in it.

'There's too much ice in here; could you take half of it out and replace it with some water, then just drop the bottle in it . . . I'll do the rest.'

'Sure.'

She takes it away to do so and returns promptly with the correct ratio of water and ice. I smile and thank her. I pop open my bottle and pour myself a glass, slowly, rather ceremoniously. I begin to attract attention and some rather peculiar glances from the regulars in the bar. It becomes apparent rather quickly that this isn't the sort of establishment where champagne is consumed so flagrantly, and that those who do are promptly looked down upon with complete and utter contempt. Random men begin to shout things at me.

'What you drinking, you fucking ponce?!'

I try to ignore them.

'Coming in here flashing your wad!'

I down glass after glass.

'You can't come in here drinking that shit!'

The champagne goes straight to my head and before I can do anything about it I find myself helplessly drunk. I'm a mess. I'm nervous, too. I fear someone might follow me out of the bar if I try to leave. It's obvious that I shouldn't have bought the champagne. Then something overtakes me, forcing me: I ask the red-headed barmaid to pour drinks for everyone around the bar. It's a big mistake. The whole bar explodes into a threatening cacophony aimed in my general direction.

'Flash fucking Harry!'

'Fucking ponce!'

'Big time fucking Charlie!'
'Who does he think he is?!'
'I've never seen the cunt before.'
'He's never in here.'
'Billy fucking no mates, innit!'

I pour another glass and down the last of the champagne in one. I ignore them. I focus on a man talking to his woman, speaking in that aggressive way drunken men seem to speak to women they're with, without them even noticing: close, leaning in, gesticulating wildly, grabbing on to her arms and waist, pulling her close to him, trying to kiss her ear in mid-sentence, roughly, not really knowing his own strength around her. She seems to be enjoying it, though. Or at least she's used to it now and it doesn't really faze her: laughing along, straightening her face when she feels she should, giggling with him, matching him drink for drink. They're perfectly content with each other. As if nothing else exists for them, just their lives, their everyday lives.

I begin to think about my own loneliness. It's a cliché and I know it's the booze sending my brain the signals to do it, but I can't help it. How I failed to love my own wife, to find happiness with her, start the family, do all the things we're supposed to do. Surely it's not hard? I mean, this man and woman have found each other. They've found happiness . . . or at least something that resembles it, something to share with each other. At least they have that much.

toledo road

She's sitting across the room from me, almost directly behind me, alone at a small table trying to read a book, or something like a magazine. I wonder how long she's been there; she could have been sitting there for hours, all afternoon for all I know, or she could have just breezed in as I was drinking my pint of water. All I know is it's definitely her, I'm sure it's her. It looks just like her: the same hair and eyes, even the same clothes. I squint, trying desperately to focus, to get a better look. She doesn't seem to be waiting for anyone, she looks perfectly content, sitting there as if no one else exists. It all looks very peaceful over there: the noise of the pub seems to have filtered away, like she's too far away for it to reach her. She's drinking a glass of wine, red. She seems settled, comfortable, at home, as if she's one of the regulars. My heart begins to beat irregularly, like something is happening inside me, something strange. She's beautiful, I can see that through the haze; so beautiful. No one else is looking at her, not even the other drunks at the bar; it's like I'm the only person who can see her, as if I'm meant to, as if she's just for me, as if a sign has been thrust in front of me, addressed to me only. I begin to shake. I step off my stool to steady my legs; it's like I could reach up and touch her, she's so close, elevated, up in front of me, sitting there, something to be worshipped, so tantalisingly close yet untouchable, completely separate from me, some kind of beautiful icon. Should I just casually walk over to her? Offer her another drink? Maybe that's what I should do? Maybe that's what anyone else would do, but I don't. I sit back on my stool and continue to gaze across at her, hoping she might notice me, remember me too, and wave me over. But she doesn't, of course she doesn't. It doesn't happen like that. It never does. It's never head-on in real life. She just continues to read whatever it is she's reading and I continue to stare at her like a lecherous drunk, for hours, as if we're both stuck in that moment.

I consider buying another bottle of champagne, but even clouded in booze something inside tells me that this isn't a good idea. Plus I have dinner with Mr Buchanan tonight, that I should really be *compos mentis* for. So I continue to do what's easiest – stare – hoping, hoping, hoping she'll eventually look up and recognise me. She looks like an angel; nothing spiritual, but something transformed, glowing, existing on a higher plateau than the rest of us. It's as if I'm looking up to her now, even though I'm slumped on a bar stool. She seems separate from the rest of the bar and I'm positive that I'm completely and utterly in love with her. It appears in me, this incredible feeling, something I haven't felt for a long time, if ever. It runs through me, fills every corner of me. Nothing else can compare to this. Nothing else can touch her. She's the most beautiful thing, angel, ghost, girl I've laid eyes on. I can feel it. It's in me now. Right now. I'm transfixed by it, I'm scared of breathing, as though if I take one more breath she'll disappear. I can't even blink. I'm scared to look away, that she'll vanish if I do.

When she looks up I want her to notice nothing but me. That's how it should be. Suddenly, something takes my eye off her: the man and woman begin to row with each other, screaming and shouting like they're the only two people in here. The group around them begins to back away, as if they've seen it all before, to give them room to argue. It's a big mistake. I quickly look back over to her, but she's gone. I suck the oxygen around me into my lungs and quickly grab my rucksack and stick. I go after her, leaving the bar in a blur of faces, shouts and screams. As I rush out of the door I'm sure the man shouts something at me. I ignore him without looking back. The cold early evening air hits me. I look left down towards the High Street: there she is, she's turning right onto it, heading south towards the sea. I walk after her, lifting up my stick so that it doesn't scrape the ground or bang into anything. When I reach the High Street I can still see her, she's waiting across the road at KFC. I hang back, just out of sight, as the High Street is quite empty and I don't want to cause alarm. She crosses the road then snakes across the High Street just after KFC. I follow her, my heart still pounding. She seems to be walking at a pace now. A young lad on a mountain bike cycles past her; he slows down, circles and cycles back to her. They seem to know each other. He's a shady-looking lad and isn't best pleased to see her. They exchange a few words before he cycles off away from her, and as he does this she quickens her step. As if she's been told to get somewhere fast. I begin to walk as quickly as I can without causing any attention. I follow her left onto York Road, alongside what look like halfway houses, bedsits, drop-in and drug rehabilitation centres. The street is empty, which surprises me as much as it unnerves me. She heads all the way to the bottom, stopping at Queensway. Ignoring the pelican crossing, she dashes across the left-hand lane and stops at the barriers, steadying herself before hopping over it to cross the other lane. I begin to jog now, sensing that she's getting away from me. She heads up the grass verge on the other side of the dual carriageway. Just as I'm about to tear out into the road I suddenly think better of it. I wait at the pelican crossing until the traffic stops and then dart over the road. I run onto the grass verge. She's gone. I look at the name of the small road behind the grass verge: Toledo Road. She lives here, on Toledo Road. I can feel it. I know where she lives. It's here. It's got to be here. I've nearly found her. I just have to find out which house she lives in.

I walk back up York Road, using my stick to take the strain. The young lad on the mountain bike cycles past me, coasting down the hill. He spits on the ground and stares at me, slowing down to take a good look at me. I grip my stick, hoping he'll pass without stopping. I look back at him and dig my stick into the road until he reaches Queensway. He heads along the wrong side of the road, ignoring the cars, towards a gap in the barrier. He heads through, crosses the other side and cycles up the grass verge to Toledo Road.

language is such a mess

I take my table at the Lobster Smack. Everything feels good, like I've spent the day reading at the beach, or something, but Mr Buchanan can easily sense that I'm more than half cut. I try to act normal, but this only makes things worse. It's obvious that I have things on my mind and that I'm unable to control the alcohol in me. I swallow huge gulps of air, one after the other, hoping it'll revive me, but it doesn't and I soon give up and just sit there. I must look a mess, but there's nothing I can do about it now.

The pub is full. I regret not stopping off at Uncle Rey's caravan first, just to freshen up, maybe have a wash, or a change of clothes. I've left my stick at the door for some reason, knowing that it won't be taken. Mr Buchanan is behind the bar, smiling. I don't know if it's for my benefit or it's just a thing he does when he's behind the bar.

'What do you want to drink?'

'Oh . . . lime and soda with ice, please.'

'Not drinking tonight, Jon?'

'Oh, no . . . early start on the caravan tomorrow.'

He walks over with my drink and a beer for himself. He sits down next to me, his body spilling over the chair.

'Mind if I join you?'

'No. Please . . . take a seat.'

'Thanks, Jon.'

'That's okay . . .'

'So . . .'

'So . . .'

'How are you, Jon?'

'I'm well.'

'And how are things with the caravan?'

'Well, yes, it's warm . . . comfortable . . .'

'No . . . I mean, clearing it . . . Your, you know . . . Rey's stuff.'

'Oh, that, yes, well . . . there's still a lot to do . . .'

'Right . . . I thought you'd be making progress by now, see . . .'

'What do you mean?'

'Well, there's no sign that you've done anything . . .'

'What do you mean?'

'There're no bin bags, rubbish, unwanted stuff . . . belongings . . . You've left nothing. It's as if nothing has been touched . . . as if you've just been living there and not really doing anything. You do know that the lease is up? Rey only paid until the end of next week . . . And then . . .'

'What?'

'And then everything will be taken away.'

'I see . . . I see what you mean . . . What if . . . ?'

'What if what?'

'What if I moved in, started paying you rent?'

'Well, no, see . . . it's being rented out to contractors for, you know, the refinery. It's closing down soon, the refinery, and there're contractors on the island to help take care of everything. It's all been booked already, contracts signed . . . We really have to get things moving here.'

'Really.'

'Do you understand?'

'Yes. Of course.'

'I know it's hard. It's difficult, I know. But I'm running a business, here.'

'A business, I know.'

'Listen, Jon . . . I know what happened is tough . . . it's tough for all of us who knew him. I know how that sort of thing . . . well, I know what it can do to a family. He was a good man. A quiet man. He spoke softly. He was kind-hearted. I doubt he ever hurt a fly in his life. He had his secrets, like us all . . . You know, he just wanted to hide . . . but I just have to think of my business . . . Something like that happening, well, it gets in the papers, people start talking . . . And then, well, you know what can happen . . . These things aren't good for business.'

'Yes, he was a good man, from what I can remember . . . And I've been working in the caravan. I've been sorting through all his tapes and recordings . . . I've even found a book he attempted to write; it's an odd thing, more about not being able to write it than anything else. It's about the truth, his search for the truth, how to put the truth down on the page, I think . . . I don't know what he was trying to attempt . . . some sort of facsimile, I think. But it's full of mistakes, errors, smudges, spills, cross-outs. All I know is that I have to edit it, get it into some sort of shape . . . to see . . . to see if there's anything worthy in it. Once I've done that, I promise I'll clear the caravan. It'll all be completed by the end of next week, honest.'

'A book, eh . . . I'd never have guessed. Something to do with music, yes . . . but a book . . .'

'I don't know what he was up to . . . some kind of moral crusade, as if he was trying to right all his ills . . . The thing is, it's all a jumble, and I can't make any sense of it. Then there're the recordings . . . The recordings, his diary recorded each year, on random days, explaining to those who'll listen . . . As if he's talking to me and no one else.'

'Maybe that's how he wanted it to be, messy like real life, over before you can take hold of it . . .'

'It's these recordings, hundreds of them, spanning decades . . . all his daily frustrations are spilled onto them . . . words, language is such a mess when you are confronted with it . . . head-on, you know . . . Him, leaning in, staring, facing the camera in his favourite chair . . . No one in my family knows they exist, and I don't know what to do with them. The ones I've watched, hours of footage, he's just so . . . angry and lost . . . and he's drunk and high on weed so much of the time that he's practically incoherent, to the point where he'll burst into song, usually something by Dr Feelgood . . .'

'Oh, yes, he liked those lads. Canvey lads.'

'It's all just a bit overwhelming for me at the moment, so I hope you understand if it looks like I've yet to make any progress with the caravan and all his stuff, there's just so much of it . . . I'll make progress, I will, I will . . .'

'Okay, Jon . . . Now, what would you like to eat? The lamb is good today.'

'I'd like the steak. I'd like the steak again . . .'

'I'll see to it . . . rare?'

'Yes.'

blackening

Mr Buchanan is eating opposite me, sipping his beer in between mouthfuls of lamb. We don't speak much now, we're too busy eating. I gaze out of the window into the darkness; the sky above the sea wall is blackening, shading gradually through grey as clouds pass into the night. My steak is good; it's huge for a start and has been chargrilled to perfection. It melts in my mouth. I know that I should be savouring each mouthful, but I don't. I wolf it down instead. My head is fuzzy and I would like Mr Buchanan to leave me alone, but there's no way of asking him to leave. He's adamant he'll eat with me. I mentioned that he might have work to do, but he wouldn't have any of it. Even my silence hasn't put him off. He's here for the remainder of the meal, that's for sure. I like him if I'm honest. I like his face. It's the sort of face that looks like it's lived many lives. A friendly face – wrinkled, weathered, trustworthy, the lines on his face like a map of territory I already know.

After my steak I order sticky toffee pudding and Mr Buchanan has the butterscotch cheesecake. The pudding is good, and I feel compelled to tell him this. He waves my words away from his face, a little embarrassed, and asks the barmaid for another beer.

'Do you want another drink?'

'Well, really . . . I shouldn't . . .'

'Rubbish . . . Stacey, give the man a brandy, a double . . . On me, my treat . . . In fact, this whole meal is my treat. I don't want you to pay for a thing while you're here, okay . . .'

'Mr Buchanan . . .'

'Ach, it's Robbie . . .'

'Robbie, that's really kind of you to offer, but . . . it's okay, I can get this. Allow me to pay for this . . .'

'Never!'

'Please, I can more than afford it . . .'

'I wouldn't dream of it . . .'

'That key . . . Well, Uncle Rey, he left me something . . .'

'Yes, the key . . .'

'He's left me his entire life savings . . .'

'Jackpot! . . . I'm sorry . . . I'm just trying to lighten the mood . . .'

'It's okay . . . It's just that I'm confused . . . Why me? Why did he leave it all to me?'

rerum vulgarium fragmenta

After I finish my brandy I thank Mr Buchanan for the meal and company and make my way back to Uncle Rey's caravan. The blackness outside unnerves me a little, the moon is hidden by dark, thick cloud and it's frighteningly black. I fumble for my torch and then remember that I don't have it, so I use my stick to feel for any obstacles – stones, little puddles, anything that might cause me to stumble – along the sea wall. Up ahead of me there is a giant break in the clouds, stars are visible beyond it. I look up to where I accidentally found Saturn through the telescope. I begin to feel dizzy; it doesn't make walking while simultaneously looking up that easy. I dig my stick in with each step. It's a strange feeling, looking up, knowing that Saturn is up there above me, somewhere, up there among it all. The fact that all this is happening in real time, right now, is quite hard to believe: the birth of new stars, the death of old, the planets orbiting, the expanding blackness of the universe, the quickening of it, the existence of space and time itself.

It's all too much. It must be, as I suddenly fall. I roll to my left, down the grass embankment, towards the barbed-wire fence encircling the caravan site. I manage to keep hold of everything as I tumble down, crashing against the fence, upturned, on my back, gazing back up at the stars again. I stay here for quite some time, the world spinning above me, looking up at it all passing by again and again and again, the sky widening, spinning, everything contained within the blackness, a spinning that pulls me in. It takes me all my strength to break away from it and drag myself up, with the aid of my trusty stick, to my feet.

Back in Uncle Rey's caravan I find his laptop. I'm surprised the site has its own Wifi connection. The first thing I do is google Toledo Road, Southend. I want to know if there are any B&Bs or hostels there, but I'm out of luck. All I find is some information about how Toledo Road, before it was a road, used to face what used to be a river, down to the estuary, its bed now Queensway. The river existed way before the urban development that's now Southend, way before the fishing villages, when it was just farmers' fields. I find it strange that it's Queensway, the ugliest of dual carriageways that follows the exact route of this river to the sea. Toledo Road sits on its left-hand bank, looking down, southwards towards the sea. I click on a few more links, one for Toledo in Spain: a town that also overlooks a great river. I also find out that a Toledo is a double-edged Spanish sword. There's nothing else online that might help me find her house, or flat, or whatever it is she's doing there. Absolutely nothing.

I soon become bored with the internet; not even the temptation of some porn can keep me interested. Instead, I shut down the laptop and walk over to the vast collection of tapes, CD-ROMs and DVDs. I pick up another DVD at random and put it into the machine.

Rewriting Aeneid #122 2003

I read something by old Petrarch today that made sense to me, which is remarkable because nothing else seems to these days. It's a beautiful line or two . . . It really hit home, made me shudder, hit me in the gut. It's from his sonnets . . . sonnet 14 to be precise, from his *Canzoniere*, or better still, yes I prefer this . . . from his . . . Re . . . *Rerum Vulgarium Fragmenta* . . . as they were originally called . . . the Fragments of Vulgar Things . . . Isn't that just beautiful? You know, both ugly and ordinary, just beautiful because of that, the everyday vernacular . . . Vulgar Things, that's what I'll call it . . . My new moral maze, all those random words piled into boxes on disks, on memory sticks . . . My rewritings . . . My attempt truthfully to right all my wrongs, to spill soot-like ink onto the white paper, filling the blanks, being the blanks, turning white into black, that's all I can do . . . To hide away from a life of excess, to recreate a new moral code for you and my family, to do right by myself, to struggle to do it, to fail to do it and knowing it will always be . . . that's what Vulgar Things will be . . . Ah, Petrarch, here's what I read . . .

[He pulls up a book from his lap, so that it can be seen on camera, his eyes just visible above it. He reads slowly.]

Seeking for ever in whatever place . . . Some crudely copied shadowy hint of you.

[He places the book back down on his lap. He stares into the camera. His eyes well up with tears. He wipes his eyes.]

Isn't that just beautiful? Isn't it? . . . Oh, those words, those words, they seem so true to me and yet whatever I say, whatever I write, it doesn't, it collapses under the weight of its own inauthenticity . . . No matter what I do, I'll never be true to myself here . . . A shadowy hint . . . Crudely copied . . . that's me all over . . . And just to think of it, of her, the centre of all this for me . . . I remember when I first saw her, my own Laura . . . She was with him, I couldn't even touch her if I wanted to, he brought her to me, home to meet our parents. I was younger, I was insignificant, an age of no importance. She was beautiful, she was so, so beautiful . . . and I loved her there and then, I loved her from that moment I'm sure of that . . . I swear I did . . . and I knew I always would. I was trembling, I was sure she could see me trembling. I'd never seen such beauty, such elegance . . . The way she smiled at me when we were introduced, I could barely stand up, but I did. I managed it, half respectable, but still an idiot, a fool, a moron before her . . . it was like her very essence had been injected into me. This new love I felt was coupled with an immediate suffering, the thought that she wasn't mine to love . . . The thought that she didn't love me . . . It was that sudden. That's how it hit me. I shudder recounting . . . that's how Virgil put it, anyway . . . it's too much to bear . . . it was real and I didn't know what to do. But my Laura, I can . . . I can see you now . . .

[He picks up the book and reads from it again. His voice trembles and stammers.]

I'd see the snowbound roses of her lips quivering . . . and that glint of ivory that marbles the onlooker . . . Every reason I'd see wherefore my joy outstrips the pain of it . . .

[He holds the book tightly to his chest.]

Maybe this is where I should leave it? Yes? No? Simply take leave of this world tonight? Here in this wretched caravan . . . My worthless fucking life, crippled by its own excesses . . . Maybe that's what I should do? Disappear into the blackness of night . . . To look back, never to return . . . You see, I've always wanted to be truthful, I've always wanted to bring truth's mystery back up to the light of day . . . yet I've never been fucking truthful, how could I? Who the fuck do I think I am? Oh fucking God, I've wanted to tell everyone the truth . . . the truth . . . But I've always failed, turned my back on it, kept it hidden . . . all those times I've been so close . . . so fucking close to it and I've backed away at the last minute . . . I'm nothing but a coward . . . Nothing like Aeneas the True . . . Nothing like him. Oh to be truthful, oh to sing the fucking truth . . . This duplicitous sham of a life I live, fraught with the excess of shameful abandon . . . I could have been so true to her, to my Laura . . . and to him . . . I could have been so truthful to him.

[He stops to pour himself a glass of whiskey. He takes a long gulp from his glass. Finishes it, then takes a quick glug from the bottle before refilling the glass.]

That's the aim . . . to be truthful, never to deviate, always to rewrite, to reveal the truth I've hidden from view all my life . . . And if I can't do that, well, I'm fucking nothing . . . and oblivion awaits me.

MONDAY

all colliding

I leave Uncle Rey's caravan without any breakfast and head straight for Toledo Road. I arrive in Southend quickly and seamlessly, like a somnambulist waking up in a desired destination. It's early and the road is quiet, except for office workers making their way to Southend Central Station to begin their daily commute into London. I momentarily think about the job I've just lost. I'm happy, that's how it feels. The idea of sitting in that office with those people sickens me. London seems like a fading memory to me, like a fading dream. I'm happy to have escaped their clutches, even if it might only be for the duration of my task at hand. It doesn't matter to me now, right now this minute. Nothing does. Even this morning, when I stumbled off the sofa and back into the same clothes, I remember thinking nothing, absolutely nothing, just going with the flow, and enjoying the peculiar lightness of it for a moment, before my urge to see her again truly kicked in.

It doesn't matter at all, now. Especially the thought of that office, of the life I used to lead. All that is behind-hand now. All that matters is finding her again – seeing her, speaking to her. The thought of seeing her, catching her glance, that's what I want. It's real. It's a real feeling: knowing that she lives somewhere along Toledo Road. I can feel it. It's up to me to find her, to wait for her there for as long as it takes.

She's beginning to haunt me more than I can imagine. It's like

I've been programmed to do this, or something, as if some force is controlling me. I have three perfect images of her floating behind my eyes: the pier, the creek and the pub by the station. It was her each time; the same girl, the same image of her. When I eventually do stop to think I realise that something is bothering me: it's something about the way Mr Buchanan acted last night over dinner. He seemed eager to get rid of me, I think. Like something was troubling him.

Another thing's bothering me, too: the recording of Uncle Rey I watched last night. He seemed different, less manic, more in control. Now that I am away from the recordings – his voice, his words, his face, the eyes looking directly into the lens – now that I am away from all that, it strikes me that something other than the struggle to articulate his book must be happening in each of his recordings: each must reveal some sort of clue. There was this 'Laura' for a start. Who is she? What's the connection between her and Uncle Rey? Then, just a moment ago, as I was waiting to cross Queensway at the pelican crossing, it occurred to me that Uncle Rey had been talking about my father. It was Father who brought Laura to him. Even before I reach the other side of the road I realise that Laura is my mother. Which is odd; she's someone I hardly think about usually. Not that much, anyway. I haven't seen her since I was a child, for a start. I can't think what Uncle Rey is trying to say. It's weighing down on me, but it's all got to wait. I have to find her first, before any of that.

I look at my phone. It's early. Early enough for me to spend the majority of the day waiting for her to appear, if that's what it takes. And I'm confident she will. It's a matter of waiting. I'm just like a fielder in the slips in a test match: waiting for the event, the moment everything suddenly slots into place: positioning, geometry, trajectory, sight, observance, all colliding, all joining as one to form the event. Just as I put my phone back into my rucksack it begins to vibrate; a text message from Cal:

how's it going? been ringin you all nite. C.

I look at my missed calls: Cal has indeed been ringing throughout the night; strange that I missed them. I count nine missed calls from him in total. I try to forget about it. He'll only want to know how the clearance is going. I've other things on my mind right now. I decide to call him later in the evening, after I've found her and made sure she's safe.

I walk up the grass verge between Toledo Road and Queensway. I set my stick down on the grass below a large cherry tree and sit down. For some reason I look up at the sky through the branches: a thin veil of grey cloud is covering it. I think about what I saw last night: the constellations, the planets, all swirling around in the night sky. It's strange to realise that they're all still there, behind that thin layer of grey cloud, swirling above me as I sit here on the damp grass. Something grips me and I suddenly want to know if Saturn is up there. I need to know that everything is still in its correct place, just beyond and out of reach, just where it should be. The thought of it all disappearing is too much to bear. It all seems so fragile, too unstable, as if some fall or crash in the universe is imminent. I've had similar thoughts at different times throughout my life, of course. This is nothing new.

I grip on to clumps of grass, as if I'm holding on to the entire earth, thankful to the force of gravity for keeping me from drifting off into space. I grip on to the clumps of grass as tightly as I can, just in case it all goes wrong and things begin to fall; in case we're all suddenly flung off, in some massive jolt, some crack, all of us spewed out into the cosmos. I hang on for dear life; convinced in doing so I'll remain rooted, firmly attached to this rock, while everything else unfixed shoots past me, out into the vastness, a great surge of things disappearing in an incredible whoosh.

This sudden sense of ill-ease is eventually soothed somewhat by the well-timed appearance of a cat, sniffing my stick. I didn't notice it at first and it made me jump. I let go of the clumps of grass, which in turn startles the cat. It skips off towards another tree to my right. From the safety of this tree the cat, a tabby, observes me,

93

assessing if I'm a threat, something with food, or just something odd to look at for a short while. I call out to it.

'Phssst phssst phssst.'

Nothing. I call out to it again.

'Phssst phssst phssst.'

It decides to saunter over to me. I hold out my fingers for it to sniff before it decides I'm okay. The cat circles me a couple of times, meowing back to me, and then curls up by my side, all sleepy, purring, ready for a nap. It makes me feel like napping too, but I know this could be disastrous, so I straighten my back and make sure that I can see all the houses on Toledo Road. I count ten in total. Ten houses that she could be in. Although some of them could be divided up into flats, which would make things a tad more complicated. It still seems feasible, though. I feel content that I'll find her at some point. I stroke the cat and wait for her to appear. While the cat begins to doze I gently look at the name tag on its collar. It's called Homer. I wonder if it's named after the father of the Simpsons or after Homer the Greek poet. I smile and hope it's the latter, but something intrinsic tells me it's most probably the former. In any case, it doesn't really matter. It's a lovely little cat, hanging around with nothing to do like the rest of us.

Homer begins to purr loudly now. It's a sound I've always loved. I grew up in a house without pets. It wasn't until later on in life, when I moved in with my then partner, before the marriage and all that followed, that I began to understand the need for domestic pets. It took me a while, to be honest. She had a cat. At first, I would simply keep my distance, but slowly and surely it won me over with what I now recognise are universal cat tricks. It wasn't long before I began to allow the cat to sleep next to me at night, when my partner was away on long business trips. It was only then that I appreciated the comfort of a cat's purr: that shared primordial moment, the feeling of complete and utter oneness, contentedness with everyone and everything. The whole universe purrs when cats are happy, I'm sure of that.

stranded

I must have dozed off, too, because suddenly Homer isn't here any more and the air around me is busier and colder, and the traffic on Queensway to my immediate left is louder, too. I stand up, my bones creaking and my legs stiff. I lean on my stick and check the time on my phone. I am angry with myself, even though I've only been asleep for about ten to twenty minutes. I know that anything could have happened in that amount of time. She could have come and gone from any one of those ten houses, she could have been bundled into a waiting car, walked her dog on the grass verge all around me, screamed for help from her bedroom window, anything, and I'll have missed it. I want to shout out, to swing my stick at something, but I think better of it. Maybe I haven't missed her? Maybe she's at any one of those windows this very moment, looking down at the big cherry tree above me, at the entire grass verge, at me? Wondering to herself why the man from the pier, or the creek if she saw me, or the pub, is now sleeping on the grass verge across from her house? Maybe that's what has been happening while I've been asleep?

I look at each of the houses, staring in through the windows to see if I can detect any movement, any signs of life. It's no good, it's too light, each window is like a mirror, reflecting back a wash of green and grey. I stand here, my stick sinking into the grass under my weight. I need to be less conspicuous, to hide from view, but there's nowhere to hide. It's like I'm stranded. A scrap of litter, detritus buffeted from pillar to post.

signalling

Now I'm distracted by the same thin layer of grey cloud above me again, separating me from everything else beyond it, shielding me, keeping me rooted, covering me like a protective blanket. I want to pull it down from the sky and wrap it around my shoulders, take it with me wherever I go. When I look back over to the row of houses something has changed dramatically: she's standing there, on the doorstep of the house with the big brown door about to shut behind her. It's her. It looks like her. The same hair and eyes, the same beautiful face, the same languid stance. I'm sure it's her, my very own Laura. I name her on the spot, without hesitation. It seems natural to do so. My beautiful Laura standing before me. My heart's thumping now. It really is, I'm not just thinking this, I can feel it in my chest. I stand perfectly still, my grip tightening around my stick. She walks down onto the street, shutting the garden gate behind her. I walk down the other side of the grassy slope, towards her road, skipping over the iron railings, about ten metres behind her. I follow her up to the lights and over Queensway, onto York Road, heading up what used to be the steep right-hand bank of the river looking southwards towards the estuary.

Halfway up York Road, just before the car park on the right, opposite the row of Chinese cultural centres and restaurants, a man shouts out from a window in one of the many drop-in centres, hostels or halfway houses at this end of the road. Laura waves at him, signalling for him to come out and speak with her. I hold back just out of view, behind some parked cars. The man appears across the road, dressed in a pair of jogging bottoms, white trainers and nothing else. He's muscular but skinny, covered in scars and tattoos, some of which are clearly prison tattoos. He swaggers towards her with both hands down the front of his jogging bottoms, a smile revealing both blackened and missing teeth. She hugs him when he reaches her, they both laugh about something, gesticulating wildly, then her face becomes serious. From where I am watching it looks like he begins to act out some kind of fight or altercation, some kind of attack or beating that it looks like he might have been involved in. He's feigning kicks and punches, laying in to an imaginary figure, demonstrating how someone, maybe him, smashed something, a bottle maybe, over someone's head. She remains stoic throughout the anecdote. When he finishes whatever it is he's saying she gives him another hug and walks away, while he swaggers to his front door, just up from me on the other side of York Road. He tucks his hands down the front of his jogging bottoms. I'm not sure, but I think he glances over at me before shouting something to her in a thick local accent, something about her 'nice arse'. She turns around, laughing, and gives him the Vs, a big smile spreading across her beautiful face. I begin to walk after her again. I want to turn back and hit him with my stick. I feel nauseous thinking about what he might very well have done to someone recently, and the way he shouted after her and the way she responded turns my stomach. She's too beautiful for someone like him. I can't believe that someone as beautiful as her could know someone like him. It just doesn't make sense. It sickens me. It really sickens me to the core.

a photographic list of dancers

She walks left along the High Street towards Royal Terrace, where she turns left again and continues down past the Palace Hotel and through the cemetery at St Peter's Church. Before I know it we're on Lucy Road, at the top end next to Rossi's ice-cream factory. Lucy Road is the centre of Southend's sleazy nightlife, a back alley that runs parallel to the neon-bathed Golden Mile. By day it's barren, filthy-looking, dominated by a huge litter-strewn coach park. I follow her down the street, and I count each of the desperately named nightclubs as I pass: Chameleon, the Liberty Belle, Papillion Music Bar, Bar Blue, Talk Nightclub, the Lounge, Chinnery's, Zinc Bar, Pockets Bar (snooker), Route 66 Bar (pool), and finally Sunset Exotic Dance Bar. It's at this bar that she stops, ringing the buzzer on a big black door by the side of the main entrance. She lights a cigarette with a match, flicking it onto the road. A large man opens the door, thick with muscle and fat, shaven head and tattoos covering his pallid skin. He gives her a long hug and she follows him inside. Is she a stripper? Is that what she is? I pull out my phone from my rucksack and immediately google the bar to see if they have a photographic list of their dancers, but I can't really find anything other than a few generic shots of girls, all of them blonde, looking suggestively into the camera. Maybe she's going inside for an audition? But why would he hug her like that? Strangers don't hug like that. I walk up to the big black door and put my ear to it. Nothing. Not a sound. I spot her match on the road and pick it up. I sniff it, before putting it in my wallet.

I decide to wait for her on the other side of the road, in the coach park, just behind a large white van. I stand there for a couple of hours. At least it feels like a couple of hours; it's certainly a long time. It might be longer. Nothing. Nothing at all. No sign. No opening of that big black door. Nothing. I figure she's either still in there, or she's used another exit. It's hard to tell. I don't really feel like waiting much longer, and besides, I'm famished. I really am. It feels like I've been awake for days. I need to eat, to rest, to regain my strength. Even if I don't see her again today, I now know where she lives, that's the main thing. And now I know where she possibly works, I can visit the Sunset Bar tonight, when it opens. If she works here, she'll be dancing tonight.

painting the sky

I walk out onto the esplanade on Golden Mile in the direction of Thorpe Bay and Shoeburyness. The sky is wide and the sea is flat. Kite surfers are gliding by, out in the estuary's mouth, and in the grey distance beyond a huge container ship is interrupting the horizon, slowly making its way into the estuary.

As I walk past the multicoloured beach huts at Thorpe Bay I catch up with an elderly couple ahead of me. They're talking loudly and are blissfully unaware of my presence behind them. I decide to hold back, worried that if I do pass them I might give them a fright, especially with my stick. My stomach is tying itself in knots with hunger, I should really carry on past them. I can see Uncle Tom's Cabin, a café in the distance. I should head straight there, but I can't ignore their conversation.

'You've always been awkward . . . ever since I first met you.'

'Why's that?'

'Remember the wedding dress?'

'What about it?'

'The palaver we went through . . .'

'Well . . .'

'Well, that's when I knew I was about to marry an awkward bastard . . . sometimes I can be bothered, sometimes I can't. I've been like this all my life, you know that with everything and everyone, and it's getting a lot worse the older I get . . . and I'm getting old . . .'

'What? . . .'

'I said . . . it's getting worse the older I get . . . It's like yesterday with that poorly pigeon, why wouldn't you let me take it home?'

'I'm not having a pigeon in the house.'

'But I could have made him better . . .'

'They're filthy creatures.'

'We're filthy creatures . . . we have cats in the house, full of fleas and things . . .'

'Cats aren't pigeons.'

'I bloomin' hate those cats . . .'

'What have you got against our cats?'

'I've had to put up with them for too long, always hanging around, scratching, falling off the furniture . . . I can't stand them, Elsie . . .'

'Why haven't you told me this before?'

'I'm telling you now.'

They both stop: agitated, facing each other to carry on the argument. I walk by them without being noticed. The old man looks tearful, I think. I don't look back at them. I think it's best I leave them there, behind-hand. Instead I look down over the multi-coloured beach huts; the tide beyond them has gone out and the brown mud is beginning to dry out in the faint sunlight that's just started to seep through the thin veil of grey cloud. People are already out on the mud, walking in pairs, fours, larger groups and alone. I follow their footprints out into the estuary until they meet up with the feet that made them, out towards Mulberry Harbour, the old concrete harbour wedged permanently in the mud. Men are digging for bait, following the receding tide, children are running around, flinging the mud at each other – I can just about see them, rolling around in it, making strange little structures with it. Pools of sea water have gathered where the bed naturally dips, creating temporary eco-systems to be disturbed by curious children, fathers and sons, friends. It's tempting to go out there and join them, all I have to do is take off my shoes and roll up my jeans, my stick would support me, but it's not a good idea, I've nowhere to clean up afterwards for a start. I have to keep in tip-top condition for tonight. I have to look as good as I can. So I continue along the esplanade, out towards the peninsula of Shoeburyness, my stomach rumbling along the way, my stick click click clicking in a peculiar rhythm.

being wrong

My mind goes back to Uncle Rey again. I'm beginning to feel a little guilty. I really should have made a start in sorting through his papers and belongings. People are counting on me to do a good, thorough job. But all I can really think about is Laura, my Laura, his Laura. I feel as though there's no fixed point any more, except my obsessions, those recordings, the telescope, the things that need to be packed away and hidden from view. But the more I try to hide things, or, better still, ignore them, the more things are revealed. Why am I so fixated on the image of Laura? Why do I go on listening to these urges? What, or who, am I trying to save? What a complete and utter mess. Just like Uncle Rey, I have nothing to cling on to any more. It seems to me that if I let go of this Laura, like he did his, like him I'll regret it for the rest of my miserable life. This is my lot. This is all I have. There's nothing else for me.

I have to find her, that's all I know. But first I must eat; my stomach is turning and turning, it feels like I haven't eaten in weeks. I need sustenance to get me through the day. If I am to find her again tonight, to save her from whatever it is she's frightened of, whatever it was she was too afraid to speak about on the pier, then I have to do it on a full stomach. My strength has to be up. I have to feel fit and strong, ready to tackle anything that might be thrown my way. It has to be this way, for her as much as for me. If it even is her, I mean the girl from the pier. I might have it all wrong. I could be wrong, I mostly am. I've spent my whole life being wrong, feeling wrong, making the wrong choices, doing the wrong things. This could just be another repetition, the same thing . . . I simply don't know.

It's way too much to think about right now anyway, so I banish these thoughts from my mind and concentrate on the sound of my stick click click click clicking with each of my steps. Its rhythm soothes me. I feel like I'm making progress once again. It doesn't take me long to reach Uncle Tom's Cabin at the end of the beach at Thorpe Bay; an ugly little building dwarfed by a recently built sea wall that obscures any chance of a view out into the mouth of the estuary.

if you want anything

The café's empty. I sit at a table by the window, with a view of the sea wall. I take comfort in knowing it's keeping the estuary and its surging currents away from me, keeping it all 'out there' where only the container ships, oil tankers and the odd Thames sailing barge can take it on. Inside the café everything is still. In here there are no currents to contend with. I order a full English breakfast and a large mug of tea. I mix some white pepper into it, something I haven't done for a long time, remembering how I like the peppery aftertaste.

When the breakfast arrives it's huge. I take my time eating it. My stomach welcomes each forkful gladly, and I can feel the blood returning to my veins under my skin. Before I know it I'm contemplating a short walk out to Shoeburyness to see the old Second World War anti-aircraft gun casements. I haven't seen the gun casements since I was a child. I want to know how much things have changed out there, if at all.

Just as I'm contemplating the sheer immensity of the concrete gun emplacements, the power that used to be fixed in position there, the door to the café opens, sending white light across the floor. I nearly jump out of my skin. A large, bearded man enters the café, who looks the spitting image of Mr Buchanan, so much so that I have to convince myself more than once that it definitely isn't him. As I dip some of my buttered toast into the yolk of my fried egg, I watch him. The resemblance is uncanny. The man orders a mug of coffee and gammon and chips, then walks over and sits down at the table directly next to mine. Almost immediately his mobile phone begins to ring. The tune is tinny, but familiar. I soon realise, just in time, that it's a Dr Feelgood track. I'm not sure which one, but I'm convinced it's the first track I'd listened to in Uncle Rey's caravan that first night. It's the same geometric guitar riff.

'What?'

[. . .]

'What's that got to do with me?'

[. . .]

'He should have done it.'

[. . .]

'Well, that's not my problem, is it?'

[. . .]

'When?'

[. . .]

'Fuck off, did he?'

[. . .]

'When?'

[. . .]

'You're joking, what's he on?'

[. . .]

'It's not the first time.'

[. . .]

'Listen, I've told you before. One phone call and I've got fifteen of Bethnal Green's finest to sort his lot out. Seriously, if he thinks he can just come down here and fuck around like he has been, then on his fat head be it . . . the cunt.'

[. . .]

'It's not my problem . . . But . . . I . . . I know . . . Listen, if he wants one, tell him he's got one.'

[. . .]

'I don't care.'

[. . .]

'I couldn't give a flying fuck.'

[. . .]

'No.'

[. . .]

'No.'

[. . .]

'Listen, fuck off, what part of "no" don't you understand? He's fucking trouble, a fucking nuisance . . .'

[. . .]

'No. I've told you.'

[. . .]

'Fuck off.'

[. . .]

'Fuck off.'

He slams his phone down on the table and takes a large gulp from his coffee, which makes me flinch – it must be scalding, but it doesn't seem to affect him. He looks around the café for some time, until his gaze finally settles on me. I look away immediately, hoping he will too.

'Never nice to hear, is it?'

'Pardon?'

'A phone call like that, when you hear a phone call like that . . . Never nice to hear, is it?'

'Oh, that, oh, I wasn't listening . . .'

'Well, I was loud enough to hear. So I apologise for that. Never nice. Never nice at all, that.'

'No, really, it isn't a problem.'

'Just come in here for some peace and quiet, I bet.'

'No, well, yes . . . no, not really.'

'Always good to escape, isn't it?'

'Pardon?'

'You look like you're in hiding . . .'

'I don't know what you mean . . .'

'You, in here . . . away from all that . . . you look like you've had enough, that's what I mean.'

'Oh, well . . . I was just out for a stroll . . . I was hungry . . .'

'Long . . . stroll . . .'

'Pardon?'

'I've been behind you all the way, from Royal Terrace, all the way to here . . . Long stroll.'

'Yes, oh, well, I like walking . . . I prefer it to driving.'

'Is that why you have that big stick?'

'I suppose so . . .'

'Can come in handy a stick like that, eh?'

'What do you mean?'

'Well, it's hefty . . . you could do a man some damage with a stick like that . . .'

'I use it for walking . . .'

'Always useful, just in case . . .'

'Yes. I suppose . . .'

I tuck into my black pudding and then look at stuff, nothing in particular, on my phone. I don't feel like talking to him and I hope he gets the message. He continues to stare at me while he chews on large chunks of gammon.

'I think I need a stick like that.'

'I bought it on Canvey.'

'That makes sense.'

'Well, people like walking sticks, I guess.'

'I saw you before Royal Terrace, actually . . .'

'Oh . . .'

'Yeah, near York Road . . .'

'Oh . . .'

'You were asleep, I think . . . flat out on the grass.'

'Was I?'

'Yes.'

'Are you sure it was me, I mean . . .'

'I never forget a face.'

'Oh . . .'

'You waiting for someone?'

'Now?'

'No, on York Road.'

'No . . . No . . . Just having a rest.'

'You want weed, brown, coke?'

'Pardon?'

'What do you need? . . . A woman . . . man?'

'No, no, no . . . None of that, that's not why . . . No, I'm not
into any of that.'

'You sure?'

'No . . . Thanks . . . Really . . .'

'All right.'

He stuffs more gammon into his mouth, like he's in a rush to
leave, but he isn't and I realise that this is just the way he eats his
food. Chips and gammon, the bits that miss his mouth, fall back
onto his plate and the table, which doesn't seem to bother him, as
he just picks up the bits, stuffing them into his mouth with his
hand.

'If you ever need anything I can always be found, I'm always
knocking around . . . York Road, out here by the wall . . . get a lot
of men out here, wanting certain things . . . You know what I mean
. . . You just give me a shout next time you see me, if you want
anything . . . You only have to ask.'

'Oh, right . . . yes.'

I eat my food as quickly as possible. I swig down my peppery
tea and take my empty plate to the man behind the counter. I
give him the money and he takes it without smiling. I'm not
sure he heard our conversation. I think about saying something
to him about it but I think better of it as the man eating the

gammon is staring at me again. I wave goodbye as he gives me a wink.

ejected and abandoned

I head along the sea wall towards the garrison, towards the Second World War gun casements. It's an eerie place out here. The sky stretched out, like I'm walking into it, and the sea over the wall is almost black in the distance.

I walk around the first of many gun casements: a smattering of thick-walled, concrete structures that still seem to maintain a sense of permanence and importance. I peer inside where the huge guns used to be, hurling shells out into the estuary. It's quiet and it's hard to imagine how loud the guns must have been. Now it's bathed in silence it doesn't seem right, although I wouldn't have it any other way. Now, the silence, as odd as it may seem, is comforting.

I look over to my left, where the old barracks must have been. An old parade ground and mess houses have all been bought by a developer, and people – families, young professionals – are beginning to move in, buying into something that doesn't exist any more. The whole place seems dead. I feel like I'm intruding, like I've gatecrashed a funeral. It's like I haven't just arrived but I've been spewed here, ejected and abandoned, here on the ness, for the elements to chip away at me until finally I crumble. It's a strange feeling: being stuck out here at the first point of defence; the barracks and garrison just slightly hidden from view. It's hard to ignore this place, nestled comfortably here by the sea, Sheerness and the hills of Kent out across it on the other side, wider, freer, the sea less restricting out here. It's hard to imagine the numerous rivers and outlets gushing into the estuary at Foulness – large arteries pumping fresh water into its salty depths, a huge black river before me. It doesn't seem real.

I walk down onto the beach below, a tangle of grass, concrete and shingle, where I walk to the water's edge to trace the shape of the land better from the ness and beyond. I stand here. Fixed, rooted to the spot. There's no point walking any further. There's nothing else I can say.

something snaps

I can smell the sea now that I'm walking in the opposite direction. My stomach is full and I feel energised. I've decided to return to Toledo Road immediately, to knock on Laura's door to see if she is there, to find out if that's where she lives, and if she remembers me. I want to be sure that it's her: the girl from the pier, the one who wants me to know that she's in trouble. Surely that's what she wanted out there, to tell someone, anyone. It just happened to be the right person . . . me. If I ignore her plea, then what's the point in all this? This strange quest to find her? It's no good, there's nothing else for me to do, I just can't get her beautiful face out of my head. I know that if I don't at least try, she'll haunt me until the day I die. It's the right thing to do: I'll just calmly knock on her door, that big brown door, and if she doesn't answer I'll just calmly ask if she is there, and if she is I'll introduce myself, she'll remember me. I'll take her away to the island. We'll watch the stars together at night and listen to that low rumble of the passing ships' engines as they float by just beyond the sea wall. She'll be safe out there, away from any danger, from everything and everyone.

Voices interrupt my thoughts: I can hear them on the other side of the wall, more than three it seems, talking energetically.

'Did you fuck her?'

'Course I did.'

'What's she like?'

'Her pussy . . . what her tits like?'

'She's fine, bruv.'

'What's her pussy like?'

'She sucked me off, near Sainsbury's, in the fucking bushes where Acky fucked Michelle Taylor. She sucked it right there.'

'She's well fit . . .'

'I wanna go, too . . .'

'She'd fuck anyone . . .'

'Not you, you skank . . .'

'Too much fucking cheese there . . .'

I listen, the sprawl of Southend seafront ahead of me, leading me on. The group of teenagers hop over the sea wall just in front of me, now the voices are real, one by one, four voices in total, dropping in front of me as if they've just fallen from the sky. I step to my right over to the cycle lane to allow them to pass but instead they circle me like an angry swarm of wasps. They're laughing at my stick, egging each other on.

'What you gonna do with that stick?'

'Give us your stick?'

'Leave him, let's go . . .'

'I want his stick.'

'I need this stick, it helps me to walk . . .'

'You a cripple?'

'You don't look like one.'

'Fuckin' mong.'

'Mong.'

'I'm okay, okay . . . I'm on my way home.'

'Give us that stick . . .'

'No.'

'Give us that stick . . .'

'No.'

'Fuckin' mong.'

'No, leave me to walk home . . .'

'No, you're not . . .'

Just like they say, a red mist suddenly descends. I raise my stick and swing it wildly around my head. It narrowly misses one of the teenagers' heads, and then another. All I know is that I need my stick and I want to get to Toledo Road as soon as possible. I begin to jab it towards their faces, the point of the stick millimetres from them. They back off. I go for one again, swinging the stick up and bringing it down towards their head like an axe. They manage to avoid it.

'Come on . . . Come on . . . He's fucking mental . . .'

'That nearly fucking . . .'

'He's fuckin' psycho . . .'

'Come on . . . Come on . . .'

They half jog past me, as close to the sea wall as they can. I allow them to pass. Once they're at a safe distance they begin to sling insults at me until I can't hear them any more. Two of them stop and do some sort of hand signal before turning away. I'm in some form of shock, shaking, my breathing heavy and erratic. I've never reacted that way before; I usually walk away from confrontation.

As I continue to walk a large pebble smashes into shards at my feet. I turn around – the teenagers are throwing them at me; some of them narrowly miss, others fall way wide of the mark. The teenagers are laughing, hurling obscenities. I quicken my pace away from them, without looking back again, pebbles smashing all around me until I'm out of range. After a while they are dots in the distance. I continue to walk quickly, heading as fast as my short legs will take me towards her, energised, unafraid and in search of her, my beautiful Laura, heading to save her from any darkness, to bring her back from the depths of night, back up into the light of day.

short circuit

Toledo Road is busy when I eventually arrive. A removal van is causing havoc for two cars that are trying to get past and up onto nearby Hilltop Road. The driver of the removal van is refusing to back up to allow them to pass, informing them in no uncertain terms to 'back up' themselves and 'fuck off back down the other way'. People are hanging out of windows and standing on porches watching. All except the house with the large brown door. I look in through the windows, half hiding behind the thick trunk of the cherry tree on the grass verge. The blinds are half closed so it's hard to detect anything, but I'm sure I can see some movement inside. As the drivers all begin to shout at each other – one, the driver of a small Nissan Micra, seems to have taken it upon himself to step out of his car to have a go at the removal van driver – I slowly walk down the grass verge towards her house. I walk across Toledo Road as a fight breaks out: pushing and shoving more than anything. There are three buzzers at the door, a total of three flats inside the house. I stand there looking at them, the mêlée erupting on the street as more drivers step out of their cars. I ring all three at the same time; whoever lives here can all answer the communal door together. Nothing. I press them again. Still nothing. Then I press each buzzer one after the other, waiting a few seconds between each, worried that in pressing them at the same time the signal might have short-circuited or something. This seems to work, as I can soon sense some movement in the communal hallway. After a few more seconds the door slowly begins to open. A man greets me in just a pair of boxer shorts. He's trim, muscular and covered in tattoos. I've clearly woken him up.

'What!?'

'Er . . . Does . . . Does Laura live here?'

'Who? No.'

'No . . . I mean, is there a girl who lives here with blonde hair, big eyes . . .'

'Lots of girls live here . . . Who do you want?'

'Pardon?'

'Girls . . . You want girls . . . You come back later, we have plenty girls for you later.'

'Wait . . . Wait . . . What do you mean?'

The door shuts in my face. It doesn't take me long to realise what he means. I feel like puking. I walk away, as the man from the Nissan Micra is running back to his car, the man from the removal van chasing after him. I walk away from Toledo Road, my ears ringing, dizzy and nauseous. I realise one thing: I know where I need to be tonight before I visit the Sunset Bar.

you must have found something

I spend the late afternoon back on the island in Uncle Rey's caravan. It's about time I attempt to start what I came here to do: to clear and remove his private belongings. I decide to start with packing his clothes into bin bags so that they can go to a charity shop. Items of clothing are scattered about his caravan where he'd left them: on tables in heaps and under the bed, in the kitchenette and bathroom, on the floor by his record collection. It takes me over an hour to collect them, neatly folding them up before putting them in the bags. I separate them: jeans in one bag, trousers in another, et cetera. While I'm folding his T-shirts I pick up one that catches my eye. At first I don't realise, but it's a Dr Feelgood T-shirt. I like it: plain black with a print that simply reads *Oil City Confidential* in white. I give it a sniff: it reeks of sweat and cigarette smoke. I throw it aside, determined to give it a wash in the sink and wear it at some point.

After I finish, I place the bin bags – twelve in total – outside by the door. If I'm up to it I'll take them to 2nd Hand Rose. I feel like I've accomplished something at last. I take a shower. It feels glorious, as if I haven't washed in weeks. I sit on the floor, cross-legged, motionless, breathing slowly, thinking of Laura, and let the cold water fall on me. I'm desperate to set eyes on her again. I know she'll be at Toledo Road, and if she's not there, she'll be at the Sunset Bar. I'm getting closer all the time. I can sense it. There's something about the guy who opened the door, like he knows I've been following her, like he's seen me hanging around. It's as if he knows just how much I need to see her. I continue to let the cold water fall on me. I crawl out onto the cold floor. There must be something I can use to dry myself. I grab some tea towels hanging over some boxes near the kitchenette and pat myself dry with them.

I wash Uncle Rey's Dr Feelgood T-shirt in the sink with some washing-up liquid and dry it immediately with a hairdryer. Just as I'm about to get fully dressed for the evening my phone rings. It's Cal.

'Jon, how are you?'

'Cal . . . Just sorting through Rey's clothes . . . I'll take them to a charity shop tomorrow.'

'Oh, nothing you can sell, I imagine . . . Anything else?'

'Yes, I found an amazing T-shirt, looks like it fits, too . . . He wouldn't mind if I wore it, would he?'

'Jon, the man was a tramp. Why would you want to wear his rags? Is there any legal stuff? You know, a will. Have you gone through his papers yet? There was a lot of stuff there, I remember.'

'A will . . . Right . . .'

'Yes . . . have you found anything like that?'

'Oh, that . . . well, no . . . I've not got to any of that yet . . .'

'You must have found something? You've been in that dump since Friday evening.'

'Well, I've been cleaning the place, you know . . . and clearing away his junk first . . . I'll get to all that stuff tomorrow . . .'

'Okay . . . Well, keep me informed . . .'

'Yes.'

'Speak soon, Jon.'

'Yes.'

What's the point? How can I tell Cal Uncle Rey's left me all his money? Everything Uncle Rey had he's given to me. How am I able to explain that when I don't even understand it myself? He'll never believe me. He'll think I forged something, or stole it, or whatever. There's no point in telling him the truth. What does the truth matter? There's no such thing. It's best to keep quiet, to keep low, to move away. And I already know who I want to come with me. I have enough for us both, to start up a new life together some-where, away from everything. As soon as I persuade Laura to come with me, as soon as I've taken her away from whatever it is she needs taking away from, as soon as my work here at the caravan is finished, we'll vanish together. It'll be like we never existed: there'll be no more work, no more phone calls from Cal, just me and her, wherever it is we choose to go.

haunting

I'm back in Southend. I need to waste some time before I go to Toledo Road. The High Street is empty apart from a few stragglers and the odd man walking from the betting shops to the pub. Just before the railway bridge I turn left onto Clifftown Road and walk up it for no other reason than it looks like the sort of side road that might house a pub. And it does, by the look of it: an old Wetherspoons, a dive, toothless old soaks and the dregs of Southend. I walk straight past it to the railway station. From here I can see another pub: a huge Victorian building, dark and elegantly decaying: the Railway Hotel. I pick up my pace and head straight for its doors. There're two men arguing outside. I stand beside them for a while, listening, then I attempt to walk into the pub, but a woman blocks my path. She must be in her late fifties. She's wearing layer upon layer of clothing and has a yellow helium balloon tied to her right wrist. She's in a world of her own, rather childlike, happily bumping into the door frame. She's smiling, singing along to some song that's playing inside, mouthing the words theatrically. In her left hand she's holding a bottle of Newcastle Brown Ale, which at first looks rather incongruous but then after a short while begins to make perfect sense. She stops in her tracks and stares at me for some time.

'I've blocked your way . . . the Tupenny Bunters are on in a minute . . . Great little band . . .'

' . . .'

'You look so much like an old friend of mine . . .'

'It's okay . . .'

'No really, it's freaking me out, dearie . . . you really look like him . . .'

113

'Really.'

'He was a dear friend ... A good, dear friend ... lived on Canvey.'

'Where?'

'On Canvey ... A good, dear friend.'

'...'

'He passed away ...'

'...'

'So sad ...'

'Excuse me ...'

I walk away. I can hear the woman calling after me but I don't turn around to look. I can't face the thought of it being Uncle Rey she was talking about. I run into Prittlewell Square and sit down on a bench facing the sea below the cliffs. The sky is dark and blackening quickly; it feels like I've reached the end of the world: nothing but the empty abyss before me. Even the cliffs are falling into it. I understand how clichéd and corny my thoughts are, how others have sat on similar benches and had similar thoughts, but I can't help weaving myself into it, into the grid of others, lost in the same void, the same space. I'm seeing and thinking it right now, so it has to be real, surely? Even if I'm not the originator. I grip tightly on to my stick, so that I don't fall away too, like the cliffs before me have. I sink back into the bench. I try to compose myself, but my head's spinning, my heart is thumping, like I've been spiked with something nasty and fear-inducing, like someone has plugged me into the grid and everything that has gone in before me is now charging through me like all hell has broken loose.

some fucking present

Toledo Road is enveloped in blackness: a thick, deep black that even the street lamps can't seem to penetrate. It's one of the things I miss about London: the street lights are brighter there, and there are more of them, too. London resists night – it's found a way of defeating the blackness. This place is continually surrendering itself to night's pull. There's no escape out here by the estuary.

At the corner of Queensway and York Road stand a group of teenagers, all of them hooded-up, milling around in silence. I slip by them on the other side of the road, crossing when the traffic is between me and them, forming a barrier of machines. I hop over the central barrier and walk up the grass verge on the other side and head straight for Laura's flat. I knock on the door without hesitation. Nothing. I knock again, this time much louder. I look over to the group of teenagers; they're looking over at me, and a couple of them walk up the grass verge towards Toledo Road. I knock on the door again. This time there's some movement behind the door. Seconds later it springs open: it's the same man from earlier. He recognises me immediately.

'You here for the girls?'

'One girl in particular.'

'Come. Follow me . . . Quick . . . In here. Come.'

I follow him into the communal hallway, waiting behind him as he opens the door to his flat. We climb the stairs. The place reeks of weed and body odour. I'm shown into a living room, where two other men are sitting on a stained sofa, both of them smoking weed, staring at the bare wood-chipped wall opposite.

'You sit. Wait here for girls.'

The man points to a faux-leather armchair by the window, its ripped arms fixed with masking tape. The lights in the room are dim and the blinds are closed. It's a depressing room. He walks out of the room slowly. There's some shouting going on in a language I can't quite put my finger on; not quite Polish, further east. It sounds like two or three men, and maybe about three girls. All of them shouting at each other in the same language. The man returns to the room and smiles at me. He clicks his fingers, then waits, clicks them again and then shouts something into the other room. The shouting stops. The two men on the sofa get up and follow him out of the room, leaving me alone. I hear more shouting, this time at the back of the flat, then a number of footsteps going

115

up some stairs into a loft. I sit staring at the floor, my stick resting against my knees.

After about ten minutes the man walks slowly into the room.

'You here for girls?'

'Well, no . . . yes, one girl . . . is there a girl called Laura here?'

'Laura?'

'Yes, a girl called Laura?'

'Eh?'

'Blonde hair . . . beautiful eyes . . .'

'Ah, blonde hair . . . Blonde . . . beautiful . . . Yes, we have beautiful blonde for you . . . you must pay sixty pounds . . . One hour sixty pounds . . . You can do what you want, yes.'

'I just want to talk to Laura.'

'Yes, blonde . . . No stick.'

'Pardon?'

'Stick . . . No stick . . .'

'Oh . . . this? . . . It's okay.'

'No fucking stick.'

'Okay . . . Okay . . .'

'You want blonde?'

'Pardon?'

'Blonde . . . You want to see?'

'Oh. Yes . . .'

He shouts back into the other room. After a short while a girl walks in to join us: heavily made-up, black short skirt, white blouse, stockings and heels. I look at her; if it is Laura then the make-up makes her look different, but I'm sure it's her. It looks like her, I think. It's hard to tell, because her hair is tied back and her lips are now bright red with lipstick and gloss, her eyes blackened with mascara. It looks like her. I'm sure it's her. It has to be her, she looks the same size. She stands there in front of me, staring at me, waiting for me to say something. She looks bored, emotionless, drained of life.

'This is her. Yes. Blonde . . . Good . . . ass.'

'I think . . .'

'Sixty pounds, boss.'

'Oh, I don't . . . I just want to talk to her . . .'

'Sixty pounds . . .'

'Right, yes . . . Right.'

I take three twenty-pound notes from my wallet. I give him the money. As soon as he puts it in his own wallet she walks out of the room. I lean forward in my chair, trying not to stare at her.

'Go . . . Go . . . You follow her.'

I get up and begin to follow her.

'Stick . . . Stick . . . You leave your stick.'

'Oh, yes . . .'

' . . .'

' . . .'

'Follow . . . Follow . . .'

'Ah, okay . . .'

I place my stick on the floor and walk up the stairs at the back of the flat, up to a small room, one of three crudely divided in the attic. I can hear the two men and a girl in one of the rooms. It doesn't sound pretty. I gag a little, trying to regain my composure, but I can't stop shaking. The girl waits for me in the far room, she points to the bed and I sit down on it. She puts some music on a stereo, some Euro-pop stuff that makes me feel queasy. Then she begins to undress slowly.

'No . . . No . . . No . . .'

She stops, alarmed, looking at me like I'm crazy.

'No . . . Not that . . . I just want to talk to you . . .'

' . . .'

'I don't want that . . . I just want to talk to you . . . Talk . . . Do you speak English?'

'Of course I do.'

'Oh . . . good . . . well . . . I just want to talk with you, I don't want anything else.'

'You can do what you want to me . . . You've got just under an hour.'

'Good . . . That's good . . . let's talk . . . Is your name Laura?'

117

'You can call me that, yes.'

'Laura, do you remember me?'

'What?'

'The other day on the pier . . . You told me they were after you . . . You looked scared. Do you remember? On the pier, by the bell?'

'What pier?'

'The other day . . . we were talking to each other . . . You told me that you weren't happy, at least I think you did . . . But you seemed scared of something . . . of someone . . .'

'Look, I don't know what you're talking about . . . Do you want to fuck me?'

'No . . . No . . . No . . . I want to talk to you, Laura . . .'

'You can fuck my arse if you want, rub your dick on my breasts . . . You'd like that, wouldn't you?'

'No . . . Please . . . I can help you. I can help you get out of here. I know it was you on the pier the other day, then swimming in the creek . . . I followed you to the strip club today . . . It's you, I know it's you . . .'

'You followed me? What do you mean you fucking followed me?'

'No, I mean, I saw you today . . .'

'I've not been out today . . . If you've followed me I will tell them downstairs, they'll throw you out . . .'

'No . . . No . . . I've not followed you like that . . . I just need to talk . . . Please, trust me, I can stop all this, I have the money to get you away from here . . .'

'Money?'

'Yes, money, we can move away from here . . .'

'How much do you have?'

'Enough to help you . . .'

'Do you have money on you now?'

'Yes . . .'

'I'll talk if you pay me . . .'

'How much?'

'How much do you have?'

'I've got more than a hundred on me . . . Look, take this twenty . . .'

'Thanks.'

'Do you remember the pier?'

'Oh, yes, the pier. Yes. Whatever, yes.'

'No, seriously . . . Do you remember the pier?'

'. . .'

'Do you remember talking to me on the pier?'

'Er . . . Okay. All right then . . . Yes, I remember talking to you on the pier, yes.'

'By the bell?'

'Yes, the bell.'

'We talked about the pigeons . . .'

'The pigeons . . . Yes, we did.'

'And Canvey . . .'

'Canvey?'

'Canvey Island, you remember?'

'Oh . . . Yes, Canvey Island. I remember now.'

'And then you said to me, you became scared as you said it, you said you shouldn't be talking to me, and that you might be seen . . . Do you remember?'

'Oh, yes, I remember now.'

'Who didn't you want to see you talking to me?'

'What?'

'You were frightened you might be seen talking to me . . . Who, who was that?'

'What?'

'Who are you scared of?'

'You have quite a few of those twenty-pound notes, yes.'

'Here . . . Now tell me . . .'

'Thanks . . . Them . . . I was scared of them.'

'Them?'

'Downstairs, them downstairs . . . I was supposed to be working, I shouldn't have been out, I should have been here.'

'Listen, I can get you out.'

119

'How?'

'We can move away . . . They'll never find you. I have enough money to disappear, to start a new life with . . . please, you've got to trust me.'

'I can't just leave.'

'Why?'

'Er . . . They'll come after me.'

'No they won't . . . they'll just find someone else to take your place . . .'

'I can't just leave . . .'

'Please . . . I think you're the most beautiful girl I've ever seen . . . I've thought that from the first moment I set eyes on you, on the pier . . .'

'Well, mister, if you think that, why don't you want to fuck me now . . . here?'

'Because it's not about that . . .'

'What's it about then?'

'I don't know . . . I can't explain it. Something is happening to me in my life and it's like I have no control over it, like I'm being controlled, like each of my footsteps is being continually written out for me . . . I just know I have to do this . . . That I have to save you . . . Does that make any sense?'

'I get this from men a lot, especially older ones . . .'

'Get what?'

'That I need to be fucking saved. I mean, what's all that about? I don't need to be saved. I can take care of myself . . . All you lonely men . . . What's wrong with you?'

'I'm not lonely . . . I'm not like other men.'

'You're all the same . . . A fucking viper's nest inside your heads . . .'

'No . . . No . . . No . . . I'm honest . . . I've never felt anything like this, for anyone . . . Not even my wife . . .'

'See . . . You're married . . . Typical . . . You're a fucking cliché.'

'I'm not, she left me for another man, she was having an affair with another man she met at work . . . She was seeing him for over a year before she left me . . . with nothing . . . I had nothing.'

'It's not my problem.'

'I am different . . .'

'I don't . . .'

'Please . . . let me take you . . . We can go to Canvey tonight . . .'

'I don't want to go to Canvey . . .'

'Please . . . Anywhere, then?'

'Stop it . . . I don't like this . . . I only have to shout and you'll be thrown out of here.'

'Please, Laura, please . . .'

'Stop calling me that . . . My name isn't fucking Laura . . . I hate that name . . .'

'But the pier . . .'

'You freak . . .'

'But . . .'

'What fucking pier? . . . I've never been on that fucking pier . . . I hate Southend Pier.'

'Please . . . I can help you . . .'

'Fuck off, you're scaring me . . .'

'Please, there's nothing to be scared of . . .'

Before I can finish what I'm saying the door bursts open and the two men from downstairs pull me off the bed and drag me out of the room. I bang my head on the door as they scramble me out. I think I black out in the process, for a few seconds or a minute or two because the next thing I know I'm sitting on the doorstep with one of the men shouting something at me, as the other pokes my stick hard into my gut before pulling me down the porch and onto the pavement, throwing my stick out onto Toledo Road. I stumble to my feet and pick it up, using it to steady myself. I run over to the grass verge and then onto Queensway without looking back at the house, stopping the traffic on the road. I run up York Road towards the High Street, through the gang of youths who were standing on the corner of Toledo Road near the phone box earlier – one of them tries to trip me up, but I somehow manage to dodge his foot. I can hear them laughing at me. I keep running, faster and faster, up the hill towards the bus station.

I sit down on a bench as the pain suddenly begins. My head feels like it's developing a huge lump at the back where it connected. My stomach is burning with pain. I'm in agony. I need to go back to the island, the Sunset Bar can wait.

path of saturn

I arrive back at Uncle Rey's caravan late. I head straight for the key to his shed. The sky is clear now and the deepest black, each star shining brighter than I have ever seen. There's something quite remarkable about them, littering the blackness, like they've just been thrown there. I set up the telescope and retract the roof with the pulley-lever. I know exactly what I want to look at. I swivel the telescope roughly to where I had pointed it the other night, hoping that it's still hanging there, somewhere among the stars. I put my eye to the lens. Nothing. I move the telescope a fraction to the left. Nothing. Then to the right. Nothing. Up. Down. Nothing. Then I look up through the opening in the roof myself; I'm sure I've got the telescope pointing in the right direction. It has to be there. I look back through the lens, focusing and refocusing, moving the viewfinder across the night. Nothing. I can't find it. I begin to feel dizzy, that same sense of vertigo, like when I first set eyes on it: Saturn, that beautiful planet. But this time, now that it's not there, it feels stronger, like I have no control of what is happening to me.

I continue to try to find Saturn, but it's not there. It can't disappear. It can't hide away like this. Things can't have shifted like that, as if nothing had ever happened. Not as much as this, not in a couple of days. I begin to feel sick, like I'm spinning out of control, the lump on the back of my head throbbing, like I'm whirling through the same deep blackness above me, like I'm vanishing too. I need to see it, to make it all stop. I want it all to stop. But it's not there. I want it to reveal itself, so that I can be sure it's still hanging there in the black of night. I look around the shed: there're some charts pinned to the wall, but I don't understand them. I pick up a couple of books, looking for 'Saturn' in their indexes. Nothing. The last book I look at has a chapter called: 'Looking for Saturn in the Night Sky, 2006–2013'. I sit beneath the gaping void of night and read as much of it as I possibly can before the feeling of vertigo takes hold of me again, throwing my eyes off the pages, my head spinning. At the end of the chapter is a chart that makes no sense to me whatsoever. I stare at it. It's quite mesmerising: a series of arcs and giant ellipses, of widening degrees, sweeping diagonally downwards, through the constellations, which I presume to be the path of Saturn in the night sky. But it makes no sense to me. All I know is that somewhere within it is not only Saturn's, but my own place in time. I stare at it, trying to make sense of it, but it's simply impossible for me to connect the chart with the giant expanse of black through the retracted roof of this shed. Again, I look at the path of Saturn depicted on the chart: spiralling downwards in a series of ellipses, turning, spinning through the years, each month, disappearing and becoming visible again. I can't help but think that I'm somehow aligned with it, mirroring its fall through time and space.

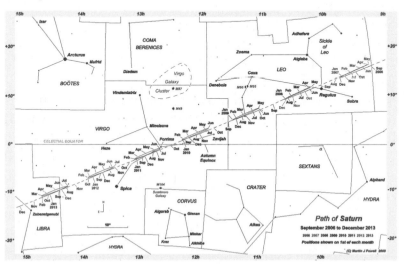

123

I can feel Saturn near. I know it is up there somewhere in the blackness. I just need to see it. That's all I need to do. I look through the lens again. Still nothing. I frantically focus and refocus the lens, even changing it for others: a x12 mm, a x20 mm and then a x25 mm. Nothing, just a blurry void. Saturn's disappeared. It's too much for me to take. I feel like screaming, smashing the whole place up, but I can't. I just can't. I simply crawl into the corner of the shed, where it's darker, where the void can't reach me, and curl up into a ball, hoping that I will disappear, too.

TUESDAY

scene/image

I awake to rain. It's pouring in on me and the telescope through the opening in the roof of the shed. I clamber to my feet, steadying myself with my stick. I struggle with the pulley-lever, trying to shut the roof as quickly as possible so that nothing gets damaged, but the books on the table are sopping wet, as are most of Uncle Rey's charts. I salvage as much as I can – which is still a lot due to the amount of stuff in here. I find a box of rags and try to soak up as much water as possible, but every time I bend down, or reach across the sopping wet floor with a rag a wave of burning pain shoots across my back, up through to the back of my head. I'm in agony. I make my way to the caravan; I need to dry out, to wash, to drink coffee or something, anything to give me the jolt of energy I need.

I struggle up to the caravan, my hands shaking, the pain shooting from the back of my head all the way down my spine. I fall into the caravan and collapse in Uncle Rey's armchair in his bedroom, staring at his record collection, hoping the pain will go away, but it doesn't. I know I have to start work on his possessions, all the legal stuff, but the thought of sifting through all his old paperwork, or packing away his records, is filling me with dread. All I want to do is watch more of his recordings. I lean over to the side of his armchair and reach into a box by the manuscript. I pick up a DVD at random. I sit there, staring at it in my hand; it's a wonder I've not seen it before, I'm sure I've not seen it before. It sends a shiver through me. How have I not seen this DVD before? It's so different from all the rest: it's got a different title for a start. I read it over and over again:

Jon #1 1976–1984

Even if the pain in my back and head was non-existent I think I'd still remain paralysed in the armchair, holding up the DVD in front of me, just staring at it as the terror begins to well up inside me. I'm too frightened to put it in the machine. I have to, I know that, but right now it feels impossible. But there's something else alongside the terror, something compelling me to do otherwise. I suddenly begin to move. I don't know how long it takes me to get up and out of the armchair and put the DVD into the machine, switch on the TV, press play and sit back down again. I stare at the TV screen, waiting for something to happen. Maybe it's blank? Maybe there's nothing whatsoever on here? Then the screen flickers, then . . .

Jon #1 1976–1984: scene/image 1

a room
a TV in the corner of the room
a child kneeling in front of the TV watching a cartoon
aged about six
watching a cartoon
just the back of the child's head
no sound
child suddenly turns around and stares into the camera
smiling
the child knows the person filming
cut to black

I recognise it immediately. It's my father's living room. Filmed a long time ago. It takes me a while to realise that the child kneeling in the room, watching the cartoon, is me. I can tell by the shape of me, the back of my head, the way I'm kneeling. I can tell that it's me. I shudder when my six-year-old self looks down the lens, smiling, beaming from the TV; my face, happy and smiling. I feel sick. Something's not right, something I didn't realise back then. I've no recollection of this ever happening, of ever being filmed in this way. I guess it must be Uncle Rey behind the camera, filming me. On one of his few visits to London.

Jon #1 1976–1984: scene/image 2

inside of a parked car
window frame and window lock of car
rain on window
cigarette smoke
through the window a high street somewhere in London
people walking
red buses
traffic
two people, backs to camera, walking down the street
a small boy holding a man's hand
the small boy looks up to the man as he looks down at the boy
the man is saying something to the boy
the camera zooms in
close shot of boy
side of small boy's face, looking up at the man who is now out of
    shot
then the man and small boy disappear from shot
camera pans back
the man and small boy have turned left off the high street
cut to black

It's me holding my father's hand. I recognise his gait immediately. The POV is unsettling, we obviously had no idea that we were being filmed and again I can't remember the day, although the clothes I'm wearing are vaguely familiar. I guess at once that it's

Uncle Rey behind the camera in his car. He must have driven to London to spy on us. I want to know what my father was saying to me. I really want to know what he was saying to me. I look safe in his company, the way I looked up at him, my father, like I was in awe. My eyes begin to fill up with tears. My first instinct is to pause the film, to phone Cal, but I can't move. I continue to stare at the screen.

Jon #1 1976–1984: scene/image 3

department store
women's clothing
racks
young boy running around through the racks of women's clothes
POV from high up – possibly from stairs to upper floors
boy soon joined by a woman
woman grabs boy and kneels beside him
stern words – the woman is clearly angry
shoppers stop and stare
the boy begins to cry
the woman holds the boy's hand and leads him through the shop
    floor
the camera zooms in after them but is blocked by a row of manne-
    quins
cut to black

Tears are falling down my cheeks. I wipe them away, shaking, glued to the screen. It's my mother I'm watching – and me again. Mother looks young, full of life, busy with it, full of hopes and dreams. Her skin is pale, and her clothes are bright. Whenever I think of her it's usually grey, her clothes miserable: browns and greens. But here, on this screen, my mother is an explosion of colour. It startles me. I've never seen her in this light before. She must have visited, or I was allowed to visit her. I don't know. It's like it never happened. I have no memory of what I have just watched. It's like another life. Another fiction. But, amazingly, there we are.

Jon #1 1976–1984: scene/image 4

a house
a window
a living room
a TV
the light flickering
a man
a boy
the boy is sitting on the man's knee
they are both laughing
watching the TV
door to the room opens
another boy walks in to join them
they all watch the TV together
the man puts his arm lovingly around the other boy
the boy sitting on the knee of the man suddenly turns around and
    looks at the camera
hedgerow
pavement
lamp post
footsteps
car
POV through car window
a house
a window
a boy is looking out from the window back at the camera
cupping hands around eyes
cut to black

A cold shiver runs through me. I think I remember this happening.
I remember watching the TV with my father, Cal joining us, and
then suddenly sensing somebody else's presence outside. I remember
seeing him, at least I think I do, running back towards his car. I'm
sure I remember it. I must have been about ten or twelve, I'm not

too sure. Ever since that day, I've always been aware of that feeling: the sense that someone is near, watching me, always watching, wherever I go. It's never left me.

I watch the entire DVD. There are about twenty or so separate images and scenes. Mostly of me and quite a few of Mother: across streets, through windows, across playing fields, during the summer holidays, right up until my mid-teens. Then: nothing. Just blackness, like the blackest of nights: without stars, without Saturn. I fall back into the armchair, wiping away the tears from my cheeks. I feel numb, like I've fallen from a great height and somehow survived. Then something strange happens: another image appears. Like a hidden track on an old CD:

Jon #1 1976–1984: hidden scene/image

inside a caravan

this caravan

the same boy

just a little older

a voice off-camera: 'Go on then . . . Go on then . . . say it . . .'

the boy: 'No . . . I don't want to . . .'

the voice: 'Aw go on, Jon . . . Just for Uncle Rey . . . You said you would, before your dad . . .'

the boy: 'I've forgotten . . .'

the voice: 'You know . . . the message to your future self . . . the message we made up for you to listen to when you're older . . .'

the boy: 'I've forgotten . . .'

the voice: 'We practised . . . Go on . . .'

the boy: 'There is no future me . . . He's a ghost . . .'

the voice: 'Just for Rey . . .'

the boy: 'He's a ghost . . . a ghost . . . a ghost . . .'

the voice: 'What do you mean . . . a ghost?'

the boy runs out of shot

the camera falls to the floor

the voice: 'Jon . . . Jon . . . Jon . . .'

Blackness

I'm shaking. I play the scene back and immediately watch it again. My own words drill a hole into me: 'There is no future me . . . He's a ghost . . .' I have no idea what I mean, or who I'm talking about. I look scared, or uncomfortable, like I want to be elsewhere. I take out my phone. I play the entire scene, but this time I don't just watch it: I film it with my phone. I watch myself through its lens: the image of me on the TV, and the caravan wall surrounding it like a frame, until the scene ends. I'm shaking. I stop filming as the TV screen turns black. I immediately re-watch the scene: this time through my phone, the scene I've just recorded. My voice sounds distant, discordant, like I'm speaking from some other place, something governed by circuitry. I look at myself, my shaky, minimised image; pixellated, fainter, a shade lighter. Some sort of digitised interference flickers across the screen, just before the moment I speak to Uncle Rey. I speak the same words in complete synchronicity, just as I uttered them all those years ago: 'There is no future me . . . He's a ghost . . .' I stop as soon as the scene ends on my phone. It feels like I've captured something, some form of truth. I stare at the blank screen on my phone. Suddenly I notice something reflected on the screen: something in the caravan, something behind me in the window in the other room. I throw my phone onto the bed: I'm sure I just saw someone looking into the caravan, looking at me. I'm sure someone's been watching me, watching this whole scene.

I get up and walk into the front room. There's more light here, streaming in through the same window. I look through it: there's no one there, it might have been a shadow caused by the sea wall, or something else: the way I was holding the phone, a flicker of light. There's definitely no one else here. I look out along the grass verge and up to the sea wall: nothing, not a soul. I walk away from the window and slump into the other armchair, still shaking. I sigh, reaching over to pick up Uncle Rey's manuscript. I begin to read it, from the beginning.

camouflage

Reading *Vulgar Things* takes up most of the morning. It's hard to follow and, if I'm honest, parts of it are complete and utter gibberish, but it doesn't seem to matter – as the gibberish seems to make sense in spite of this. Like it's supposed to be gibberish, like the gibberish is some sort of code, and only the readers who go along with it will begin to understand. The whole manuscript is a series of blackouts, the blank spaces in Uncle Rey's life, those dark moments when things became truly unbearable for him. In among all this is his vision: the idea to replicate, to rebuild, to take the past and rewrite it, to right everything he felt was wrong: to create the truth.

It feels good simply to read his text, to let it exist on its own terms: as a text, resisting the urge to edit. There are moments in the manuscript that feel utterly real to me in their telling and others that feel totally foreign. The gibberish begins to make more sense. Most of it is about Laura, his Laura, and his brother. Something had happened, something traumatic, something to do with Laura, that is never made explicit, only hinted at – camouflaged, masked and revealed all at the same time. It makes the whole thing far more intriguing. As much as his life is a mystery to me, as much as I once looked up to him because of these little mysteries – his strange ways, the strange way he was around everyone, his being distant and close all at the same time – because of this I hate him, I hate him so much right now, because of his aloofness. Why has he left us with all this stuff? This horrid detritus? These utterances, fragments and ciphers to be unravelled by me, or whoever?

And then there's the question of all this money: I feel guilty about the money, why has he burdened me with all this money? I feel like I'm falling deeper into his world: a dark, dark place in which the light of everyday life has been almost extinguished, where that last chink, which might have survived, is unable to escape. *Vulgar Things* is a mystery to me: all his thoughts condensed and interwoven with that other book, the *Aeneid*. What's the point in trying to splice them together, what's he trying to achieve in that? Why doesn't he just tell it like it is? Instead of rubbing out everything he wrote, masking it, erasing it from existence, smothering it with other, older, more classical words. Why do this? Why purposely hide everything you want to say? His words, mixed with those images of me, roll around inside my tired head, prickling behind my eyes. I can't escape them, they're pulling me in.

it's a short chapter

I must have fallen asleep, as the next thing I know the manuscript has fallen to the floor from the arm of the chair, each of its pages scattering across the worn-out, stinking carpet, random pages fluttering beneath the open window. I get up and gather them together, but it's impossible to put the manuscript back together as the pages aren't numbered. I could scream, but I act calmly, as if I'm tidying the table after a pleasant meal with friends. I look around to see if I have missed any of the pages. Then I see it, wedged beneath the coffee table and a pair of walking boots: one entire section of the manuscript, intact. I pick it up. It's a short chapter titled: 'The Underworld'. I set it aside on a shelf, away from the rest of the manuscript.

a different narrative of the same thing

I need some food. I pull myself together and head out of the caravan to the Lobster Smack. The pub is empty, apart from Mr Buchanan sitting at the bar, reading a newspaper. It takes him a while to look up. He greets me with a broad smile.

'Jon . . . Jon . . . Young Jon . . . How are we today?'

'I've felt better . . .'

'What would you like to drink?'

'Bloody Mary . . . Double vodka . . .'

'Heavy night?'

'Something like that . . .'

'I didn't see you yesterday . . .'

'No . . .'

'You busy clearing that caravan?'

'Oh . . . Yes . . . Cleared out his clothes . . . And other stuff.'

'Listen, Jon . . . Have you read more of his book? What's it called?'

'Oh, yes . . . *Vulgar Things* . . . yes, I have . . . It's a work of brilliance . . . There's this one chapter that I'm going to be working on . . .'

'That's good . . . And what about everything else? Is that all nearly done and dusted?'

'Well . . . I . . . nearly . . .'

'Here . . . a double . . .'

'Thanks . . .'

'We need it vacant by the weekend, remember . . .'

'Yes, I remember. It will be . . . There's lots of stuff . . . personal stuff, stuff that other family members should look at . . . I don't know . . . They all pretty much hated him.'

'You have a large family . . .'

'No . . . Not really, I don't know where my mother is and . . . well, my father, Rey's brother, died some time ago now. They didn't have the best of relationships, you know . . .'

'I'm sorry to hear . . .'

'You see, this is the thing . . . *Vulgar Things* . . . his book . . . Well, I think it has something to do with, it's about my father.'

'What do you mean?'

'There's just something about it . . . Not like he's apologising, but more like he's offering an alternative, a different narrative of the same thing . . .'

'Thing? I'm not sure I follow . . .'

'That's just it . . . I haven't worked out what that thing is yet, I just sense that it has something to do with my father.'

'Jon, you have to concentrate on the job at hand . . . Clearing away his belongings . . . This place . . .'

'The island?'

'Yes, this place . . . It's a strange place, it entraps people, it can do funny things to people's minds . . . It's such an odd place . . . You'd be best leaving as soon as you're finished, don't hang around here . . . get back to where you belong . . . I mean you well, I like you, you're always welcome here. Just don't get too involved with this place . . .'

'I'm trying not to, thanks for the advice.'

Silence suddenly falls between us. I take sips from my Bloody Mary. It's just what I need. We remain sitting at the bar, staring at the optics in front of us, allowing the silence to consume us. I'm in two minds: a) stay at the caravan to finish what I have to do, or b) head back into Southend as soon as I'm feeling better, back to Toledo Road. I quickly decide on neither option: I'll wait until the evening to go back into Southend. I'll finally check out the Sunset Bar, where I know Laura works. Maybe she'll be able to talk to me there, away from the flat and those men. I turn to Mr Buchanan once my mind is set.

'Mr . . . Robbie . . . Are you serving food?'

'Yes, we are . . .'

'Could I have the biggest fry-up your chef can muster? I'll pay extra . . .'

'Of course . . .'

'With a pot of tea?'

'Sure . . .'

'I'm famished.'

cliché

I stay in the Lobster Smack for a good few hours, well after finishing my fry-up – which was good – and Mr Buchanan has left the pub for a 'meeting' in Leigh-on-Sea. I drink peppery tea and a couple more Bloody Marys while reading the newspapers. I'm feeling better. The pub has filled up somewhat and I bathe in the general brouhaha.

The talk is football and recession, and something about a man who's renovated a Thames sailing barge that got caught on the rocks near the jetty. A couple of locals try to strike up conversations with me, now that they've seen me in here a few times, but I'm not really in the mood, so I ignore them. Instead I think up ways in which I can make Laura mine, but they all seem idiotic, the thoughts of a man who's lost the plot, but something in me seems to resist the feeling of humiliation that goes with such thoughts and I continue to scheme and to run through imaginary scenarios: I'd take Laura on my arm and lead her away from Southend for good.

I know my behaviour is a cliché, but I don't care, something that doesn't surprise me any more. None of it matters, by which I mean everything else other than Laura and me. Even Uncle Rey's manuscript fades from my mind as Laura takes over again: the desire to be with her, for her to look at me the way she did the first time I set eyes on her. I need her in my life, in whatever manifestation – even another fleeting glimpse of her, if that's all I'm offered. For her just to walk into this pub now. I'd die happy on the spot if she did that.

the underworld

The rain is pouring. I sit on the train to Southend clutching my stick, my pockets stuffed with twenty-pound notes, maybe about three hundred pounds in total, maybe a bit more. I must have gone to the cash point but I can't remember. In my rucksack is the chapter from Uncle Rey's manuscript, 'The Underworld'. The air inside the carriage is stuffy. I pull out the manuscript from my bag and begin to read.

The Underworld

It was a duty call, really, a way of paying my respects, when death hits you, it forces you to reconsider things, I guess thats why i went, but its never easy, people warned me along the way, like they always do, people like that, id already found the ring he'd given me when we were small, it had taken me an age to find it, it really had, I looked and I looked every where, once it was found I could take it with me, lay it by his cofin, return it to him – where it rightly belonged, Id never forgotten the day he gave it to me, when we were small, little nippers, before we were teenagers even – he'd found it by a tree when we were out exploring, it was the most beautiful thing he'd ever saw, this huge ring, golden, the image of a bough etched into it, he just found it there, as if he was meant to find it, like some one had left it there for him, just for him, only him, 'I want you to have this' he said 'why?' 'because you're my brother and it will take care of you, just like I will' I clutched it to my chest, we told no one, knowing it would be taken away from us and sold, or given away to someone else, i kept the ring with me all the time never leaving it out of sight, sleeping with it under my pillow at night, it became part of me, completely me, only my brother could take it away should he have wanted to . . .

the funeral was busy, it took me a long time to get there, I travelled by foot, crossing long distances, all the while thinking of him, wanting to see him, it was a black day, there were people i didnt want to see, to set eyes on, to speak to, but I knew she'd be there and wed have to at least acknowlege each other like you do at these occasions, it had been such a long day, such a long time, Laura, that beautiful thing who'd haunted my dreams, my days, my thoughts, i figured just being there, to hand back his ring, dropping it onto the coffin would be enough for her to acknowledge me, to just simply smile, or nod her head, it had been such a long time, its all supposed to be under the bridge now isnt it? all that stuff we went through, the boys all growing up, i would have to see them too, of course I would, what would they make of me? what would the youngest make of me? the youngest, the most perfect of all . . .

i was walking in the darkness, towards him, his coffin, with shadows all around us and nights loneliness above, there was no life ahead or within, like walking in a vast wood with no light, the sun blotted out by Saturn or moon or nothingness where black night has stolen the colour from the world, where nothing exists but him, there, dead, vanished from me and us, for as long as ever will take to die itself, hiding from me all of those things i wanted to say to him, because he knew, he knew what i'd done to him and I had never spoken of it to him, or mentioned it to any one and it was tearing me apart, ruining me inside, turning me, against my will, into darkness . . .

Before the church is a giant and shady elm tree, spreading branches like arms to greet me, to greet you, full of years, nightmares cling to its branches, false dreams, beasts prowl around it, the centaurs guard its secrets, I was struck with sudden dread, i drew my stick and presented it – but each monster was an apparition, bodiless, hot air, hollow and airy, from this tree I followed the path to the church, we all did, paying our respects . . .

i held the ring tightly in my hand, I thought I caught sight of her, my Laura, it could have been her, I was sure it was her, standing there, by the gates, black ribbons in her hair, dressed in black, cheekbones high on her drooping face, I looked back and she had gone . . .

But i knew it wasn't her, It could never be her, she didn't exist anymore, there was nothing left, like she had been torn to shreds in the hill, or just evaporated before us, yes, that's what she did when she walked out on him, on me, never telling him why, never contacting me again, she vanished from both of our lives, like that, like a ghost finally being expelled from our imaginations, Laura had disappeared, she'd beaten time and vapourised herself into perfect nothingness, becoming blackness, surrounding the night that had befallen us both . . .

mud and murk seethed in the abyss – I fell into it in going there, darker into the pitch of blackness, it was enormous and engulfing

138

and there was nothing I could do but walk towards him there in the cold dirt, the church emptying out as they laid him to rest in the mud, I began to choke, it was maddening to me, why hadn't I told him, the reason Laura left him, was because of me, but i could never tell him, there was nothing i could do to change this . . .

they were all looking at me now, of course they were, as I walked amongst them, I raised my arms, my stick, to say these words of mine, I threaten no violence, i'm here with you, with him my brother, please let go of your alarm, set it free, monsters at the gate there is no need to come forth, I am harmless, I mean you no harm, i am here because you asked it of me, I am here out of respect for what must be forgiven, the cries rang out all around me, the church-yard in blackened ruins, as if the darkness had stolen life itself from them, a death before their time, why are you here if you react to me in such a way? why do this to yourselves? i am here to speak once and for all . . .

i walked towards the hole in the ground, dug for him, his place in the universe, I watched as they lowered him, all ills must be made right this very day they said, I threw the ring onto his coffin, down with the black dirt, down into the blackness . . .

seek to know the terrible sorrow of your family, fate will allow the world merely to see him, no more, and thereafter allow him to live there no longer . . .

Oh brother, what did i do to you, I ruined you, I was the sole cause, oh brother you never knew, you loved Laura too, as did I, she wasn't to know, to blame, nothing is by her hand, oh brother forgive me, I didnt want this to happen, i didn't want you to die alone, I will take this with me, this burden, the mark, throughout my life, I will die like you, a lonely man, caught by desire, I will see to this, guide me from this blackness in your forgiveness, away from this churchyard, away from these people, guide me home, away from

139

here, oh brother, please forgive me, oh brother, he's mine, oh brother, your youngest is mine, he's mine oh brother, he's mine . . .

I stop reading. The realisation hits me hard. I shudder. It makes me stand up, even though the train is moving. I lean on my stick, like I'm wounded. An old man opposite me asks if I'm okay.

'I'm . . . Yes . . . I'm fine.'

I don't know what else to say to him. I need to calm down, to drink something strong, to eat again, to jump into the sea at the end of the pier. All the usual questions begin to litter my head, all the *whys?* and the *what ifs?* and countless images of my mother, my father, all of them flooding into me: Mother's jet-black hair, her perfume, the way she laughed. But one thing sticks: her with him, with Rey, I can't picture it, I can't see them together. It doesn't seem possible. I recall all the times people had made passing comments about how much I looked like him. I remember that he doted on me more than Cal when we were children, which always made Cal jealous, and probably fuelled his hatred of Uncle Rey. I remember that he'd always ask about Mother, and how I was, before he ever asked about anyone else. I remember everything my feeble mind will allow, piecing it all together in seconds, here on the train, as it slowly pulls out of Chalkwell Station.

failing light

As the train pulls into Southend Central Station I'm too afraid to get off it. I don't want to face anything else. But I get off anyway, just as the doors are closing and everyone else has got off. The station manager looks at me disapprovingly, but I ignore him. I waltz through the station, my stick tapping in rhythm on the platform, trying to block out what I've just read. The rain is still pouring. Before heading to the Sunset Bar I head down towards Toledo Road, moving as if programmed to do so. I feel like it's my last chance, my only chance to find my Laura, my vision from the pier, that beautiful face I can't shake from within me.

This time, instead of waiting on the grass verge, I wait directly outside the house in which her flat is, or the flat she was in yesterday. I rub the back of my head and my ribs and wait for her to appear, Uncle Rey's words swirling within me, the night beginning to darken all around me. The street lamps are murky, at least two of them flickering to my right up the street, casting a gloomy orange strobe across the wet pavement. It's dizzying to look at, so I turn my back on the pavement and stare at the front door, looking for movement within, steadying myself, trying to concentrate, ignoring the failing light.

There's somebody there, looking at me through one of the four small panes of glass. I jump back, swallowing the cold air, nearly falling. The door opens, it's Laura, it's her. I'm sure it's her: she looks different, though, without make-up and her hair's been cut shorter. It doesn't look like her, but it is, I know it's her.

'What are you doing standing outside here?'

'I'm waiting for you . . .'

'What?'

'I'm here for you . . . You remember me, right?'

'I have no idea who you are . . .'

'Last night? We spoke, we talked about stuff together . . . in there . . .'

'What? . . .'

'They threw me out . . .'

She walks down the steps quickly, looking back to the house to check if anyone is there, before whispering in my ear.

'Meet me in the Sunset Bar later tonight. I can't talk here.'

'What time? What time? . . . Wait.'

She turns and runs back up into the house, shutting the door in my face. I can smell her perfume all around me, the air is thick with it, it's strong and musky. I breathe it in so that I never forget.

pointless

In spite of the prolonged downpour, Southend is busy with shoppers and college kids taking advantage of the later opening hours most of the shops have introduced. I head towards Waterstones and then turn right onto Clarence Road where I enter a pub called Clarence Yard, which, by the look of it, used to be an old warehouse, the bar itself situated in the old cobbled courtyard that's now closed off to the elements via an impressive glass roof. A barmaid with bleached blonde hair and a warm and friendly smile serves me. I take a table by the right of the bar, up on what must have been an old loading bay. I take a sip of my cider and rest my stick against a chair next to mine.

I contemplate reading the manuscript again, but it's still too much. I've gleaned from it all I need for one day, there's no point in going over it all again. I even contemplate giving it a little line edit, changing everything back to upper case where it should be, changing a few lines, but what's the point in that? My project's changed: editing this manuscript is pointless now as it can't ever be read by anyone else.

it has to be her

I leave the Clarence Yard after a couple of hours. I feel an urge to be closer to the sea. I want simply to sit by it in the dark, but the rain's falling in sheets and I know that I've a long evening ahead of me. I walk up the High Street, sheltering in doorways from the rain along the way, heading away from the sea and the darkness and towards the Victoria, an indoor shopping mall, where I figure I can sit down and have a coffee somewhere and wait for the rain to pass.

The place is heaving. I walk through, dripping wet, dodging gaggles of teenagers, women with prams, junkies and old ladies. I find a seat at the Birdwood, a café, and order a large latte from a miserable-looking lady behind the counter. The coffee is good. From where I'm sitting I've a clear view of the two escalators that take the shoppers up to and down from the upper level of the shopping mall. I watch people as they're fed up and down from the upper level, parallel to each other, never acknowledging each other as they pass. A silent geometry surrounds me, the entire mall a complex system of lines, angles, triangles, bisectors, trapezoids, arcs, concurrent figures, grids and oblique lines. I realise that this system of geometry is mapping itself out everywhere I look, in every building, on every street, house, high street, town and city, the most rudimentary of things. Even when I look through the telescope in Uncle Rey's shed I'm looking up into the vastness of space through some kind of silent geometry, something poetic and unfathomable. Even the vertigo I feel when I think of Saturn hanging there in the blackness of space is pure geometry to me – so is its absence, those moments when I feel like clinging on to the ground beneath my feet, so that I don't fall off the earth into the same blackness. Gravity isn't enough in situations such as mine; at least the escalators seem to be defeating all this, delivering us upwards.

I gaze up the escalator as it carries a woman and a small child to the top. I follow them all the way up. It's at that moment, just as they reach the top, that I see her: Laura. On the upper floor. I'm sure it's her. Her hair looks longer, and I've only just seen her and she was wearing different clothes back then – she could have changed, I guess. She's walking along the upper level, towards the escalator; it carries her down, just her, looking dead ahead. Time seems to warp, to slow down all around me as I watch her, looking dead ahead, her delicate hands resting on each rail, gliding down towards me from above. As she hits the bottom she carries on walking seamlessly, gliding past the café to the right of my table, never blinking, staring dead ahead, floating almost.

I get up, leaving my half-finished latte where it is, carrying my stick so that it doesn't hit the floor, tightening the rucksack on my back as I walk, following her through the mall, around gaggles of college kids, mothers and their children, office workers, through the front doors and outside onto the square. It's her, it's the same way she walks, that day on the pier, the exact same walk, I'm sure. What's she doing here? Shouldn't she be in the flat on Toledo Road? Maybe she had to pop out for something? But isn't she waiting to go to work at the Sunset Bar? Isn't that what she's supposed to be doing? She doesn't look like everybody else, like she has something ordinary to do. She's walking with purpose, an apparition in the streets, a lone petal floating along the pavements in the breeze. Everything else around her blackens: the buildings, the cars, the cyclists, the people, everything darkens except her, floating, gliding along. It has to be her. I want to walk right up to her, to smell her perfume again, to hear her voice, her strange, lilting accent. It has to be her, my beautiful vision at the pier.

they kiss

I follow her back down the High Street, towards the sea, hanging back when she stops to look in Ann Summers and then New Look. I sit on a public bench, trying to look normal, like everyone else, as she steps into Greggs to buy a cheap sandwich. I do my best to look like part of the background. She heads to Pier Hill below the Palace Hotel. I follow her, closer this time, straining my neck in the hope that I can catch her perfume, something I want more than anything right now.

Just as she reaches the bottom of Pier Hill she's greeted by a man. They kiss. My heart sinks. They embrace. The man is in his early twenties, I guess, with slicked-back hair, black. He's wearing skin-tight, stone-washed jeans, trainers and a black leather jacket, zipped up closely to his chin. I pretend I'm looking out to the estuary, even though I can't really see it from where I'm standing. I even take out my phone and pretend to take pictures of the scene I can't see, all the while watching them from the corner of my eye.

After the embrace they both step back a little and become serious with each other, like they have business to do and the kiss and embrace was all an act – which it seems to be as she opens her jacket and hands the man a large, folded Jiffy bag, obviously stuffed with money. After the transaction they both turn and walk off in opposite directions. He walks away, back down towards the arcades on the esplanade, while she heads back up Pier Hill towards me. I panic and stare at my phone awkwardly, trying to act as inconspicuous as I can, even trying to hide my stick on my blind side, but it's no use, we somehow gain eye contact. I try to smile, but it comes out all wrong, nervy and suspicious, even though she simply looks straight through me as if I'm not really there.

'Hello . . .'

'. . .'

'Hello, it's me . . .'

'Pardon?'

'Fancy seeing you here . . .'

'What . . .'

'You and me . . . bumping into each other again . . .'

'What do you mean?'

'I just saw you . . . I mean . . . we just spoke at the house . . .'

'I've never seen you before in my life . . .'

'Wait! . . . Wait! . . . Toledo Road . . . Toledo Road . . . Last night, do you remember?'

'Stop following me . . .'

'But we're meeting tonight . . . remember?'

'Go away!'

'At the Sunset Bar . . . You said you wanted to talk with me, that you couldn't talk outside the house . . .'

'Stop following me . . . now!'

'But I'm trying to help you . . .'

'Stop fucking following me, you fucking pervert!'

'Please . . .'

'I'll call the fucking police . . .'

'Okay . . . Okay . . .'

I stop following her. I watch her all the way to the top of Pier

Hill, before she walks away, on to the High Street and out of sight. I stand there, looking up the hill. It must have been an act, she mustn't be able to talk to me, to be seen to be talking to anyone. I look behind me, down the hill towards the esplanade, checking to see if anyone is there, but Pier Hill is empty, the man has gone. She must have been worried he was still there, that's why she acted the way she did. I need to speak to her, to tell her everything will be okay. I look out over the estuary: yet more black rain clouds are racing over from Sheerness and the hills of Kent. I look up, following the clouds back over me. I can see a terrace behind me, above my head at the Palace Hotel. I steady myself with my stick. The terrace overlooks the entire estuary.

waxy with sweat

I leave my coat, rucksack and stick in the cloakroom, and take a seat by the looming windows. The view is spectacular, even in the fading light. I can trace the entirety of the black storm as it sweeps into Southend. Sheets of slanting rain; they hit the pier and then the amusement arcades below, and finally the looming windows separating me from their tumult, smearing each pane with grease and grime. It's spectacular: everything blurred above and below me, the outlines of familiar things distorted by the rain, everything morphing into a black-greyness that I want to reach out into and touch, such are the varieties of its textures and hues. It's hard to believe that anything else can exist outside it.

The early evening passes slowly. After the storm abates reality seeps back in through the looming panes of glass. A man and a woman enter the bar; they fall onto a sofa behind my table, near enough for me to listen to their conversation without making it obvious. I quickly turn around to look at them: the man is tall and lanky, he looks like a retired headmaster of a public school – he sounds like one, too. She's local, her voice slurring and grating, dressed in jeans too tight for her figure and a vest-top that can hardly contain her chest. She looks out of place. I'm positive the management will ask her to leave, but they don't.

'Oh, I love you, you know . . . I want to take care of you for the rest of my life . . .'

'Aw, really, that's nice . . . I like you, too.'

'I feel like I've met my soul mate . . .'

'Aw, really . . .'

'Yes, I just wish it could have happened a long time ago . . .'

'Aw, that's so sweet to say . . .'

'I love everything about you . . . But I love your body the most . . . I haven't seen a body as good as yours in such a long time . . .'

'What about your wife's? . . . I bet she's really nice . . .'

'We don't . . .'

'Have sex? . . . Aw . . .'

'No . . . We don't . . . It's dead . . . That's why you . . .'

'Aw, that's so sad . . . I'm really sorry to hear that . . . it's a shame . . .'

'But I have you now, my beautiful soul mate . . .'

'Soul mates . . . I like that . . .'

'We are . . .'

'Do you still buy your wife presents?'

'Yes, sometimes, to make her happy . . .'

'Aw . . . Nobody buys me presents . . .'

'I will . . . My beautiful . . . I'll buy you anything you want . . .'

'Really . . . Would you?'

'Of course, my love . . . I'd like to take you ballroom dancing . . .'

'. . .'

'Would you like that?'

'. . .'

'That would be so good, to take you dancing, to show you off . . . Can you dance?'

'Like on *Strictly* . . .?'

'Yes, proper ballroom dancing . . .'

'They wear lovely dresses . . . I'd need a new dress . . .'

'Would you like that?'

'Oh yes, a dress . . .'

'And the dancing . . .?'

'Oh yes . . . dancing, yes.'

'Ah, my love . . .'

'Hmmm . .'

'What is it?'

'I'd never be able to afford one . . .'

'A dress?'

'Yes . . .'

'I'll provide you with a dress, my beautiful . . . we can go up to London one day and I'll buy you one . . .'

'Aw, that's so sweet . . . They have nice ones in Selfridges . . .'

'Yes, they do, my love, my beautiful love . . .'

'We can go next week.'

'Yes, we can . . .'

'Oh, Timothy, you're amazing . . .'

'You are, too. Mandy, I love you so much . . .'

As the man says this, the woman breaks out into a fit of coughing and sniffling. I look over at her, she's clearly withdrawing from crack cocaine or something, her emaciated face is waxy with sweat and she is continuously rubbing her nose, congealed bits of white spittle congregate in the corners of her mouth, visible even from where I'm sitting.

'Hey, hey, my love . . . Shall I get you a tissue . . .'

'Oh yes, sorry, please . . . yes . . .'

When he gets up to go to the bar she immediately stops coughing and begins to text someone on her phone. When the man arrives back with the tissues, she begins to sob.

'Hey, hey, my love, my poor, poor love . . . What's wrong?'

' . . '

'Please, my love . . . What's wrong?'

' . . '

'Tell me, please . . .'

'It's . . . It's . . .'

148

'It's what?'

'. . .'

'What is it, my poor love?'

'It's my landlord . . . I owe him rent . . . Oh, I've been so stupid, so, so stupid . . . It's so hard, bringing up four kids alone, they're grown up now, I never see them, they never help, but still . . . I have no money, I didn't pay my rent for months, just so I could get through Christmas, you know, have a good Christmas, you don't think about the debt at the time, and I've not paid him . . . and now . . . and now . . .'

'What is it, my love . . . What is it?'

'He says he's going to evict me . . .'

'When?'

'Next week . . . I have nowhere to live, my ex is a psycho . . .'

'How much do you owe him?'

'. . .'

'How much?'

'. . .'

'Mandy, I love you, how much . . ?'

'Four thousand eight hundred quid . . .'

'Mandy, my poor love, it's okay . . .'

'Really . . .'

'Yes, my poor love . . . I'm going to help you . . . I'll transfer the money . . . I have the money for you . . . I have money in banks doing nothing . . . I have lots of money to help you. I can help you . . .'

'It's more like five thousand five hundred . . .'

'That's okay, my love . . .'

'Aw, Timothy, you're so kind . . . You're such a kind beautiful man . . . I'll give you my bank details, we can go to the bank . . . then we can go to my flat . . .'

'Yes, my love . . . Anything for you . . .'

I leave them to it. There's no point in interrupting him, to tell him to stop, that it's all a lie and she's simply playing him for a fool. Even when he gets up to go to the Gents, I leave him alone, it's not worth it. These things must run their own course.

149

I return my gaze to the estuary. The storm is racing in again. I can see others behind it, all waiting in line to hit Southend, these looming windows, one after the other. Now the lightning is forking from the dense clouds, hitting the water about six miles out. It's like a light show out there: the different colours of the sea – from almost black to deepest green in a flash. The bursting-full clouds drooping lower now, like everything is about to come crashing down, or a great weight is pushing it towards us. This time the rain falls even harder, so much so that I take a large breath when it hits the windows. Down below, this side of the pier, I can just about see the outline of a Thames sailing barge, struggling through the torrent. I wonder what it's doing out there in this weather at this time of the evening. It's a magnificent vessel, beautiful in design, completely unique. It looks like it's doing okay out there. I worry about it being hit by the lightning. The sight of this flat-bottomed barge makes me feel extremely proud for some reason, and I begin to feel a strange kind of emotion well up inside. My eyes fill up, for a start, and I struggle to contain myself, to hold everything back, swallowing and coughing, but I manage it, something that pleases me.

I soon notice another barge behind the first, and then another, and another. Five in total, all edging their way up the estuary in the failing light. It's a truly beautiful sight. It must be a convention, or a club. I stand up and walk towards the window, just as another sheet of rain hits it. Everything is blurred, but I can still just about make them out. I try to take some photos with my phone, but they don't come out too well. The photos look dark and murky, blurred into a wash of grey turning into deepest black, the blood-red sails of the barges just about visible in the blackness around them.

When the light eventually fades I sit back at my table and flick through the photos, about twenty-five in total. If I flick through them quickly I can trace the barges' movement along the estuary, as they move en masse. I'm struck by their blood-red sails, deeply thick red against the black of night. It makes the photos feel like a moving painting, if such a thing is possible – or better still, a vision. As if it hadn't really happened and what I was looking at was one of those ghost photographs I sometimes hear about, where someone has taken an innocent photo only to find something else has invaded the frame once it's been developed: a figure, a hooded man, whatever – it doesn't matter to me.

artificial light flickers

When I step out of the hotel the cold air gives me a hug and I curse myself for not bringing a proper overcoat. I zip my jacket up to my neck, hunching over as I walk down Pier Hill towards the seafront. As I turn onto the esplanade, right by where they kissed earlier, the multicoloured neon lights shrouding each amusement arcade glow all around me. Everything is buzzing, the artificial light flickers, I feel like I'm trapped in static, like I'm walking within a scene from a film on a huge screen.

As I walk along, through it, inside the flickering light, I notice a black Mercedes car is following me along the road. At first I don't think much of it, but then I recognise the man in the passenger seat: it's one of the men from the flat in Toledo Road. He smiles at me, nodding his head, before the car picks up speed and moves away. My heart is thumping. I dash left into a loud, bright amusement arcade. I walk around it, shaking and confused. Groups of teenagers look at me, pointing, some of them laughing, others moving away as they notice my stick. I walk up to the cashier's desk and change a ten-pound note. I try to act normal, like I would if I was in a film, which I'm not, but I feel as if I am. I wonder which machine or video game to play. Are they following me? Have they spotted me talking to Laura? Have they been following me all day? I walk up to a random machine, some war-zone simulator. I put in my money, pick up the machine gun attached to the machine and start to fire indiscriminately as soon as the action begins, holding the machine gun in one hand like I've seen it done in films, holding my stick in the other. I'm not really sure what, or who, I'm shooting at, but I continue to shoot at whatever moves. It feels good. I imagine it's the men from Toledo Road, and once they've been obliterated I imagine it's Jessica from my old office, then her boss whose name I've forgotten, and then the whole office. Pretty soon I run out of ammunition, because of my non-stop frantic shooting, and after about ten more seconds my machine gun begins to vibrate violently and blood begins to drip down the large video screen in front of me, slowly; deep, thick red, like the sails on the Thames sailing barges. Finally it obscures my view of the enemy, like a crimson veil.

GAME OVER

I take the words in front of me as a sign. I shudder and walk out of the arcade. The two words swirl inside my head as I make my way over to the other side of the road, where there's less light, sheltered by the deep blackness of the estuary. My eyes are fixed on the road ahead, in case I spot them, waiting for me in their car, 'GAME', 'OVER' swirling behind my eyes, in that strange place in my head, deep behind everything but ever-present on the surface of my eyes, 'GAME', 'OVER' as real as the light of day.

blank space between the scenes

I cross the road. Every black car that crawls along the road to my left becomes a minor obsession, as I squint, straining to see if it's them inside. I walk slowly along by the wall before the beach. I can smell the mud and the iodine, vapours flung into the air by the passing storms. I can see moody silhouettes out in front of me: three, maybe four figures. Is it them? Out of their car? No, just random people like me, out for a stroll in the rain. Everything becomes a blur again, like I've suddenly entered some blank space between the scenes, the whole set being shifted around me with each step, backdrops spliced and edited, as if the mood is being generated just for my own POV. I stop and sit on the wall. Across the road is the Cornucopia pub and behind that, just to its left, is the Sunset Bar. I've no idea what time it is; I check my phone but the battery has gone. But I can see them.

Just up the road, parked outside Benson's Guest House, is the black Mercedes. I wipe my eyes. I can clearly see it. It's empty. I figure they're all in the Sunset Bar as I can't see them through the windows of the Cornucopia, or walking along the esplanade. I understand immediately that this has created a problem for me to make contact with Laura. If they're inside the club with her, there would be no way for us to talk. It's an impossible situation. They obviously know what we're up to – why else would they show up like this? Why else would they have made their presence felt? Slowing down to acknowledge me the way they did? Why else would they be parked outside the one place in Southend I've arranged to meet up with Laura?

he won't bite

For some reason I look up at the night sky, cursing the clouds for obscuring my view. I want to see the stars, I really do. I want to know they are really there: that I exist beneath them and not caught in some other nightmare. I yearn for Saturn, my legs shaking. Just to see it now, hanging peacefully; it would be a comfort to me. Instead, because of night's presence, or Saturn's absence within it, the vertigo begins to take hold of me. I grip on to my stick, holding on to it as tightly as I can. When I look back down, a small, black Staffordshire bull terrier is playfully sniffing at my feet. It appears as if to mark the passing of time. I stroke its thick head and full muscular neck. Soon the owner joins it: a rather tired, skinny man who's missing all his front teeth.

'Fucking cold tonight, innit?'

'Yes.'

'Don't worry about him . . . Like . . . he won't bite.'

'Oh . . . I know.'

'Fucking freezing, innit?'

'Yes, the storm.'

'Rocky! . . . Rocky! . . . Come here, boy!'

'Hope it doesn't rain like that again . . .'

'Fucking freezing . . . Do you have some change for a cup of tea, geezer?'

'Yes.'

'What?'

'Yes, I do. Money . . . Change . . .'

'Really . . . Oh . . .'

I dip my hands into my pockets and give him the pound coins, nine in total.

'Fucking hell, man . . . Fucking hell . . . Rocky! . . . Rocky! . . . have you seen this? . . . Fucking hell . . .'

'That's all right, you should be able to get more than a cup of tea with that . . .'

'Fucking hell, man . . . Fucking hell . . .'

I watch as the skinny, toothless man walks off towards the pier, with his faithful companion Rocky. For some reason they make me smile. I feel like I've made some kind of difference in his life, at least for tonight. It's only nine pounds, but I figure he knows what to get with it.

part of the furniture

I head for Lucy Road. The black Mercedes isn't there any more. I breathe in the cold air, exhaling slowly. I figure with them potentially gone, for the moment at least, it's a good time to visit Laura in the Sunset Bar, like we'd arranged. The bar's just ahead of me on my left, just around the corner. The car park and refuse centre across Lucy Road on the other side is dimly lit and I suddenly frighten myself thinking the black Mercedes might be parked across there, in the darkness, lights off, watching me. I stop, frozen. I look all around me: nothing, not a soul, just some distant whoops and cheers from a group of men in the Cornucopia. The street is empty.

The Sunset Bar is open. I can hear music coming from its doorway. I walk in and pay some money on the door.

'What's that?'

'What?'

'That stick?'

'It's a walking stick . . .'

'You can't come in here with that thing . . .'

'But I need it . . .'

'Leave it on the door. With the cashier . . .'

' . . .'

I leave my stick with the woman behind the counter and clutch my rucksack tightly to my chest – they're not having that as well. The club is dimly lit, the music is loud, so loud I can't even distinguish what it is the DJ is playing. Gaggles of men are standing about, drinking from bottles of lager, all watching a girl dancing for them on the stage. The other girls are all standing near the bar, talking to the staff, waiting for the place to fill up with more punters. I can't see her. I stand at the bar and order a whiskey. I sip it slowly, not wanting to tip myself over the edge. I need to be fully conscious.

I try my best to ignore the girl dancing on the stage, but it's hard not to look as it's what everyone else, except the other girls, is doing and I don't want to draw any unnecessary attention to myself. I turn to the dancer for a few moments and then turn away, watching the men, just in case the men from the black Mercedes are here. Most of the customers are in their early twenties, though some of them, those at the back, are much, much older. It's strange, I've never hung around with other men in packs, and the thought of drinking with a large group of men in a strip club turns my stomach. It's obvious to me that they have no idea what they are doing, they just seem to be going through the

155

motions, doing what the man standing next to them is doing, acting like other groups of men they have seen in other bars. Most, left to their own devices, away from the pack, would shrivel up in a place like this.

Soon, one of the dancers, a tall, skinny girl with a strange accent, possibly South American, walks over to me.

'Would you like a private dance?'

'Well . . . Well . . . Er . . .'

'Are you shy?'

'Erm . . .'

'I won't bite you . . .'

'I'm waiting for someone . . .'

'Another girl?'

'Yes.'

'Who?'

'Laura . . .'

'Laura?'

'Yes, Laura . . .'

'Are you sure?'

'Yes.'

'What's her stage name?'

'What?'

'Does she work here?'

'I just know her as Laura . . . She said I could call . . . She told me to meet her here, that she'd be waiting for me here . . .'

'Laura?'

'Yes.'

'Nobody works here called Laura, darling . . .'

'Are you sure?'

'What?'

'Are you sure?'

'Yes.'

'But . . .'

'Are you sure you don't want a private dance?'

'Yes.'

She shrugs and walks away. I watch her return to her group, she says something about me, but I don't mind. One of them points at me, I smile, she turns away, saying something back to the girl I was just speaking to, then they all look over at me and I have to look away myself. When I return my gaze they're all still looking at me. I don't know what makes me do this, but I raise my glass at them all, in a moment of personal defiance. I turn away again, happy. The lights at the back of the room dazzle my eyes. I step back to the far wall and lean on it, nonchalantly, like I'm part of the furniture. I decide that I'll wait for her here, leaning against the wall at the back of the club feels right, I feel safe and comfortable, like I don't care who speaks to me or what I hear. I know Laura will appear, she needs help, she's in trouble, of course she'll turn up, she needs me. Maybe she's hiding from the men in the black Mercedes too? Maybe that's why she's late. I sink back into the wall. I close my eyes and listen to the music, then the music drifts and I concentrate on the thud thud thud of its beat through me, inside me, then my head drops, then my whiskey glass drops . . .

Then it hits me: what if the men from Toledo Road are in this club? Part of the club? Own this club? I straighten up, scraping the shards of glass by my whiskey-stained shoes over to the wall out of harm's way. I walk over to the bar, shaking, and try to look through a door behind it, to see if there's an office there, or somewhere they could be watching me, waiting for me: nothing. It's not a film, I remind myself. It's not a film. This is real, right? I try to calm myself. Nothing. I wait for Laura and order another whiskey.

aggressive behaviour

The bar is busy now. Before I know it I'm having to queue at the bar for another drink. The bar staff are obviously used to the crowd, but I'm not; people are bumping into me, standing on my shoes, and I'm having to apologise for things I haven't done. I become increasingly frustrated, as more and more people jostle to get served, an elbow here and an arm there to block other people's paths. Eventually, I'm served. I order a double whiskey, so I don't have to go back. I try to stand where I was before, where I had a nice view of the entire bar, but it's impossible to get over to that side of the room. So I stay where I am, close to the bar, surrounded by eager drinkers, all of them male.

Almost immediately a young lad, covered in tattoos, all up his arms and neck, begins to talk to me.

'What's that?'

'This, it's my rucksack . . .'

'I didn't think they let schoolchildren in here . . .'

'Pardon?'

'Are you a skater?'

'What?'

'What's in it, your fucking homework?'

'Homework . . . Ha . . . Yes . . . Homework . . .'

'It looks fucking stupid in a place like this.'

'Oh, it's just a bag.'

'A fucking rucksack . . .'

'Oh, well . . .'

'Are you a faggot, or something?'

'What?'

'Take it up the shitter, do you?'

'. . .'

'Pussy.'

'. . .'

I push through the crowd, my heart pounding. I head to the other side of the long bar. Luckily, a girl starts to speak to the lad and he doesn't follow me. He's unsettled me, though, and I begin to shake. I can't stop it. I look over to where the lad was standing – he's taken the girl over to his friends, who all look the same: chequered shirts, high collars, short hair parted to the side, bottles of beer. He's laughing along with them, his arm around the girl. He seems happy, in spite of his aggressive behaviour towards me. Maybe that's his idea of humour? A good night out? Accusing random men of being homosexual? I sink back against the wall, in a corner near the door, where it's darker and I don't stand out. I gulp my whiskey down, forgetting my plan. It goes straight to my head. I take another gulp and finish it, my insides burning; there's nowhere to put the glass, so I put it by my feet. When I straighten up to look around the bar a rush of blood fills my head, it feels like my brain is swelling up, drowning in whiskey, it makes me dizzy, but I manage to control it. As I refocus I notice Laura is standing in front of me with a big smile on her face.

'You're here . . .'

'I'm drunk . . .'

'I didn't think you would . . .'

'I always keep my word . . .'

Her hair's tied back, or combed back and pinned with something, I don't know. Her face is heavily made-up: black eye-liner around her large eyes, almost like it's smudged on purpose. She's wearing a flimsy top and a short skirt, which could have been underwear for all I know. I figure she's arrived here by car, or maybe she's been here all this time, somewhere in the bar, as she looks untouched by the elements outside. Her smile soon fades and she grabs me by the arm.

'I need to speak with you . . .'

'Right.'

'Come with me . . .'

'Right.'

She pulls me through the crowd, holding on to my arm; we walk through the group of lads, the guy with the neck full of tattoos stops what he's doing and watches us, as she escorts me into the Ladies. I turn around to look at him just before the door closes after me and we step into a cubicle; he's staring at me, a mix of jealousy, curiosity and hatred in his eyes.

'In here . . . In here . . .'

159

She shuts the cubicle door behind us.

'We'll get caught . . .'

'Ssssshhhhh . . .'

She seems nervous, jittery, her eyes darting to and fro.

'I need to speak to you . . .'

'What is it? . . . What's wrong?'

'I'm in trouble . . . You were kind to me . . .'

'In the flat?'

'Yes.'

'I knew it was you . . .'

'I'm in trouble . . .'

'Who with?'

'Them . . .'

'Who?'

'Those men . . .'

'From the flat?'

'Yes.'

'What's wrong? What've they done to you? Are they holding you against your will?'

'I'm in trouble with them . . .'

'What is it?'

'I need money . . . To get away from them.'

'Yes . . . Yes . . . Yes . . . we can go . . . we can both get away from here . . .'

'No, that's not safe, I need to get away first, on my own . . . Then you can come.'

'Where do you need to go?'

'To Tirana . . .'

'Where's that?'

'In Albania . . . I need to get back there as soon as I can . . .'

'You need me to help you?'

'It'll cost money, I have no money . . . I have to pay money to people to help me get back, to take me, good people . . .'

'How much?'

'. . .'

160

'How much do you need?'

'I need three thousand eight hundred . . . That's how much. It's so much, I don't know what to do.'

'Pounds?'

'Yes . . .'

'I can help you.'

'Can you?'

'Yes, I can. Of course I can.'

'I knew you would, I knew you would . . .'

She leans over, throwing her arms around me. She kisses me on the lips, pressing her body up against me. I stand there, gripping on to her waist, not sure if I can let go.

'I can get you the money tomorrow . . . We can meet . . . On the pier . . .'

'Yes, the pier . . .'

'Where we first met . . .'

'What?'

'The pier . . .'

'. . .'

'The bell . . .'

'. . . The bell, oh . . . yes, the bell . . .'

'Meet me by the bell at 3 p.m. tomorrow . . .'

'The bell, 3 p.m., yes . . .'

'I'll give you the cash.'

'Yes, the cash, oh the cash. Yes, you give me the cash tomorrow . . .'

'I'll follow you, I'll come after you, after you are home and safe . . .'

'Yes, when I'm settled . . .'

Her hands are all over me, grabbing me, squeezing me. She's breathing heavily.

'Yes.'

'We have to go, you have to go, we can't be seen together . . .'

'Yes, okay . . .'

I walk out of the cubicle and out into the bar. She follows me a couple of seconds later. I push through the group of lads again, ignoring them, staring down at my feet. When I look back up I notice the men from the black Mercedes at the door. They've already spotted me and are looking over. The man from the passenger seat begins to grin.

'You've got to go . . .'

'. . .'

'They've seen us . . . You've got to go . . .'

'. . .'

'Say nothing.'

it all happens quickly

I'm shaking. I walk over to the door. The man is still grinning at me. He blocks my path. He stops grinning.

'What she say to you?'

'. . .'

'What you doing here with her?'

'. . .'

'Why you here with her?'

'Let me through. I need to get through. I'll call the bouncers . . .'

'No good.'

'Please . . . I haven't done anything wrong.'

I try to push past him, but he grabs hold of my arm and pushes me up against the wall. The bouncers at the door look away, talking among themselves.

'What you fucking say?'

'I didn't say anything . . . Honest . . .'

'What she fucking tell you?'

'Nothing . . . Nothing . . . Honest.'

'What you fucking doing here?'

'I was asking for a bar job . . .'

'A bar job? . . . A bar job?'

They all begin to laugh. He lets go of me. I walk to the counter for my stick. The woman hands it over without looking at me. I do my best to remain calm. When I turn around the men are all facing me, blocking my exit again. One of them tries to grab my stick, but I pull it away just in time. Then the man who pinned me up against the wall throws a punch at me, I think, and I thrust the stick in his face at the same time. It all happens quickly. He falls to the floor, screaming in a language I don't understand, blood pouring from his eye. I swing the stick around like a lunatic. I can feel the heavier end hitting things, but I don't know what, heads, limbs, walls, I haven't a clue. I don't hang around to find out, either. I push through the bodies, frantically swirling and jabbing my stick at anything that moves or is in my way. Just as I step out onto the pavement, something hits the back of my head, probably a bottle. It causes me to stumble onto the road, my rucksack swinging around my neck. I stumble to my feet and run as quickly as I can up Lucy Road, past the clubs and burger vans and up towards Rossi's ice-cream factory and the back of the Palace Hotel. I don't look back, but I know they're all running after me.

just the silence

I turn right through the car park, onto Herbert Grove, past the dilapidated row of guest houses and then left onto Chancellor Road. Just before I turn again I look back; they aren't far behind, a huddled mass heading towards me, two or three of them running at high speed. I figure the others must be in the black Mercedes somewhere, so I decide to get off the road. I turn left and dive into the cemetery at St John the Baptist Church. I'm suddenly enveloped in blackness, I feel at home and soon my eyes grow accustomed to the change in light. I weave along the path, gravestones and sarcophagi all around me. I run into the corner and hide behind a huge grave displaying a bust of a bearded, bespectacled man. I lie down in the long, wet grass behind him. I act like I'm dead, clutching my stick to my chest as tightly as I can, trying to slow down my breathing, directing it down into the earth.

I can hear their footsteps behind the crumbling wall separating the cemetery from Chancellor Road. I hear them enter the cemetery; they're out of breath, wheezing, talking to each other, then shouting and arguing. They stick to the path – I can hear their footsteps on the gravel, heading through the cemetery, out towards the other exit by the Palace Hotel. I wait. Dead in the blackness of night. Waiting for however long it takes to convince myself they've gone. I sit up in the grass, the large bust above me. For some reason I look up at him and thank him. I'm sopping wet all through. I pull the slugs from my arms and legs, wipe down my back and front and walk on to the path to find a bench to sit down. I sit on the hard bench until it feels like my clothes have dried out, although I know they haven't. I get up, convinced it's safe enough to venture out of the cemetery.

I walk out the same way I entered, onto Chancellor Road. It's deathly quiet, empty and cold. I walk up towards the Royals Shopping Centre and then take a left, following the road around to the High Street, turning left again to head back down to the seafront and the Palace Hotel. I stand at Pier Hill beneath the Palace Hotel, staring out at the pier, just visible within the blackness of the estuary. I take out my phone to capture an image of it, but I remember the battery has gone and put it back in my pocket. It must be late, maybe around 3 a.m. or something like that. I look up into the sky just as the clouds break around the moon, and my first instinct is to get back to Uncle Rey's caravan, to look through his telescope, just to see if Saturn has returned, but the trains will all have stopped by now. Silence, that's all I have. I listen, I wait, hoping to hear it out there: that rumble, that low grumbling of a cargo ship's engines, reverberating underneath the water all the way to my feet: but nothing, just the silence, and the moon, and no way of knowing if Saturn is up there, hanging, waiting for my gaze. I turn around and walk up the hill to the reception doors of the hotel. I've still got money in my pockets.

we understand that, sir

A young lady and a grey-haired man are sitting behind the reception when I walk through the sliding doors. I walk towards them. It doesn't occur to me that I'm clearly drunk and sopping wet, grass-stained and mucky from the stint next to the grave.

'I need a single room, just for tonight.'

'. . .'

'Please . . .'

'We're, I'm sure we're . . . let me see . . . yes, we're fully booked I'm afraid, sir.'

'Well, I'll have a double room, then?'

'. . .'

'A double room, for tonight only . . .'

'Okay, right, sir . . . I'm afraid we are fully booked . . .'

'What . . .'

'Yes, he's right, we're fully booked.'

'What about a family room?'

'We're fully booked, sir.'

'Oh . . . I get it, right, I'm sorry . . . yes, I'm a mess . . . Sorry, I'm locked out of my house . . . I have money, I'm good for the money . . . look . . . seriously, just look . . . I was in here earlier, drinking in the terrace bar . . .'

'We understand that, sir . . .'

'. . . but we're fully booked, like he said, sir.'

'It's a Tuesday night . . .'

'Like I say, sir . . . We fully understand your . . .'

'Who comes to Southend on a Tuesday night . . .'

'. . .'

'. . .'

I walk back out of the reception. Just as I turn left I hear a loud screech of tyres: it's the black Mercedes, I'm sure it is – but I don't look, I run. I run as fast as I can, without looking, turning left again, down Pier Hill, across the road at the bottom towards the rusting iron legs of the pier. I head up a side road alongside it, then turn right, running underneath the pier. There's no one in sight. It must have been another car.

'Who the fuck is that?'

The voice startles me. It comes from lower down towards the sea, down among the pebbles.

'Who the fuck is it? Jimmy, is it you? Jimmy?'

Just as I'm about to run off again a bright light shines directly onto my face, so that I can't see anything. I raise my arms up like I'm under arrest, dropping my head to shield my eyes from the blinding white light.

'Oh . . . it's you. What the fuck are you doing down here? What's with that fucking stick?'

The voice switches off the torch and I watch as an emaciated, toothless face emerges from the blackness. At first it presents itself as a floating head, which is soon followed by a hand, then another, then long, thin arms and a gangly torso, skinny legs and big white Reebok trainers. I immediately recognise the man before me as the homeless man with the dog, Rocky. The one I gave nine pounds to.

'What the fuck are you doing here? You're not with that fucking church are you?'

'No . . . No . . . Hi . . . I'm . . . I'm lost.'

'Lost?! . . . Lost?! . . . Do you hear that, Rocky? Geezer says he's fucking lost . . . This is the underworld. We're all fucking lost down here.'

'I got split up . . . Well, I got into a spot of bother, with some men . . .'

'Did they follow you?'

'No . . .'

'Get the fuck away from here if they did, there's nothing I can do to help you. We don't need any nasty business down here.'

'No . . . No . . . They didn't . . . I lost them, hours ago, up by the cemetery . . .'

'Come with me . . .'

I follow him down into the blackness. He leads me to where four of the pier's iron stanchions are grouped together. Tarpaulin is tied around them, wrapped a few times it seems, making a natural windbreak and shelter. In between the space created by each post is a cardboard enclosure, built up on each side with pallets. Above this space is another piece of tarpaulin that forms a roof. It's quite a large space, much larger than I first think.

'Come in . . . Come in . . .'

I follow him inside; the cardboard floor is covered with sleeping bags and other belongings. There's a woman huddled beside a lamp eating a sandwich; Rocky sits down next to her. She looks up at me.

'Who the fuck is this?'

'Don't be fucking rude, Sandra. This is the geezer who paid for the scran you're eating.'

'Hello . . .'

I sit down next to Rocky. The dog raises its eyes to look at me and then closes them again, letting out a sigh.

'Do you want a sandwich?'

' . . .'

'It's fresh, it's from the sandwich man . . . he sells the cheap stuff the shops are throwing out.'

'Yes . . . I need, yes, that's very kind.'

I've forgotten how hungry I am. The woman pulls two slices of white bread from a bag and puts a slice of processed cheese between them. She squeezes the slices together and hands it to me, leaving her grubby fingerprints all over it. I don't care.

'Says he's been in some trouble . . . with some other geezers . . .'

'Has he . . .'

167

'Yes, they chased me down from the Sunset Bar . . .'

'The strip club?'

'Yes . . . I don't know what I'd done to upset them . . .'

'Well, it's our turn to help you . . .'

'Thanks . . .'

'That's all right . . .'

'This town can be like the Wild West . . .'

'Not as bad as Tortuga . . .'

'Where?'

'The island . . . Canvey . . . People living in disused railway carriages on that shithole . . .'

'That's where I'm living, where I've got to get back to . . .'

'Ignore her . . . It's not as bad as that.'

'Why do you call it Tortuga?'

'Sinbad, innit . . .'

'Full of fucking pirates . . .'

'You can get anything there . . . anything you want.'

'. . . for a price.'

'Why are you both living here, then?'

'. . .'

'Under the pier?'

'Not been the same since I injured my groin and leg.'

'He got macheted last year . . .'

'They nearly took my fucking leg off . . .'

'Besides, we can fish here . . . Spends his time fishing, off the end of the pier.'

'We've had good catches, too . . . There's more in that water than in that fucking town, that High Street . . .'

'You can't drink it though, love.'

'The water?'

'Yes, all that blackness out there, enough for everyone, but not a drop to drink . . .'

'It's why we're wasting away . . .'

'How long have you both been here, under the pier?'

'Dunno . . .'

'Dunno . . .'

'Maybe a few months, I dunno.'

'Yeah, a few months . . . It's not as bad as it looks, down here no one bothers us. Everyone's scared of the sea at night. First few weeks I thought we'd be drowned in the night, but it doesn't reach us here, the sea, we're just above where it reaches, even in storms at high tide . . .'

'No one knows we're here . . .'

'Plus town is rough . . . York Road and all that . . . I never go there without Rocky . . . He protects me, see, you know, with my leg, it's hard to defend myself. All I want is a quiet life now, and down here that's what we get, don't we?'

'Yes.'

'We're going to stay here until I'm all better . . . Just fishing, and waiting for things to get better.'

'Things will get better, won't they, my love?'

'Of course they will . . . The sea is keeping us healthy, people like him are keeping us healthy . . . There're not many people like him, all those horrid people . . . Where do they think we should go? Eh? The fuckers . . .'

'I can give you more money . . . I can help you both . . .'

'No . . . No . . . You don't have to do that . . .'

'How much would you give us?'

'How much do you need?'

'Twenty pounds . . .'

'No, sixty!'

'One hundred pounds . . .'

'I'll give you . . . sixty . . . eighty . . . here, take it . . .'

'Fuck . . .'

'Fuck, thanks, mate . . . I told you, Sandra . . . I fucking told you he was a good one, I fucking told you!'

'It's okay . . . Really . . .'

'I can buy new fishing tackle with this, and clothes . . .'

'You need it more than I do . . .'

'Mate, no one has ever done anything like this for us before, no one. I don't know what to say to you, geezer . . . I've had, we've . . . It's been so hard, we've . . . I never had, well I did, but my real father, you know . . . my blood father, he didn't want to know . . . He left my mother and me and I was brought up by my mother's boyfriend. Now, you know, I don't have many memories of my blood father, except for one night, when he threw me out of the house, into the yard, and I had to sleep underneath some bin bags by the shed. He said I had to prove myself to him, to see if I was "man enough" . . . just to be his son. So I lit a fire in the yard to keep me warm and during the night it spoke to me, the flames fucking spoke to me and for that moment I felt like a god, higher than my father, higher than everything he stood for . . . Well, I've been searching for that feeling all my life . . . but it made me fucking realise something . . . My blood father, he wasn't fit to lace my boots, he didn't deserve it. The real hero of this story is my real dad, my mother's boyfriend, who took me in, who took me in as one of his own . . . he took me in . . . Loved me . . . But he got sick . . . cancer in his liver took hold and eventually sucked the life out of him . . . But now I know, see, now I know what a real father is, it's the man who takes you in, no matter who you are, and gives you shelter . . . But now he's dust . . . It's all turned to dust . . . And we're all among it, the dust, here in Southend . . . Southend has given us nothing, there's no one to help you, except the sea, the sea helps us, we live for the sea. Down here we're safe, away from everyone else . . . I just wish I could make things better . . . I feel useless most of the time, I feel like no one can see me, that no one knows I'm here . . . But I've been here longer than them all, geezer . . . I have. I know everything about them, I know everything they've done, what they say, I listen to them every day. I can hear everything they say and the best part about it is they never see me, they don't even know I'm listening, they don't care what I'm doing. I'm like everything else in their lives, I just slip by, part of the make-up of everything that passes them by, the stuff that happens while they're sleeping, safe in their beds. I never meet them head-on, and even if I did, after I'd gone they'd never remember me. I find it all so funny, so fucking funny, geezer . . .'

'I guess I'm one of them . . .'

'You're not one of them . . . You're different, there's something special about you . . . and I'm not saying that because of the money . . .'

'I don't know about that . . . I know somebody who is, though . . . But I can't reach her, she's too far gone, into the blackness . . . I've tried to help her . . . Hopefully I'll help her tomorrow, but . . .'

'What?'

'I just wish . . .'

'What?'

'Oh, it's nothing . . .'

'What? Is she your lover or something? Is that why you've been chased? . . .'

'No, I hardly know her . . . I don't know her . . . I don't even know if it's her, but I'd rebuild my entire life for her, just to be with her . . . It's like one moment she's real, like now she's real and the next she doesn't even exist, and I don't know what to do about it. That's what's so incredibly beautiful and tragic about the whole situation . . .'

'I'll tell you what, geezer . . .'

'What?'

'After some kip – there's a spare blanket over there – you come fishing with me tomorrow, that'll sort your head out . . . Best thing there is . . . Fishing . . . Sorts a man's life right the fuck out . . . I do all of my best thinking when I'm out on the pier, fishing. Everything goes away. I'm a fucking king out there, geezer, I tell you, a fucking king . . .'

'Oh, I can't . . .'

'You must, you fucking must . . .'

'I can't . . .'

'. . .'

'. . .'

'You see . . . I don't want to forget . . .'

171

Sandra begins to wrap the bread and cheese back up while he rummages around for my blanket.

'Here . . . This'll keep your knackers warm . . .'

'Thanks.'

I wrap the blanket around me; it reeks of wet dog and sweat. I don't mind though, as I'm starting to really feel the cold. Rocky curls up beside me, intrigued and happy with the new guest. I use my rucksack as a pillow and grip my stick as tightly as I can. I thank them both for the sandwich and fall asleep pretty much immediately.

WEDNESDAY

first train

I wake at first light, the sun not even above the horizon. The birds are singing for the new morning above the pier. If it wasn't for the horrible stench, the fact that I've just woken up hung over in a homeless couple's makeshift home wouldn't seem as horrific as it does, but the thick stench makes me gag a few times and I'm worried I'm going to be sick. I sit up and look through a gap in the black tarpaulin at the waves just a few metres from us, down a natural slope on the beach. The others are still sleeping. Rocky, the obvious perpetrator of the stench, is snoring, while the tooth-less man and Sandra are cuddled up as if sleeping here every night is the most natural thing. I reach for my stick and pull myself to my feet. I check my bag, and immediately feel bad for doing so; everything is there that should be.

I tiptoe out; out onto the pebbles. I walk from under the pier, up the beach a bit, towards the main drag. I turn and look out across the estuary: a couple of fishing boats are making their way back to Old Leigh, bobbing along, past the pier and down into the rays. I watch them for a moment, the chug chug chug chug of their engines just about audible above the seagulls following them back to shore. When they are out of sight, and the sound of the seagulls and engines has faded, I walk back up to the esplanade and make my way to the station, hoping I don't have to wait long for the first train.

another box

I arrive back at Uncle Rey's caravan in good time. If I'd got back last night I could have searched for Saturn in the night sky, even though there was a thick layer of cloud. I'd have waited for a break, for my chance. Instead, feeling quite sick, I let myself into the caravan, determined to finish the job I've been sent here for.

After plugging in my phone near Uncle Rey's armchair to charge, the first thing I do is take 'The Underworld' out of my rucksack and return it to the rest of the manuscript. I'm sure that I'll never read it again. I let out a sigh, which causes a gag reflex. I bring up some fluid into my mouth and immediately swallow it again. It burns the back of my throat. I run to the tap at the kitchenette and drink some cold water; it helps a little, but not much. I feel terrible. The next thing I do is walk over to the majority of Uncle Rey's recordings. I search for the most recent one I can find. There seems to be a gap in his recordings: from about 2004 to 2006. I find a batch from 2006 to 2010 in a box by his TV, but little else on the shelves among his vast record collection. I contemplate putting some Dr Feelgood on, but my head feels like it's split in two, so I think better of it. I can't be ill today, of all days.

I rummage around in his things, collecting from about the place the empty beer bottles I'd not cleared up. Then I notice two boxes, both smaller than an average shoe box, on the top shelf of the bookcase, pushed back against the wall of the caravan. I pull over the armchair and stand on it to reach them. I pull them down and sit on the armchair. They're covered in dust and have obviously not been touched for a long time. I open them; each box is filled with broken jewellery: gold and silver. It feels like I've discovered some lost treasure. Most of it is junk on closer inspection, and I'm not sure it's really worth much money. Then I find a gold locket and chain in the second box, buried deep down underneath all the costume stuff, in the corner. I pull it out, like a magician pulling something out of his mouth: the chain is long, much longer than at first anticipated. I open the locket to find a picture of Mother inside, taken before I was born, no doubt. Her hair longer, her face thinner than I remember, dressed in the fashions of the day. I close the locket and put it in my rucksack. I feel betrayed. I close the boxes and continue my search in the bedroom.

I look everywhere: in each drawer, the bottom of his wardrobe, on each shelf. Eventually I find another box underneath his sagging bed. Again, it's labelled.

For Jon #7 2013

There are no other CDs, tapes, DVDs et cetera, nothing else, no other boxes, just the one CD with the same label as the box. Where were the other six? Did the other six even exist? This must have been the last recording he made. I begin to tremble, walking over to the TV in the living room, pulling the armchair from the bedroom back in front of it and placing the CD in the machine. I press play immediately. The screen is black for an uncomfortable amount of time before it begins.

For Jon #7 2013

I never wanted you to have to listen to this, Jon. But I made it anyway, just in case something like this was going to happen. I guess I knew it was always going to happen. I knew you'd find out, I knew how curious you'd be . . .

    [He takes a long, hard drag from his rolled-up cigarette. His eyes are blank, staring. The wrinkles in his face fold each time he sucks deeply.]

This isn't the way things were supposed to be, this isn't the way they . . . they were supposed to happen. I was supposed to finish my book, hoping that one day you would read that and we'd . . . Well . . . You would read that and we'd never have to speak about it. But here I am . . . speaking to you about it.

    [He takes a swig of whiskey from a bottle by his side and then gets up slowly from his chair and walks off-camera, out of the frame. The rattling of tablets in a bottle can be heard.

He sits back in his chair, slowly, running his gnarled hands
through his grey hair.]
I don't know who I am any more, you see. I know I once loved
. . . I loved well . . . I was good at that, I know I was, people told
me . . . But where . . . Where has it got me? Eh? . . . Eh? . . .
Where? . . . Laura was everything to me, she was a beautiful
woman, my beautiful woman, she was mine . . . Mine . . . I can't
say that enough, I can't. What would be the point in not telling
you this? If I think back, I can still smell her perfume. I can smell
it now . . .

[He takes a deep breath which makes him burst into a hacking
cough.]
I never wanted to hurt you, Jon . . . Or to make you feel that I
never cared . . . Things were hard, you know. But Laura, she meant
so much to me. Have you ever known . . . no, felt . . . . have you
ever felt beauty in your life? I do hope you have . . . Even though
it didn't last I still count myself one of the lucky ones, the lucky
few, if that makes any sense, I don't know . . . But how could I be?
. . . How? . . . How could I be there for you throughout your life
like a real father should, how could I? I didn't know how to cope,
what to do, who to speak to . . . I couldn't speak to anyone, all I
could do was remove myself, to keep away, to do the right thing
. . . I wanted to, though . . . I thought about you every day, planned
and schemed to make you mine, thought about every possible way
. . . I begged and begged and fucking begged Laura, I mean . . .
your mother, to come away with me, but it was no use, she wouldn't
listen, she wanted nothing to do with me . . . and who can blame
her, the things I did, everything I did, the way I . . . I couldn't
convince her . . . There was Cal for a start . . . And your father, I
mean, my brother . . . it would have torn things apart . . . So I simply
hung around on the sidelines, you must have noticed? I watched,
I watched you all from afar, I mapped everything you did, recorded
it all, layered it in film, in memory, digitised it . . . I watched, I
adored, I watched from a distance . . . Oh, Jon, I never thought
Laura, your mother, would just walk away from us all. From you

and Cal. I never thought that would happen. I never thought she'd be capable of such a thing.

[He gets up again and walks over to the camera to adjust it. Zooming in a little, so that when he sits back down his face almost fills the screen. He has picked up a book, too. His face is tense, his eyebrows furrowed into a wrinkly V. He reads the book for a bit, nodding to himself, flicking through it. Then he stops and looks directly into the camera for about six to ten seconds.]

I'd see the snowbound roses of her lips . . . Quivering . . . and that glint of ivory . . . That marbles the onlooker . . . every reason . . . I'd see wherefore my joy of life outstrips . . . The pain of it . . . I shout exultantly . . . That I am kept into this elder season . . .

[He looks back at the book. A smile almost appears on his face. But it disappears. He begins to cough again, taking another swig of the whiskey to quell it.]

His words . . . His words seem to make sense to me. His words always have, because I loved her. I loved that woman and I've never been able to get rid of this . . . It's never left me . . . There was a time, a darker time than this, when I thought I could save her, take her away from him, from her life, convince her that a life with me would be better, that I could make her happy . . . Oh, Jon, that's what I wanted . . . A happy life . . . That's all anyone wants, right? . . . Not to be stuck in this elder season of pain and regret . . .

[He stops. Takes another swig of whiskey and wipes his eye with the back of his hand.]

You see, I tried to write all this down. That would explain everything to you, all my pain, everything I have been through, the reason why you breathe . . . But the words wouldn't come, and if they did, then they came all jumbled, and they didn't look right, or sound right when I read them back to myself, they sounded second-hand, far-fetched, and what I wanted to do was write a new morality for myself, as truthfully as I possibly could so that you would understand one day . . . of myself, for myself . . . something that would correct my actions, reflect them the right way . . . But I failed, my whole life I have failed to write this book for you . . .

[He sets the book down on his lap and then leans over to the side of his chair to pick up his manuscript, waving it about in front of the camera.]

Vulgar Things . . . That's what it is . . . the common voice . . . that's all I wanted. A common voice . . . This book to sing the truth . . . I wanted it to reveal everything, in a clear and beautiful language . . . But I failed to do that, and I've spent my entire life talking into this thing, because of it, trying to come to terms with it, trying to work things out, talking, talking, talking, in the hope that one day something real would appear, you know, that crystallised moment when I speak reality . . . I've waited a long time, a whole lifetime, but nothing, reality has eluded me . . . it doesn't exist, it doesn't fucking exist . . . It seems easier this way now, things just seem easier, sitting here, talking into the lens, nothing really to disrupt me . . . and then it hits me, you, you listening, watching me, that's the true reality, I've created reality for you, not for me . . . And it feels different, like these aren't words, like what I'm doing is automatic, and it's not like the writing, nothing like the writing, the stupid sitting down with a pen, my vision already clouded by the thought . . . before it hits the paper . . . ink leaving its mark . . . my mark . . . It's not like that at all . . . That's what I like about it, it feels better this way. It feels like me. Digitised me, overlapped and recorded me, like I've aborted order, proportion . . . Like when I look up at the sky now, it's the skull, but when I try to write the sky, how the sky is, it doesn't feel like a true representation of the sky, it's still stuck in here, in my skull, it still exists as the sky up there, and not on my page. But here, this representation of me, this overlapping of sound and image, this ghost, this is real, this is really me. The ghost is reality. The sky, you see, the sky I try to write, it seems to be without any plan . . . like a painting begun without a preliminary sketch. In my wayless way, my unending failure to capture everything begins and ends right here . . . But it has made me a lonely man, a failure too . . . A man who yearns for his Laura in the night . . . I've got to leave this behind, and this, these recordings, seem to be the right way to go about leaving things behind . . . And if you are listening to me now, I'll have known, in some future now, that I'll have made the right choice . . .

[He picks up the book again. Leaving the manuscript on the arm of his chair.]

There was one memorable night . . . When she was here, when I took her here, before I decided to move here permanently . . . at the end of the jetty . . . I'll never forget this, I've got it taped here now . . . The vision of her, my Laura, swimming by the jetty . . . the fire inside me no wind could extinguish, nothing could rattle this from me, nothing . . . By the jetty, the image of her pale skin, pale moonlight . . . The pale skin . . . When I suddenly saw this, the fire within . . . Nothing could remove it from within . . . I watched her there, pale skin in the gloom, in the black water . . . I saw here there, alone. She could have gone, but she stayed, breasts, the dark gloom around her pale skin, her breasts, in night . . . It was at that moment . . . I knew, I knew . . . I knew what it was, I knew . . . I knew she would soon go, all those horrible fucking things, and still she let me come to her, to lie down by the jetty, the warm night, a blanket, under the pale moonlight, my head on her lap, her warm breasts, her heart beating, my heart beating . . . we lay there together until the moon disappeared, the sea tickling our toes . . . That was the only moment, and then it was gone . . . she was gone . . . He came in the morning, to take her back home. There's a fire within me, the same fire, it still burns . . .

[He drops his head. Rubbing his hands through his grey hair.

Then looks up again, holding on to his book tightly.]

Now it's silence. All is silence. As if nothing else exists. The night. The dead black night.

[He lifts the book up and reads from it.]

Perhaps, from uttermost annihilation . . . we'll see some new . . . Strange, marvellous thing arise . . . and our suffering we shall know, was not in vain.

[He throws the book across the room.]

My son . . . My beautiful son . . . I hope you learn to forgive me?
I hope you'll one day understand? I'm recording these moments,
so that you'll understand.

[The screen fades to black.]

it feels wrong

The first thing I do is get up from the armchair and look behind
the TV in the direction he threw the book. It's there. It's still there
on the floor, tangled in the wires. I lean over and pick it up: it's
the collection of sonnets by Petrarch. I flick through its pages
noticing where Uncle Rey has written notes and underlined certain
lines and stanzas. I close it and put it in my rucksack. I sit back
down in the armchair and phone Cal. It takes him a while to
answer.

'Cal . . .'

'Jon . . . What is it?'

'Oh . . .'

'I'm kind of busy . . .'

'Can you talk? . . .'

'What is it?'

'It's important . . .'

'Okay, okay . . . What's the matter?'

'Well . . .'

'What? . . . What?'

'I don't really know how to tell you this . . . It's all rather complicated . . .'

'What's happened to the caravan?'

'It's not that . . .'

'What is it then?'

'It's Uncle Rey . . .'

'What about him?'

'Well . . . He's . . .'

'What?'

'He's . . .'

'Stop fucking me about, Jon . . . and fucking tell me what's going on out there . . .'

'He's . . . my . . .'

'Just fucking spit it out . . .'

'He's been writing a book . . .'

'A book? A book?'

'Yes, a book . . . a novel . . .'

'So fucking what? Big deal . . . Is that it? . . . Jon, I'm fucking busy, I've meetings all day . . .'

'It's about morality, I think . . . and truth . . . An apology, a failed apology . . .'

'Jon, great, that's all really great . . . Tell me about it at the weekend when you're back, okay?'

'Sure.'

'Have you nearly finished?'

'Yeah . . . packing stuff into boxes. All the legal stuff in his briefcase . . . The belongings will all be ready to be picked up on Friday . . . There's a lot of rubbish . . .'

'Just make sure it's all sorted out . . .'

'Sure.'

'Bye.'

'. . .'

I don't know why I didn't tell him. It just doesn't feel right over the phone. I figure there'll be plenty of time to explain to him what has been happening in Uncle Rey's life, why he was the way he was, his affair with Mother, that I'm his son, all that stuff. I sit back in the armchair, running my hands through my hair. His son, I'm his son. It doesn't feel right, it feels wrong, alien. I'm more than uncomfortable with the entire situation, everything that's gone on. It all feels like a sham. I sink into the chair, trying to think about other things. And then it suddenly hits me: did Father know? Did he learn the truth before he died?

181

motionless

I get up out of the armchair and put the record player on. Dr Feelgood fills the empty space again. I turn the volume right up and open all the windows. I walk to the telescope in the shed. I can still hear the music, even when I close the door to the shed behind me. I look at the charts, now that they have had time to dry out. I look at the dates. It says that Saturn should be visible right now. It was there all along when I was frantically searching for it the other night, it was there while I was sleeping under the pier last night; it should be here at this precise moment. It's out there now, above me, hanging there in the blackness, waiting for me to locate its presence again. My stomach begins to knot and I suddenly feel sick. I stare back at the charts, the music filtering in through the gaps in the wood of the shed. I let it in, the vibrations filling up the space all around me. It swirls around me. I drop to my knees, my head falls back, the blood draining from it. I begin to feel weightless, light-headed. It's the freest I've felt in a long time. I stay like this: motionless, on my knees, my head tilted back, my arms hanging limply by my side, each fingertip heavy with blood, for as long as I can stand it.

drift along with them

It takes me a long time to withdraw the money from my bank. I take out four thousand pounds in total. Three thousand eight hundred for Laura, and two hundred for me. Even though I've changed clothes, had a shower and a haircut, the cashier at the bank still grills me for all I am worth.

'It's not that you look like a conman, Mr Michaels, it's just that I have to take every precaution necessary when someone just walks into the branch, without prior warning, and requests an amount like this; a lot of money has been flying in and out of your account these past few days, Mr Michaels, and we have to be sure you are who you say you are. I hope you understand?'

The cashier counts and recounts the money. When he's finished I ask him to put Laura's money into a separate envelope. He hands me the cash: I fold my money and put it in my pocket and then take the envelope and put that in the inside pocket of my jacket. I walk out of the bank, my stick in hand, rucksack on my back, out onto the busy streets. I look about, left and right, up and down the road; I'm worried they're following me, but no sign of the black Mercedes. I can sense them; I know they'll be looking for me.

whispers

Now the café is full. I'm even having to share my table with another person: a man, clearly mad, who reeks of cat piss. He keeps mumbling to himself.

'Pressing hard . . . Pressing . . . Hard . . .'

Office workers, random people and college students are queuing impatiently at the counter. I watch and listen to them all, picking out words from the general fuzz of conversation, switching my attention from table to table, looking out of the window just to check he's not waiting outside, scrutinising every black car that pulls into the side road up to the High Street. I'm a nervous wreck.

'Ends thou . . . Ends thou . . .'

I single out the bored woman behind the counter as she shuffles to and fro, flitting from table to table when she has the chance to clear empty cups and plates, wiping the crumbs from each surface, dumping the cups and plates onto her plastic tray. Then running back to the counter to serve another customer. She has the look of Laura, slimmer though, with longer hair. Blonde, with the same angular cheekbones, the same Slavic features: stern eyes, tight-lipped. I begin to think about what I should do if it's all some kind of trap, if she is in with the men from the black Mercedes and they're simply using her to get to me for whatever it is they want from me.

'Creep . . . Creep . . . Creep . . . Creep . . . Ends thou . . .'

What if the men are waiting for me at the end of the pier? What then? I put my hand in my jacket, checking the money is still there. What if I'd inadvertently stumbled into something real? Something I shouldn't have? I hear about this all the time on the news, some man in the wrong place at the wrong time. I think about abandoning the whole thing. That's what anyone else would do, I know that. But Laura is driving me on, she makes me stronger, the image of her, what I can do for her. It's stronger than anything those men can do to me. This is what draws me to her: the sight of her face when I turn up, handing her the money, helping her get out of this mess, this life with these horrible people. And little old me, the person who can help make this happen, the person who can make that small difference, to help turn it around, to take her away from danger.

'Disappearing . . . Mist . . . Whispers . . .'

It's not like I've made a habit of such behaviour, I've never really been an altruistic person. There was a time in my life when the comfort of others mattered, but it didn't last long. That was when there was someone else in my life more important than me. I would have done anything for her. When I think of my marriage now this is the thought that rises to the surface, and it sickens me, it sickens me to the core. I would have done anything for her . . . but I didn't. Maybe you can love someone too much without realising it? Maybe too much love can suffocate a person? Maybe that's my problem: I smothered her? I killed her own love for me? In any case, it's left me with nothing but my own life. A life that makes no sense to me whatsoever.

'The . . . Gift . . . Whispers . . .'

no sense at all

The caffeine is charging through me. I walk through the shoppers on the High Street, down towards the sea, the pier. The crowds seem to be melting away from me with each step, even when a dog on a lead takes offence at my stick I simply glide past it without much effort. Suddenly, I see her: Laura. She's walking with him, the man from the flat on Toledo Road, from the black Mercedes. I'm sure it's her; it certainly looks like her, the same hair, cheekbones, the same gait. They're in conversation, even though he's talking to another person on his phone. I hang back a little, aware that I'm catching them up too quickly. I walk to my right, by the shop windows and doorways. I follow them down the High Street. They remain in deep conversation, all three of them, all the way, these two walking quickly and gesticulating to each other. I imagine the voice on the other end of the phone is walking along another street, heading for the pier, too, gesticulating into thin air.

I'm sure it's Laura. They turn right onto Alexandra Street and enter the Old Hat, another café bar. I wait where I can see them without much danger of them noticing me, just across the way, down an old mews by an air-rifle shop. I can see them at the bar; they order what looks like a shot of vodka each, downing it in one. Then the black Mercedes pulls up outside the bar. I step back and wait for a few seconds. When I look over I catch them getting into the car, before it screeches off along the one-way system, towards the High Street.

I'm sure it was her. It had to be her. Who else could it be? They can't all look alike, whoever it was the men had working for them. It doesn't work like that; the customer demands choice. It makes no sense for all the girls to look the same, no sense at all.

pushing against us

I walk to the pier. I'm hoping there'll be a lot of other people around, just in case. I'm determined to be with Laura, just to see if she's all right. I can't control what I'm doing. I walk without looking, quickly through the throngs. To my relief, when I reach Pier Hill, I can see the pier is already busy with people walking along it and queuing for the train to take them slowly to its end. I look around, just in case the black Mercedes is parked up on Royal Terrace or down on the esplanade. It seems safe, normal, as if everything that's happened to me has been some terrible hallucination and everything is real again.

I pay my money to the man in the hut at the gate to the pier. I walk slowly, trying to blend in with everyone else. I'm met by gusts of wind, huge williwaws charging down the pier, which nearly knock me off my feet. I step into it, struggling, digging in my stick, until this too becomes normal, real, and I begin to find each step easier to manage. The tide is in and the grey water is choppy, attacking each stanchion of the pier below. It feels like the entire estuary is pushing against us and at any moment the foundations of the pier will give way to the sudden tumult and fall down into its depths, but I don't care, I'm sick of nightmares and know that if I reach the end of this pier everything will be okay, just Laura to protect now, to guide back to shore.

About halfway along the pier I see a baby seagull, hobbling along the planks as a group of maybe four or five other, bigger seagulls mercilessly swoop down to take pecks at it, attacking it, bombing down from a frantic queue above. I try to shoo them away but it's no use, they dive at the baby seagull from all angles, and so quickly that I can't really see where they're coming from, or determine which one will be next, and besides, they're diving from a safe distance. The whole scene is over before I can do anything else to stop it, ending as quickly as it began: the baby seagull dead on the planks, tufts of down blowing in whorls around its limp, splayed wings and plump breast. The racket drifts away as the group of seagulls fly off, seemingly happy with the result.

I walk over to the dead baby seagull and pick it up. It's still warm, its downy feathers wondrous to the touch. I place it aside, near to a bin, out of people's sight. I think about dropping it into the sea, but this feels wrong. Then I suddenly change my mind a couple of metres up the pier, worried that the poor thing will be thrown out with the discarded kebab and fish and chip wrapping in the bins, so I walk back and pick it up again; a few people are watching me but it doesn't matter and I gently drop it into the estuary. I turn away before it hits the surface. I don't need to see that.

Maybe this event with the baby seagull will affect me in some way I'm not aware of? Maybe its cruel death will numb something inside me for ever? I don't know. I'll never know. All I know is that I'm walking along the pier outside myself. Looking at myself, observing everything I do: each gesture, each turn of my head, each blink of an eye. Looking inwards, oblivious to the things ahead of me: the crowds, the huge grey sky, the murky depths below, Laura waiting by the bell.

looping at intervals

She's leaning on the rail, waiting, looking out to sea, her back to me, facing the widening mouth of the estuary. I hesitate as soon as I spot her and stop walking. I watch her for some time: elevated above me on the second platform of the pier, the perfect pedestal. She looks completely at ease, like someone away from a busy work schedule, happy and content. She looks beautiful, like she's waiting for a lover, or just enjoying the great expanse of space before her. Elevated high enough – up above everybody else on the pier – to appreciate the vista before her. Then I notice something else: she's wearing different clothes from when I'd just seen her with the man. She's wearing skinny jeans and some sort of army fatigue jacket, zipped up close to her neck. She's wearing a rucksack on her back, too. Just like me. I regain my step and walk towards her, so that I can get a closer look. Just to make sure that it's actually her. As I get closer I notice that although her hair is still blonde, it's now shorter again, and seems to be styled differently than it was the last couple of times I'd seen her. How did she have the time not only to change her clothes but the style of her hair in the short amount of time it has taken me to walk to the end of the pier, not to mention how she then got here before me? It's possible, I think. I have been dawdling: she could have walked right past me on the pier when I was watching the baby seagull. It has to be her, it is her, but she keeps on changing every time I see her. I walk towards her. It has to be her, she's the only person who knows to meet me at that exact spot at this exact time. I pull out my phone, I look at the time: we're bang on schedule. Instead of putting my phone away, I stop and lean on the rail. I point my phone at her and begin to film her. I want to capture her, to keep the reality of her in my pocket, to take it with me, to view it whenever I see fit. I frame her just off-centre, so that more of the pier is in shot, and she takes up a tiny space in the top right-hand corner of the frame. I leave it recording for about one and a half minutes and then stop, putting the phone back in my pocket.

The image of the dead baby seagull falling to the depths of the grey water suddenly hits me. I stagger a little and have to dig my stick into the planks beneath my feet for support. It gets stuck between two freshly repaired boards. I yank it out with all my might and continue to walk towards her. I look up at the sky, at the grey clouds, knowing that Saturn is somewhere up there, with me, hanging above me, keeping me rooted. I need it to be there right now, just the thought of it there, just behind the clouds. My thoughts of Saturn are quickly dashed by a group of seagulls above me again, not the usual shrill, ear-splitting racket, more of a wail, as if they are mourning the recently departed baby seagull, like women at funerals in the Middle East: wailing in unison, grieving for all to witness, to record and to register. I watch as they whorl around me, elliptical, looping at intervals, swooping downwards in arcs: as if mimicking Saturn's slow, repetitive trajectory through space.

three thousand eight hundred

I walk towards her. With each footfall I'm sure it's her. I run through everything I'm going to say to her: how she'll react, where I'd take her, where we'd go to get away from everyone and everything. How I'll take her to the island, no one would think of looking for us there. I just have to convince her that I am doing the right thing, that all this, everything I am doing, is for her.

I walk up the pier, past the new cultural centre, up the steps to the RNLI office, onto the top deck, above the crowds, towards the bell, where she is waiting. She has her back to me. Annoyingly, there's a group of children playing loudly beside her. The children's yelps and screams are irritating the men fishing on the deck below us. I look over the edge to see if I can see the toothless man from last night, but there's no sign of him or Rocky. I turn back to Laura to find that she's looking at me.

'You're here . . . We have to be quick . . .'

'Laura . . .'

'You've got the money?'

'I'm so happy you're here . . .'

'Money?'

'Yes . . . Yes . . . I've got it, but . . .'

'But what?'

'I want you to consider a different plan . . .'

'What do you mean . . . I need the money, that's why you're here, right?'

'I can help you . . . More than my money can . . .'

'Please . . . I explained . . . I need to go home, things are not safe for me here any more. I'll contact you . . . When I know it's safe.'

'You'll be safe with me . . .'

'I'm not . . . We're not safe . . .'

'Listen to me . . . Jesus, I wish those kids would shut the fuck up . . .'

'What is it . . . Where's the money?'

'I've got it . . .'

'Give it to me, before they come . . .'

'There's no one here . . . just these . . .'

'Give it to me . . . Quick . . .'

189

'All right . . . All right . . . Will you just listen to me, once you have it?'

'Just give it to me, please . . . You're the only person who can help me . . . You're good, and kind . . . a kind, kind man.'

'Okay, Laura, okay . . .'

'I'm not who you think . . .'

'What?'

'Nothing . . . Laura's a nice name . . .'

I pull out the envelope from my jacket pocket. I think, although I'm not sure, it's the first time I've seen her smile. I can't describe how wonderful her smile is, it's as if the pier, the darkening sea below, the sky above become charged with electric light, a real fizzing presence of light, of joy, charging around us. This is exactly how it feels, how I will always remember this moment, happening exactly this way, always.

'Is it all there?'

'Yes.'

'Three thousand eight hundred?'

'Yes.'

'Can I have it?'

'. . .'

'Can I?'

'. . .'

'What is it? . . . Time is running out . . .'

'Please . . . Please . . . I just want to remember this moment, I wish I could capture it some way . . .'

something hits

It happens quickly. I'm stunned, frozen almost, barely able to process what is happening: two of the men come at me from behind, knocking me to the ground. My stick rolls along the planks. I grip on to the envelope. They pull me up and throw me against the rail, I hit it hard and it knocks the wind out of me. The children run back down the steps to whoever it is they're with. I catch eyes with one of the children as he looks back, a red-haired one, who looks directly into my eyes like he's just about to witness my execution, wide-eyed, excited and petrified, unable to stop looking. I don't want to be the subject of this boy's gaze, I want to be on the island with Laura, planning our escape, planning whatever it takes to feel part of the world around me.

Something hits me hard in the stomach: a fist that brings the bile up into my mouth. They pin me back, holding my arms away from my body. They spot the envelope in my hand. I struggle to keep it out of reach, but one of the men lunges for it, gripping on to it with me. We wrestle with it until I feel another fist under my ribs, forcing a reflex in me to let go of the envelope . . .

fishing

Nothing ever happens how you expect it to. The man isn't holding on to the envelope tightly enough and it tears immediately, its contents fluttering into the sea air like a shit card trick: each note, one after the other, arcing, out of the envelope, over the rail and into the sea. There's an almighty scream as the notes float, as gently as a bunch of petals, each stained with a lifetime's grime, down into the sea. The two men let go of me to lean over the rail, helpless, wailing in their own language, as the men fishing below, leaving their rods behind, jump over into the depths to collect as many of the notes as they can, the strongest of them, including the toothless man from last night, pushing other swimmers out of the way, stuffing the wet notes into pockets and down their trousers in a delirious frenzy. I break free and run over to my stick, picking it up, running, running, running away from the scene. I run all the way along the pier, back towards the shoreline, back towards Southend. Away from them, from Laura, from everything. They can fight it out among themselves. The money doesn't matter to me. I just want to find my place, I just want to feel real again.

Once I reach the gate to the pier I collapse into a heap. A crowd of people gather around me: some just to stare, others offering me help and comfort, but I can't see them, only hear their voices, as the blackness descends all around me, their voices penetrating into me.

'Are you all right?'

'Do you need an ambulance?'

'Give him some water.'

'Give him some room.'

'Loosen his jacket.'

'I know first aid.'

'He needs air.'

'Are you okay?'

'What's happened?'

'Can you see us?'

'How many fingers am I holding up?'

'What's your name?'

'What's your name?'

'What's your name?'

'Where do you live?'

'Do you know where you live?'

'Can you tell us your address?'

'Okay, lift him up.'

'There . . .'

'Place him on his side . . .'

'Up . . .'

'One . . . Two . . . Three . . .'

'Okay, move back, please . . .'

'Mind his head.'

'Okay, shutting the door now . . .'

to the ground

I awake at Southend Hospital A&E. I don't really remember much about my collapse on the pier, except I fell to the ground quickly, and with some considerable force. All I know is that it probably saved me from the two men. The doctor says I can leave as soon as I feel fit, so I get off the bed and grab my belongings.

'Where's my stick?'

'Here, Mr Michaels . . .'

'Thanks.'

'Take plenty of rest . . . Drink lots of water . . .'

I feel embarrassed. I want them to leave me alone. I thank them and walk out of the hospital, feeling groggy, horrible and confused. I head back to the island.

random drawers

I begin with the CDs and records, leaving his Dr Feelgood collection alone. I pack everything I can into boxes, twelve in total, and stack them up against the wall away from the shelves. It feels like the caravan is about to tip over, I stamp about a bit, just to test that it's okay. It is, so I carry on. I walk over to a desk and filing cabinet by Rey's old bed. I stand there for a while, staring at it. Something's not right: it's too quiet in here, too quiet for a task as mundane as this, so I walk over to the Dr Feelgood collection and pick out an album at random. I pull the record out from its sleeve and give it a wipe with my arm. The caravan is soon filled with the sound of the guitar. I put the other record, the one that was sitting on the record player, into its correct sleeve. Then I walk back over to Uncle Rey's desk. I open random drawers, each of them containing a lifetime of stuff that holds no meaning to me now. I don't know where to start, so I just pull things out, not really sure what I'm supposed to be looking for. There are no more boxes to put all this stuff in, so I ram it all into a large black bin-liner. It's mostly bank stuff: statements and letters spanning decades. In the top drawer of the filing cabinet, next to the desk, is a bunch of handwritten letters, all tied together with some parcel string. I undo the string and begin to look at each of them; it's hard to read Uncle Rey's spidery handwriting, but I just about manage to work out who they are addressed to: Mother. Some of the letters had reached her, but she had sent them straight back it seems. I look at the postmark, its ink fading: Bournemouth. The other letters hadn't been posted at all; Uncle Rey must have given up sending them. I am immediately struck that he kept on writing them regardless, but the feeling soon passes. I gather each of the letters together and put them into my rucksack. These letters are my only clue, the final pieces in the jigsaw to Mother's whereabouts, should I ever want to find her.

The rest of the drawers are full of newspaper clippings, mostly of significant military and terrorist events – the Falklands War, the first Invasion of Iraq, 9/11, et cetera. I read some of the headlines. All I feel is an overwhelming sense that life has passed me by. It has been there, things have happened, but I've been looking the other way, wherever that is. Nothing has slapped me across the face and woken me up from slumbers I haven't been aware of; all that suffering, all that commotion and I remained asleep, each event passing me by, my life a series of silent alarms.

The clearout carries on into the evening. The caravan looks odd, everything in boxes and bags, just the record player spinning more Dr Feelgood against the wall by the empty shelves. I decide to clear out the telescope and everything that's in the shed the next day, so that I can have one final attempt to view Saturn later in the evening. As soon as the task is finished my thoughts suddenly return to Laura. Even though I should phone Cal and contact Mr Buchanan, I begin to think about her, that maybe she was put up to it: the failed robbery, the money and the lies, maybe this was everything she wants to run away from? Even though I know it's not true, I still plan to pay her a visit at Toledo Road the next day.

it stops

I sit back and listen to the staccato guitar riff bouncing off each of the empty walls. It feels like the entire caravan is shaking, rattling in time with each fractured chord. I stand by the filing cabinet, rocking back and forth, my eyes closed, my hands passively by my sides, the music cutting into me, fragments and snippets of lyrics slicing into me, parts of drums, harmonica, bass and guitar. It swirls around me, revealing its make-up in geometrical shapes, lines, arcs and ellipses, circles, oblongs, triangles. It's mathematics. All flashing, strobing behind my eyelids. The voice and guitar morphing discordantly. All of it wrong. All of it out of sorts, but somewhere within all this I know there's perfection waiting. I know it's there. I can feel it. I don't want it to stop. I want the record to keep playing, over and over, manufactured in some way so the needle can keep returning to the beginning, over and over again, so I can remain where I am, here, cocooned in a whorl of sound, protected, away from the world, enclosed, away from everything . . .

It stops. The needle reaches the end of the record, resetting itself, ready for another play. I open my eyes. Stuck in imperfection, I can't take any more, so I leave the record like that, just as Uncle Rey had done: the record on the turntable, waiting for someone else to start it again. I walk back over to where *Vulgar Things* is by the armchair, thumbing through it, flicking the edges. I place it on the coffee table in the centre of the caravan. I look over it: it looks just right sitting there, it feels like it's sitting in perfect symmetry with everything else: the geometry of the room, the caravan, the site, the island itself: dead centre. I leave it there, knowing I never need pick it up again.

bags and boxes

I walk out of Uncle Rey's caravan. The evening light makes the sea wall seem to move with me, or flicker beside me, as if it's made of flimsy stuff, a temporary structure, like a caul or veil. I walk through the gate and up the grass verge to touch the wall, pressing against it, palms out, flat against it. Pushing and pushing, just to make sure. The cold, reinforced concrete sends a shiver through me. It feels solid, safe and immovable. I walk along it, the jetty down to my left. I try not to think of Uncle Rey and Laura, my mother, down there all those years ago, but it's hard not to. I shut my eyes, I don't want to see it. I walk like this, feeling my way with my stick, all the way to the Lobster Smack to see Mr Buchanan.

As usual he's sitting at the bar reading the paper. The man in the Dr Feelgood T-shirt is sitting next to him. The pub is busy and all the tables are full; the smell of food is too enticing to ignore and I look for somewhere to sit, where I can eat and have a private conversation, but it's no use. Mr Buchanan looks up from his newspaper and waves me over, pointing to a free stool next to his. It's as if he's been expecting me.

'Curry night.'

'What?'

'It's always this busy on curry night . . .'

'Oh . . .'

'You here for something to eat?'

'Well . . . Yes . . . But I also need to speak . . .'

'Yes, good . . . we need to speak about the caravan . . .'

'Yes . . .'

'Is it all clear?'

'Yes.'

'Wonderful . . . Wonderful . . . This is on me, tonight's on me . . . For all your hard work.'

'Thanks.'

'What you having?'

'Oh . . . I'll have the Lamb Dupiaza . . .'

'Good choice, good. It's a hot one.'

'That's okay.'

'What do you want to drink?'

'Oh, a pint of Staropramen, please . . .'

'I'll serve it to you myself.'

Something feels wrong. I can sense it. It's as if he knows something I don't, or that he's preparing me for something, some bad news, by acting like everything is fine. I sit on the stool. The man in the Dr Feelgood T-shirt looks up from his pint and nods to me.

'Nice T-shirt . . .'

I look down at myself. I'm still wearing the same T-shirt.

'Oh, this . . . it used to be Rey's . . .'

I immediately feel like I'm doing something wrong: wearing a recently deceased's clothes out in public. It doesn't feel right. I want to go back to the caravan and change into something else, but it's too late. Mr Buchanan walks back around the bar with my pint and places it in front of me.

'Here you go, Jon. I wanted to bring it to you rather than serve it to you across the bar . . .'

'Thanks . . . Robbie . . .'

'I've ordered your food.'

'Really, thanks . . . I can pay, you know . . . Please . . .'

'No . . . It makes me happy.'

'Okay . . . okay . . . Thanks.'

'So . . .'

'So . . .'

'Is the caravan all packed away?'

'Well, yes, everything's in bags and boxes. I'll arrange a van to take it all away on Friday . . . It wasn't too bad . . . you know . . . Just his personal things . . . Letters and video recordings . . . messages . . .'

'Messages?'

'It's hard to believe what he did to himself, you know . . . It's easy to forget about something like that . . .'

Mr Buchanan remains silent for a while. He shuffles on his stool and coughs a few times to break the silence, but it's obvious that he's either a) trying to stifle some urge to tell me something, or b) he's got absolutely nothing to say to me, now my job is complete, at all. I wait for him to speak. I've all the time in the world now, it seems. It doesn't matter to me either way, I tell myself. What has happened has happened and there's nothing I can do to change things. I look across the bar, over the heads of people sitting down to eat, towards the windows. The light has faded, the blackness is washing in from the estuary. I've only been on this island for a week and already I recognise about 80 per cent of the regulars sitting around me. I suddenly turn to Mr Buchanan.

'You knew, didn't you?'

'Pardon?'

'You knew . . .'

'Jon, I don't know what you mean . . .'

'You knew all along . . . about what he did . . . The reason why he cut himself off from everyone out here . . .'

'Jon . . . look . . . I really have no idea . . .'

'You knew.'

'Okay, yes . . . Something, I knew . . . a little bit of what went on . . .'

'You knew about me?'

'About him and her . . . it was a long time ago . . .'

'What do you mean?'

'Them coming here . . .'

' . . .'

'They came here, surely you know that now . . .'

'The jetty . . .'

' . . .'

'Tell me exactly what happened . . .'

'I thought you knew?'

'Tell me . . .'

'I thought everyone knew . . . Your father . . .'

'What about him? . . . Tell me now.'

'Okay . . . Come with me . . . Trish, we'll have our food on the captain's table, right . . .'

Mr Buchanan escorts me over to an empty table at the back of the bar. It's a large round table that's hard to notice if you're unfamiliar with the layout of the pub. We sit down, facing the whole bar. We're silent again, until the food arrives. I'm famished and tuck in to the curry, which is really good and just what I need, not even looking up from my plate to see what Mr Buchanan is doing.

'It was a long time ago. You know, they were all young . . . I was young, I didn't know the full story. They looked like a normal couple . . . I thought they were newlyweds, you know. Honeymooners used to come to the island back then, would you believe it . . . to this place, to walk the wall, to enjoy the air . . . it was a well-visited place back then, this island . . . Not like now . . . now, well, you know what it's like now, nothing left of the old place now, it's all gone, all the things that brought people here, as beautiful as this place is, people don't see it now . . . I just thought they were on holiday, I thought they looked like a beautiful couple, young and in love, here for a beautiful adventure. I didn't know what was really going on. I didn't see any of that. I mean, how was I supposed to know? . . . Jon, I thought you knew? She didn't . . . She wasn't supposed to be here . . .'

'. . .'

'He brought her here, Jon . . .'

'What are you trying to tell me?'

'She wasn't supposed to be here . . . He brought her here . . .'

'What . . . he kidnapped her?'

'. . .'

'Robbie . . . Tell me . . .'

'Yes . . . he brought her here . . . He brought her here against her will. I didn't know, I wouldn't have let them stay if I'd known . . . I wouldn't have let it happen. It just . . . well . . . you know, Jon . . . It just looked normal . . . Such a bonny couple, really . . .'

'He kidnapped her . . .'

'She was here against her will . . . he kept her here, in that caravan. I didn't know, none of us knew . . .'

'What was he . . .'

'They would go for walks, we would see them by the jetty, she never tried to tell anyone, or to get away . . . when she could have done . . .'

'How long did this go on for?'

'A couple of weeks . . . I don't know . . . he just paid me the money to stay.'

'What are you trying to say . . .'

'I don't know, Jon . . . I don't know.'

'What's that supposed to mean?'

'He held her captive, held her prisoner . . . this was a long time ago, before CCTV, and mobile phones, she had no way . . . he held her there, captive I guess.'

'What happened?'

'He . . . what do you mean?'

'How did she escape?'

'A man came . . . Rey's brother . . . your . . .'

'Dad?'

'Yes . . . he came to the site. There was an almighty fight. Your father beat Rey to a pulp . . . he took her back with him. I didn't know she was his wife, I knew nothing about the affair . . . It was an ugly scene. Rey refused hospital treatment and he locked himself away . . . We didn't see him for weeks. I never saw your father and mother again. It wasn't until months later that I talked to Rey about what had happened . . . He was a broken man, told me that he never wanted to leave the island, he never wanted to go back. I asked him about it . . . but he wouldn't really talk, like he was just acting out the words, he just said that he could never "love" anyone again . . . that his "moment in time" was finished . . . And I believed him . . . I believe those horrible events were the result of him loving her too much . . . if that's possible . . .'

'He's a fucking rapist . . .'

'No . . . No . . . No . . . I don't think it was like that . . .'

'He's my fucking father . . .'

'. . .'

'I'm the product of his "love" . . .'

'. . .'

'How do you think that makes me feel? . . . Knowing something like that . . . My poor, poor mother . . . it ruined her . . . No wonder she left us, no wonder she took the chance to start all over again, he never left her alone, he stalked her all his life . . .'

'Jon, I . . . I mean . . . I just . . .'

'I'm cursed, fucking cursed . . . listen to me, no one must ever find out about this. Not even Cal, no one . . . if they come asking . . .'

'Okay . . .'

'No one.'

We eat the majority of our meal in silence, except for a few banal observations about how tender the meat is and how hot the spices are, but that's about it. My head's spinning and I'm unable to block the sound of Uncle Rey's voice from my mind: all those words he'd failed to write down, to say, his truth, everything he'd failed to set right, his new morality, his stupid yearnings for atonement, the abject failure of all this, haunting him throughout his entire life, as he slowly drank and smoked himself towards madness. That one event: that 'moment in time' with my mother, destroying him for good, because he got it wrong, because his desires got the better of him, because of his selfish ways, his lack of self-control. It's all there, whirling within my head, because he is me, he created me, and there's nothing I can do to escape this: him, the living memory of him. I have to finish it, I have to put an end to everything he left behind, it's up to me to extinguish him from existence, every trace, every *thing* that is his. Only I know this is impossible, he's left his mark, his trace in the world. Me. I'm the smudge, the black mark, blackness itself. I'm his detritus, and that's all I'll ever be. He tears through me, he's boring into me every second, he's in me now. I can hardly look up from my plate.

'Jon . . . I'm so . . .'

'Don't . . . Please . . . it's okay.'

it all becomes visible

Now I'm back in Uncle Rey's caravan. I slowly walked back here after I'd thanked Mr Buchanan for the meal and his hospitality and then shared a drink with the man in the Dr Feelgood T-shirt, who drunkenly quizzed me about my own T-shirt.

'I'm not really a fan . . . this was Uncle Rey's T-shirt . . . he was a fan, not me.'

I sit at Uncle Rey's desk and take his letters to Mother out of my rucksack. I stare at them, I scrutinise the address, wondering if she still lives there. There's no point in reading them, I don't think, I know the sort of stuff that he'll have said. I can feel all that within me. I put them back in my rucksack. Then I begin to clean the caravan, starting with the bedroom, then the small bathroom, the kitchenette and the living room. I don't stop until the place is spotless, horrified at the amount of dust that has accumulated over the years. It seems only in death that dirt and grime become visible, in death we see how things really are: everything, each speck of dust, each smudge and build-up of matter, grime, shit and waste, it all becomes visible, we see it immediately and it horrifies us. Living things are filthy and it's only when death confronts us that we finally see ourselves for what we truly are: accumulations of filth. It's why we cleanse our dead when we prepare them for burial or cremation. There's no such thing as sin, just dirt.

need to move closer

After I'm finished I walk out to the shed. I pull all the charts off the walls and roll them up, wrapping elastic bands around them, stacking them in the corner. I pick up the book with the chart tracking Saturn's progress in the night sky. I stop what I'm doing. My breathing is heavy and I feel light-headed. I roll back the roof with the pulley-lever. The cold air immediately hits me, the sky is black and clear up there, a carpet of stars reveal themselves. Saturn is somewhere up there, hanging in the same blackness, silent, waiting. I can feel its presence. A small jewel in the night, a yellow-brown marble, the rings hovering around it, a protective field.

I set up the telescope, fixing it into position, slowly and carefully, pointing it up to the section of the sky where I'd last stumbled across Saturn. I put my eye to the lens, but it's out of focus. I fiddle with the lens for some time, sharpening and re-sharpening the image, until the abyss above me brings everything together: stars and constellations becoming visible, as if the blackness has willed the universe to acknowledge my presence. I feel like I'm going to fall into it, as if something is about to pull me through the lens towards it, into it, falling into the same incredible blackness. I begin to feel nervous, the same vertigo-like feelings. I need to find Saturn, to see it, to make sure it's still there: just to witness it hanging there, out there, coming through the night towards me. I delicately move the telescope across the night, sharpening and re-sharpening, my breathing quickens as I pull more of the oxygen around me deep into my lungs, the night air entering me, the same blackness filling up my lungs, fusing with me, as I sink deeper into it. Suddenly I realise I have the wrong lens in the telescope: a x6 mm instead of a x12 mm. I'm seeing too deeply into the night sky, I need to move out, outwards, allowing more of the vast night into the lens, deeper. I quickly change the lens, the blackness as sharp and as crisp as ever. I slowly move the telescope to the right, millimetre by millimetre. It feels like I'm about to pass out.

Saturn suddenly appears. It slips into view, like a trick, some sleight of hand. I focus in on it, sharpening the reflected, upside-down image, shaking a little, its back rings higher than the front, its entire southern hemisphere tilting towards me, like a gentleman tipping his hat. Saturn's declination thrills me: the way it hangs there in the blackness, leaning towards me, for me.

I imagine I'm the only person in the world looking at it right now. I focus in as much as I can, trying to determine each of its seven rings, as much as the lens will allow me before it blurs. Saturn simply hangs there, mysterious in its splendour, frightening and beautiful, a maddening sphere of gas, so real before me it feels like I can reach through the telescope and touch it. It seems to confirm everything; my entire existence: each blemish, spot and milky swirl on its surface representing some mark of me.

I stare at Saturn through the lens until my eyes begin to hurt, making slight adjustments in accordance with the earth's rotation and movement. But something isn't right. It doesn't feel right all of a sudden. Everything is reduced to this yellow-brown marble in the night, everything is sucked into it. My eyes begin to water, and it becomes harder for me to focus on the image, so I take out my phone and turn on the camera so that I can film it through the lens. It strikes me that I've never thought of this before. I line up the eye of my phone's camera with the lens of the telescope, and look through the screen of my phone at the image: at first I'm confronted with blackness, then something incredible happens as I begin to film: Saturn comes into view, a shadowy apparition of what I've just seen through the original lens, a pixellated, digitised version, overlapped and over-layered, a recorded image seen in the present. It's truly beautiful, like a work of art. Truly real.

I stop recording after one minute and fifty-three seconds. I laugh. I re-watch the recording immediately. I laugh at everyone who's lived a life unaware of its presence, its brilliance in the black night, those who live never looking up at things, never reaching out, afraid to question, afraid to learn finally that there are no answers and there never will be. Things just go on, hanging there in the blackness, surrounded by it, but they go on, things go on, everything goes on.

i know this won't last

Later on I walk to the creeks below Canvey Heights. The stars seem low in the blackness above me. I can see their reflections in the murky water below. The moon, just up behind me, is low over the estuary, too: yellow, brown, as if trying to emulate Saturn itself. I sit down by the remains of the old concrete barge, stuck rotting in the mud. The air is strangely warm and still; I can hear movement in the water, gentle laps on the muddy creeks. I look up into the dense night, out towards Southend: I can see bats wildly fluttering around, in a swooping figure of eight; beyond them I can see the outline of the old church in Leigh-on-Sea; and below that, the tall masts of the sailing and fishing boats anchored in Old Leigh, along the cockle sheds, deep down into the estuary. Their silhouettes float like black ghosts, or black paint marks on some sombre canvas. I want to capture what I am seeing. I take out my phone and try to take a picture and then some footage, but it's too dark. Just like in Uncle Rey's book, I know this is impossible anyway, I don't know why I even attempt to do it, so I sit and stare, filming anyway. I try to take in every minute detail: the smell of the mud and wild lavender, the blackness, the yellow-brown moon, the wet earth and tough grass beneath my feet, the sound of the water lapping against the mud, the stillness . . . filming every moment.

I know this memory won't last, but it doesn't matter. I know that one day most of it will be formless, dumped in some barren recess of my mind, something almost forgotten. I know that now. It doesn't matter. The moment has been digitised. I'll still have that. Uncle Rey's words are spinning within me. I find it impossible to grab hold of them, it's as if I've disturbed them in my reading of *Vulgar Things*, spilled them out of their container, where they had been put away. It's as if I've stumbled across a wasps' nest and accidentally kicked it, but instead of running for shelter and the safety of a locked door, I've simply remained and attempted to fight off each and every pesky wasp one by one. I'm finding them hard to shake off, they're everywhere, they're buzzing inside me, like a rotten virus. I feel contaminated.

It strikes me as a normal thing to do: to shed my clothes, to step down the muddy bank of the creek and dip my toes into the cold water before sinking into it and fully submerging myself, swimming out into the middle of the creek. I float there on my back, looking up at the stars, the blackness all around me. It feels like I'm weightless, floating in nothingness, like I'm hanging around with everything else in the universe: spinning, expanding, out here among it all: the stars, the planets. Saturn, the fertile planet. Its yellow glow binds me together with Uncle Rey, the island, Laura, everything that has happened to me, for ever entwined with everything Uncle Rey tried to forget, to write out of his life. That one day, like it or not, I'll forget my own way.

I float on my back, cast out, sown, planted in time. But I don't want to be rooted here, on the island, with all these people, I want to end what Uncle Rey had tried to begin. I want to destroy everything he's sown. I need to set light to his work, to reduce it to ashes, send it back to dust. I want to free it, to set it off into the universe – each strand, each particle and molecule of it. It's all I can think of. I swim back to the muddy bank, clambering up the side, trying to retrace my own footsteps. I slip, caking myself in mud. I pick up my stick where I left it and use that to pull myself up, digging it into the mud for support. Finally I reach my clothes, just as it starts to cloud over. I walk back to Uncle Rey's caravan carrying them under my arm. I know what I have to do now.

THURSDAY

some kind of happiness

A slanting beam of sunlight wakes me. It shoots in from the window and tickles the toes on my right foot, which is hanging out of the blanket because I'd been too warm during the night. I lie here without moving, allowing the warm sunlight to creep up my leg as the earth turns on its axis. I watch the dust motes, thousands of them: all hanging there, spinning, darting, floating about in their own peculiar fashion. Then I realise they're floating all around me, they're everywhere, and the earth is just like them: a dancing dust mote in space, light and time. The thought both frightens and exhilarates me.

I shoot up off the sofa. I'm still caked in mud from last night's impromptu swim in the creek, so I walk straight into the tiny shower room. Even though the water is freezing I simply stand there letting it wash all over me. I watch as the bits of mud, grit and grime swirl down the plug hole. Everything is spinning, or floating about, all around me, yet, like in my view of Saturn last night when I watched it back on my phone, everything is still fixed, stationary, hanging in time. It's a truly remarkable feeling to possess first thing of a morning, something I've never experienced before.

I dry myself off and walk into the kitchenette to fill up a pint glass with cold water from the tap. I gulp it down in a couple of swigs. I feel refreshed, brand new, like my blood is running through my veins at double its usual pace. I walk to the toilet and piss, then

I take a shit. I sit there happy before flushing the chain, wiping my arse and opening the small window to let in some fresh air. I spray myself with deodorant and then put on some underwear and the same clothes I was wearing last night. They don't seem to smell too much. I wipe off the mud, which has now hardened on my jeans and T-shirt. I pick up my stick and step outside, breathing in the fresh, salty air. I dig my stick into the grass: it's not too soft, good for walking. I nip back into the caravan, grab my rucksack and the keys, lock up and head out, following the sea wall, through the gate, along the grass verge, out towards the Labworth Café for some breakfast.

I order a full English breakfast with an extra portion of black pudding, buttered toast and a cup of tea. I pop a pinch of pepper into my tea, just how I like it now. It's a glorious meal. My table is in the corner, near the last of the big windows that overlook the estuary, away from the other customers. It's good to feel disconnected from them. I take out my phone and watch the footage of Saturn I recorded last night about four or five times, before watching the footage of the black night out by the creeks, and then finally of me, the young person, staring back at me, saying those things again and again. It feels real. It looks real. It's as real as I'm alive. After I finish the meal I pull out a scrap of paper and a pen from my rucksack and begin to write down all the things I'd like to say to Laura. I figure she'll be back at Toledo Road. I need to say these things, to help me shut her down, to close whatever connection it is I've convinced myself I have with her, to ask her one more time, to make sure it wasn't some scam and I'm not some poor victim, or, worse still, target. She must be wondering what happened to me on the pier. Or where I appeared from and disappeared to? The way I've appeared in her miserable life? Telling her she's beautiful, she's this, she's that. Telling her I can save her, how I can tip the earth's axis, so that she'll fall into a better life, an existence where she'll always be happy, closer to me, closer to some kind of happiness.

I want to tell her that I'm not bothered about the money, that there's more where that came from, that money isn't important to me. I hope to convince her that we don't need money, that we can just exist together, somewhere else, hanging together in nothingness, like everything else around us, hanging together in the ether of our lives. It's a simple wish, and I immediately wonder why other people haven't reached it. It seems funny to me now that people should want to live all huddled up together, fighting it out en masse, in what little space they can afford. What's the point in that? There's more to it than that, surely? All you have to do is look up into the blackness, up into the night: there's enough space for everyone. What are we all so frightened of that we feel the need to huddle together around the fire of our lives?

the voices float by

I walk to Southend. Familiar territory now. There's nothing to look at any more. Nothing much to see. All I can do now is listen to the world around me, listen to the breeze, listen to the sea as it crashes onto the pebbles, listen to the seagulls, the traffic, the children playing, the lovers arm in arm strolling ahead of me. I listen to them all now, every last one of them. The voices float by, in varying tones and pitch.

'He's never called . . .'

'. . . there were fifteen of the fuckers . . .'

'Not my fault . . .'

'M&S, then coffee . . .'

'OMG!'

'OMG!'

'OMG!'

'Really . . .'

'. . . underneath where the oil goes . . .'

'I'm not paying . . .'

'I've always eaten like a man, I can eat what I like . . .'

'. . . the bus . . .'

'FUCK OFF!'

'Cunt, he is . . .'

'I fucking lost them . . .'

'Come back here, Mandy, now . . .'

'Don't you touch that . . .'

'Down by the pier . . .'

'. . . it's too long . . .'

'Down by the pier . . .'

'If it's sunny . . .'

'. . . the pier's too long . . .'

'I sat by the pier . . .'

'There was nothing else to do . . .'

'We had a nice walk that day . . .'

'. . . to London . . .'

'The pier . . .'

'. . . the pier . . .'

'. . . . . the pier . . .'

'. . . . . the pier . . .'

I can't make out the faces, just their words, so many words: remainders, snippets, fragments. Their centre is Laura, where we first met, where I first saw her by the bell. I can see it on my right, as I walk along Cliff Terrace: the pier. I even look out for her, but it stretches out too far into the estuary for me to distinguish one figure from another. I head towards Toledo Road.

i had it in me

I don't understand. I'm underneath the cherry tree looking over at the house where Laura's flat is. The windows are all boarded up for a start, upstairs and in the flats below. The front door is open, off its hinges, and a group of men with clipboards are hovering around the doorstep, collecting things, recording things. Some other men are carrying things into an unmarked white van and a lady is cordoning off the house with blue and white tape. The quiet professionalism is hypnotising. I stand and watch the whole oper-ation, whatever it is, for about half an hour, as neighbours pop out of their houses to stare and gossip with other neighbours standing in the street. Some of them attempt to talk with the group of men with the clipboards, but they ignore them and carry on with their business.

There's a man on his own, writing stuff into an iPad or some-thing, near some other people talking on mobile phones and scrib-bling furiously into spiral notepads. The police are here, too, guarding the scene, dealing with angry drivers who can't get through the road. I watch it all unfold, as if I'm witnessing the penultimate scene from a bad film. I lean against the cherry tree, digging my stick into the grass, and begin to write my own obser-vations down into a notebook, and filming the whole scene with my phone. I hadn't realised until this moment that I've been writing things down, recording what I'm thinking, what is happening and what I've been doing. I've been writing stuff down all week, it seems, as I flick through the notepad, looking at all the random scribblings that I've no recollection of doing: fragmentary stuff I'm not aware of, writing it all down in fits, in starts, words trailing off, hitting culs-de-sac. When I eventually stop writing and filming I walk over to the man in the road who's also jotting things down.

'What's going on?'

'The usual . . . It was pandemonium last night, apparently . . .'

'What?'

'Two gangs . . . guns, knives . . . Eastern European . . . Bloodbath, about three or four dead, including two women . . . All this over some money and girls, I reckon. Turf war or something, people smuggling . . .'

'Women? . . .'

'There's talk of sex trafficking . . .'

'Laura . . .'

'What?'

'. . .'

'Fucking . . . This place . . .'

I walk away from the empty flat. I feel numb. I shouldn't have come back. I shouldn't have gone to the pier to try to help her. I should have made sure she was okay. I could have done something about it like phone the police. I could have changed her mind. I had it in me, I should have done something when I had the chance. I tried, I tried, but it wasn't enough. I looked into her eyes. I spent too much time looking, when I should have acted, without words, without my pathetic gaze. That's what I should've done.

moving away from me

I walk along the pier, all the way to the end, to the bell. I look up the estuary, out from its gaping mouth. I want her to be here, gazing out at it with me. I wish there had been some mistake, like she got the times wrong, or something, but I know that it's just wishful thinking. A large container ship comes into view beyond Shoebury Boom, just on the horizon. It gradually grows bigger, inching towards me, along the estuary. I'm in awe of its power, its stature. It amazes me how it keeps from toppling over. Its presence is immense as it slowly moves towards me. It looks unmovable, like nothing can touch it, that it can do anything it wants. It takes a good twenty minutes to reach me, until it's parallel with me and the end of the pier. I reach out with my stick, as if I can simply touch it. It's colossal, gigantic. It's like a miracle before my eyes. I quickly turn around, to see if there's anyone else near me, but the end of the pier is empty. Even the fishermen below seem to have disappeared. I'm in awe. There it is: that rumble now, that deep, deep, constant thump thump thump thump thump of the engines. I can feel it in my toes, reverberating through the sea, the sea bed, the mud, the stanchions; it's reached me finally, that beautiful, almost inaudible rumble that makes my whole body tingle.

The ship doesn't take that long to pass my line of vision, beyond the pier, towards the island there and on through to Tilbury. It seems to be moving away from me much quicker now, far more quickly than it took to arrive. Everything seems to be moving away from me; everything seems distant again, too colossal to pull back, to shift; everything is moving, except me. I'm stuck, it seems, watching it all slide away.

nothing can be deciphered

I walk back along the pier for the final time. There's no reason for me to return now. There's nothing for me here in Southend any more. It's all been taken away. I walk through the streets, my stick clicking at my heel. Everything is sounds, voices, buzzing around me, nothing is distinguishable, nothing can be deciphered, everything is cryptic, it makes no sense to me, nothing is recognisable, words pass me by, sounds whorl inside my head, but they puzzle me, there's nothing I can do with them, they fizz inside me, disappearing, ending in a *pffft*, filtering through me, passing through me back into chaos. I can't stop any of it, no matter how hard I try. It all becomes interference, static, a cacophony; a looping, rising madness that I can't stop. I shut my eyes, trying to force it all out of my head, but it doesn't work. I feel it's something I was once receptive to, something in which I had no choice, I simply picked it all up somehow. I simply let it all flow through me, picking out the bits I needed, that's all I could do with it. That's all I can ever hope to do with it. Now, it's simply noise.

speak quietly

Now the island is quiet. People pass me by in silence. I head to the southern side of the island, towards the jetty. I want to sit there, to watch some more ships glide by. Listening for that rumble, watching, waiting finally to leave things behind. As I walk past the huge oil containers just off Haven Road I spot the man in the Dr

Feelgood T-shirt walking towards me, about one hundred yards ahead of me. He's spotted me too, as he's already waving at me. I wave back with my stick. It doesn't take us long to reach each other.

'You're still wearing it, then?'

'. . .'

'The T-shirt . . .'

'Oh, yes, the T-shirt . . . Uncle Rey's . . . yes.'

'Those were the days, you know.'

'Sorry . . .'

'Back in the seventies . . . back in the days of the Canvey Club . . . When life was new, angry, when we had bullets to bite . . .'

'I can imagine . . .'

'I knew him, you know . . .'

'. . .'

'I knew him . . .'

'Who?'

'Rey . . .'

'Oh.'

'I saw him . . . I was with him the night before . . . You know . . .'

'Oh . . .'

'We drank whiskey looking up at the stars through that telescope of his . . . He was in a terrible state, but I had no idea . . . you know . . . that he was planning something as horrible as he did . . . We drank and talked all night . . .'

'What did you talk about . . .'

'You . . .'

'. . .'

'We mostly talked about you . . .'

'. . .'

'I knew it was you . . . When I first saw you, off the train . . . I recognised him in you immediately . . .'

'Oh . . .'

'You know . . . He . . .'

'I have to . . .'

'No . . . Wait . . . He . . .'

214

'He wasn't a good man . . .'

'He worshipped the ground you walked on . . . You have to believe me . . .'

'It's too late, though, isn't it . . .'

'He wanted things to be different . . .'

'He slipped away from me, out of view . . . His life is meaningless to me.'

'Yours wasn't to him . . . in fact, you're the only reason he went on, the only reason he remained . . . He lived in hope . . . That's what he said to me . . . He lived in hope that you'd accept him as your father, that's what he said . . . That's what he wanted to tell . . .'

'Well . . . He had a funny way of showing it . . .'

'There's no right way of . . .'

' . . .'

'He wanted you to accept him . . .'

' . . .'

'He wanted you to acknowledge him as more than . . .'

'Just stop it now . . . He's gone, no trace after tomorrow . . . for good . . . As much as you know him, as much as all the time you spent with him, listening to his bullshit, you never could, or will know him as much as I do now . . .'

'But . . .'

'But what?'

'He . . . He said something . . .'

'What?'

'He knew you'd come again, he wanted it to be that way . . . He . . .'

'What?'

'He said . . . "Tell him, tell him to speak quietly and to carry a big stick . . . that's all he'll need." That's what he said . . . He said it's a quote, but I've forgotten who he said it's from. He told me to tell you this, he kept repeating it over and over . . .'

'Do what . . .'

'Speak quietly and carry a big stick. That's what he said.'

'I don't . . . I don't think I understand . . .'

'That's all he said to me, he made sure that I remembered the quote . . . He knew how bad my memory is, so he told me over and over, so that I'd be able to remember . . .'

'For this moment?'

'Well, yes . . . I wanted to tell you in the pub, or visit the caravan, but you were always talking with Robbie . . .'

'Here . . . In the middle of this road?'

'That's all he wanted to tell you . . .'

'On this wretched island?'

'I don't know what else to say . . .'

'. . .'

'Wait . . . Sorry . . . Wait . . .'

I forget about the jetty and continue towards the Lobster Smack, leaving him standing in the road. I should speak to Mr Buchanan one last time, just to say goodbye, to thank him. There's so much more I should ask him, but there doesn't seem to be a point to it any more. It would just prolong everything, when what I really need to do is move things on, away from all this. One day I know that I'll finally look back at all this, I'll read my notes and re-watch all my recordings and I'll be able to make sense of it all, but it seems such a long way off at the moment.

is it all finished?

To my right, the oil refinery towers over me: tall chimneys, the gargantuan oil containers, brimming with the stuff. I want to submerge myself in it somehow, to sink slowly into it, its blackness engulfing me, a blackness I'd be unable to escape from, never to be found, sunken, returned, lost in its gloop, where I'd remain, entombed for aeons, eventually broken down into particles and matter, used to power giant engines on ships, machinery, fuelling the big bangs of industry. I would return to where I came from: the blackness of night.

I carry on walking, as quickly as I can. I need to finish what I started. I head straight for the Lobster Smack to see Mr Buchanan. Just as I'm about to walk through the door to the pub my phone begins to ring. It's Cal.

'Hello . . .'

'Jon . . .'

'Cal . . .'

'Is it all finished?'

'What?'

'Is it all finished?'

'What, sorry, I can't hear you, it's breaking up, the signal is breaking up, where are you?'

'I'm at Stansted . . . Just got back . . .'

'Right, okay . . .'

'Is it all finished?'

'Yes, Cal, it's all finished . . .'

'Oh good . . . Just remember to label all the boxes correctly, okay . . .'

'Sure, Cal . . .'

'We've got to go . . .'

'Cal, I need to . . .'

'Our car is here . . . We've got to go . . . I'll phone you tomorrow . . .'

'Sure . . .'

' . . .'

' . . .'

it doesn't feel like an ending

When I walk into the Lobster Smack Mr Buchanan greets me almost immediately. There's a broad smile across his face. He adjusts his wire-framed glasses and pats me on the shoulder.

'Jon . . . Jon . . . I didn't expect to see you today . . .'

'Oh . . . I just . . .'

'I thought you'd be in Southend . . .'

'I have . . . How did you know that?'

'Oh . . . I guessed . . . I just figured that's where you'd be . . .'

'Well, I don't need to go there any more, there's no need for that, there's nothing for me there now . . .'

'Well, you must be ready to go back to London tomorrow?'

'Yes . . . yes, I am.'

'Must be a relief?'

'To go back there?'

'Yes.'

'I don't know . . . I might take a holiday, or something . . .'

'Well, at your age I suppose you can still go wherever you want . . .'

'Yes . . . I guess I can . . .'

' . . .'

'Mr . . . Robbie . . .'

'Yes?'

'Is . . .'

'What?'

'Is he still alive?'

'What do you mean?'

'Is Uncle Rey still alive?'

'What?'

'Is he?'

'No . . . No . . . What are you talking about . . . What . . . Why do you think . . . What do you mean?'

'It's just that I have this feeling . . . In my gut . . . That he's been talking to you all . . . You know, since I've been here, that he's staged it all and you're all in on it . . . Like he's looking over me, or creating things for me, so that I'll, you know . . . Forgive him, or something . . .'

It just hit me really, like that, I hadn't given it much thought, and there's no real reason to have reached such a far-fetched conclusion, but something in Mr Buchanan's eyes, something in his staged reaction piques my interest. I'm convinced he's covering something up, like there's something else he isn't telling me.

'He's as dead as Dillinger, lad.'

'Something isn't right about all this . . . It's like . . .'

'What?'

'It's like it's all been staged . . . I can feel his presence . . . Like he's there wherever I go, watching me, recording my every move with some hidden camera . . .'

'But he's dead, Jon . . .'

'I feel like he's watching us now . . .'

'It's natural to feel this way . . . It's a big loss, and a sad one, under these circumstances.'

'It just doesn't feel right, like you know something . . . like you're hiding something from me . . .'

'Jon . . . Jon . . . This is ludicrous, there's nothing to hide . . . Rey was a sad, lonely old man . . . who'd lived a life of regret. He was a truly sad man, that's all there is to it.'

'I just want an end to it . . . it doesn't feel like an ending . . . it just goes on and on and on and on . . .'

I'm starting to get angry, frustrated. I seem to be shaking my stick aggressively. Mr Buchanan backs away, just out of harm's way. I stop when I see him doing this and walk over to a table to sit down. He follows me after a slight hesitation, putting his hand on my shoulder again.

'Nothing ends, Jon . . . You know that as much as I do . . . all it can do is go on . . .'

I sit with my head in my hands. I can sense Mr Buchanan fumbling around for something behind me.

'There is one thing . . .'

'Pardon?'

'There is one more thing . . . Something I didn't tell you . . .'

'What . . . What is it?'

'He gave me a letter.'

'For me?'

'No . . . For . . .'

'Who?'

'Your mother . . .'

'Oh.'

'He gave it to me the morning before he . . . You know . . .'

'Where is it?'

'He wanted me to post it to her, he just told me to post it . . . Nothing else . . .'

'Did you?'

'No . . .'

'Why?'

'I don't know . . . I must have forgotten initially . . . and then after what he did, I just . . . You know . . .'

'Where is it?'

'It's here . . .'

I put the letter in my rucksack with the others. Mr Buchanan offers me some lunch as an apology. We eat rare steak and share a bottle of Burgundy. He asks me about London and I tell him that I might sell up and leave, that there's nothing for me there either. All the while the letter to Mother is burning a hole in my rucksack. It must be the final thing he wrote, to Mother, his final thoughts. I'm itching to read it, but I remain calm, savouring each mouthful of the steak and fine wine.

'There're a few things I'd like to ask you to do . . . I can leave you the money . . .'

'Certainly, Jon . . .'

'Could the telescope and everything else in Uncle Rey's shed, the charts and maps and stuff, be sent off to me, here's my address . . .'

'Sure . . . Of course . . .'

'And there's a bunch of Dr Feelgood records, could you send them to my brother Cal? His address is here. He doesn't live that far from me.'

'Yes, sure . . . Is there anything else?'

'No . . . I think that should be it . . . The rest will be taken care of . . . I'll drop off the money and keys with you at some point tomorrow afternoon. Could you make sure everything is sent tomorrow morning . . . I'll leave the records in the shed.'

I finish my glass of Burgundy and shake Mr Buchanan by the hand. He smiles at me, but I don't feel like smiling much. I thank him for everything, grab my stick and rucksack and walk out of the pub. I climb up the grass verge, up onto the sea wall, over the iron steps and out onto the jetty. The tide is out, revealing the rocks and pebbles, the muddy flats on which the seagulls and oystercatchers are gorging themselves on whatever it is they find out there. I find myself a suitable rock to sit on, down the steps, on the shore. I open my rucksack and take out the letter. I look at her address. I stare at each letter of her address, the place where she's been all this time, for most of my life, living her own life away from the world. I open the envelope.

My dearest Laura,

I hope you dont mind me calling you this still? It just seems right, okay? I guess its how I rember you, how I will always remember you and our short life together. These thoughts I have of you, they well within me, surge, they spring from within me, succeeding the last, they breed self-sorrow, that I wish to shed, I wish to leave behind now, I have shed too many tears, each day these thoughts have haunted me, the closer I get to this day. I just wish I had the wings, so I can soar to you, my spirit freed of sorrow for everything I did to you – all of it through love for you, my love for you. Must it prove so fruitless? Must I strive in vain, Laura? I yearn for the day we can meet again, fearful of it at the same time. But I fear this hope is to late, its someone elses domain. Yet theres just one thought in me that pleads: who supports you now with words and love? I must tear from my heart these dead words from our youth, they are rotten, they strangle me, they pull me down, closer to the earth. I have gazed upon you from afar for to long now, I have dreamed your charms towards me in ecstacy. I have wished for this the whole of my life, picturing your beautiful face, whose beauty sets my heart ablaze. This flame within me has remained throughout my bitter, ugly life, my vulgar days without you, and all of the nothingness you left me with – but this flame, this beautiful

flame has brought me nothing but ill, now its time for loftier realms
to direct my will. Everything sinse you has whirled around me –
those days when I kept you, when you were mine to treasure, just
for those few days, you were mine, Laura, you were mine. You must
understand that my actions, as treacherous as they were, were born
out of my love, my desire for you. Look where these torments took
me: rising into vulgar nothingness without you. Lost in sublime
reverie. I am sick with it now, I am sick with regret.

There are other thoughts that mingle within me, which have
compelled my heart towards these lousy passions of mine, my
feverish heart, growing within me all these years – in the hope that
we will one day share the same grave, shed of flesh and temptation,
where we can live side by side in the silence together.

This shadowy desire splits my poor mind. Shadowed now, were
no other thought can grow. The seasons pass me by now without
concern, I live, have lived through them, writing for you, unable to
reach you, recording all my words for you, unable to right all the
wrongs I made. And you know how bad I am with them . . . words
I can barely spell correctly. My heart grows softer, basking in your
flow that radiates from these eyes of yours I carry with me each
day, that beautiful image I have of you. I cant allow these thoughts
to leave me, to let them drift amongst the rocks at sea, that
dangerous terrain. So I sit here confronting them, writing to you,
one final time, confronting the end head on, the full stop of my life,
in haste, unable to tie the noose that I hope will defeat me.

I know myself, Laura, I have failed to learn anything, let alone
the truth, I am held by my love for you, I have left honour behind,
I have entered a dark place, a dark wood of something, self-harm,
all of that, ridicule and delusion. The stronger my desire for you the
stronger my shame, and the louder my head screams blame, shovel-
ling my way in heaps. Its all my fault, and for this Im sorry. And
no matter how many years have passed, my pathetic little life, my
grey hair, where death now feels my true lot, I don't look for
tomorrow. I look back, I look back at you and I fail. My loss is our
past, I marvel at this failing, looking back at you in the darkness of

my life. I have cast sail towords you, the leeway seems good towards death thinking only of you.

Such then, I am a song to you, a song of sorrow and regret. A song, like me, that must perish. Death, my old friend, hears me, offeres me company. It seeks me and I seek it, never forgetting you, never able to harm you again, and all because I loved you to much, all because my desires run away with me.

Read this letter, my beautiful, as one final look back towards you, one gentle look at your fair face. Your beauty, your body whole – one last gaze at that smile of yours whose wounding grace has soothed my death . . . all my hope is ended. You were my queen of the earth, decended from above in starlight, where you comforted me, the evil race of men and dogs. In my death I will burn within you. I was yours utterly . . . my heart cant take any more, I showered you in my desire, I sent you my words, my heartfelt words of sorrow and regret, these words I hope you'll one day read, as broken as they are, as shoddily put together as I have made them, so youll know that I am eternally sorry. In this darkness, in death, my death, I offer you this, for always . . . untill the wind blows my words away.

Always
Rey

I fold up the envelope with the address and put it in my rucksack with the others. Then I rip up the letter I've just read and fling it into the air. The wind carries each piece, like petals, out towards the water's edge, where they land in the black water to be carried out into the sea. I stay at the jetty until the sun begins to fall behind the oil refinery, the sky quickly darkening, the failing light twinkling on the choppy black water. Uncle Rey's words long since washed away, sucked down into the silt and the shit, where they will remain, breaking down into particles, back to their own source, where his words will live again, somewhere else, in something else, living and dead, on and on, never ending, never going anywhere. I look out over the water, it feels like it's about to rise up above me, like a giant duvet about to be pulled over my head. It's comforting and frightening, I let it wash all over me before picking up my stick and rucksack and walking back to Uncle Rey's caravan for the final time.

BACK IN THE NIGHT I LAY DOWN BY YOUR FIRESIDE

twinkling, silent, beautiful

I sleep for most of the day. There's nothing else to do. My sleep
had been fitful with nightmares. I'd ended up drinking myself
into unconsciousness, after I'd packed away the contents of the
shed, taking extra-special care with the telescope and all its lenses
and spare parts. I labelled everything, including the box of Dr
Feelgood records for Cal. Mr Buchanan was very kind and sent a
member of staff to collect it all and take it to Southend to be
posted. I gave him a big tip, but I can't remember how much. At
some point in the evening Cal phoned me and we argued about
Uncle Rey.

'You only sent me here because you couldn't be fucking arsed
with him . . .'

'I had work . . . A trip . . .'

'You fucking hated him . . .'

'So did you . . .'

'I didn't, I might have . . . Well, I might now, but I didn't then . . .'

'Yes, you did . . . You hated going to see him . . . You thought
he was creepy, with all his cameras . . . we all did . . .'

'Have you ever done anything for anyone instead of yourself,
Cal?'

'What are you fucking talking about, you fuck-up . . .'

'You have no idea who Uncle Rey was . . .'

'What's that supposed to mean?'

'. . .'

'I said . . .'

'I know what you said . . .'

'Well . . .'

'You'll never understand . . . you'll never truly know who he was . . .'

'He was a fucking bum . . . An alcoholic . . . a loser who lived off the state, taking whichever handout was offered him . . . A fucking sponger, who was left money by parents he hated, soaking it all up, taking whatever he could from whoever he could . . .'

'He was lonely . . .'

'Did you know Dad used to send him money?'

'. . .'

'Well, he did . . . Every fucking month . . . that's how much of a loser Uncle Rey was.'

'You have no idea, Cal . . .'

The argument lasted a good half-hour or so, the whole conversation going nowhere as usual. I ended it.

'I'm moving away . . .'

'Oh . . . That's . . .'

'I'm selling my flat . . .'

'Well, the market's not in good shape, a bit better, but not good . . .'

'I don't fucking care about the market, Cal . . .'

'Right . . .'

'I'm going to find Mother . . .'

'. . .'

'I know where she is . . .'

'. . .'

'So, that's where I'm going . . .'

'Let her rot, she ruined Dad's life . . . She left us . . .'

'Cal, she's never left us . . .'

I put the phone down at that point, I think. I can't really

226

remember. There was nothing else to say. I remember walking out of the caravan and through the gate up the grass verge to the sea wall. I wanted one last look at the island. I scrambled up onto the wall. I faced northwards, looking across the island towards Benfleet. The sea was a black void behind me, a blank space, the sky above me blacker. I traced the island, following the contours formed by street lights, out right over to Canvey Heights, and then left across the island again, over towards the oil refinery. The whole island before me: twinkling, silent, beautiful. I left it at that.

title page

The afternoon is rather uneventful, except for a walk to the High Street for some provisions, including a can of petrol and some matches. I sit in the armchair, waiting for the sun to disappear. The caravan is empty, everything that's needed to go has gone. I look out of the window every now and again to check the light, the moon slowly revealing itself out above the estuary. Night falls suddenly, although I may have dozed off again, I don't know. I get up and step outside, to take in the air, to bathe myself in the blackness. I stand there, facing the caravan, taking it all in, everything that's happened, everything I've heard. For the first time there are no other voices other than my own thoughts, not even Uncle Rey, Cal, or Mr Buchanan. Nothing. I take in a huge, deep breath and step back into the caravan. I pick up *Vulgar Things*, the only possession I have left in the caravan, and place the whole manuscript back in the centre of the room, dousing it in the petrol. I take the title page and screw it up into a ball, the petrol fumes filling up my lungs as I breathe heavily in excitement. I begin to douse the rest of the caravan, the kitchenette, the shower room, the bedroom, in the petrol, leaving the empty canister on the manuscript in the centre of the room. I pick up my stick and rucksack, the vapour from the petrol making me feel a little nauseous, checking that the letters, locket and address are all safe in my rucksack. I smile and walk outside.

beacons all around me

It's funny: I feel like Cal is watching me. Like he's just about to pop out at any moment and try to stop me. But he doesn't. I take out the box of matches and light the screwed-up title page; the flame takes hold quickly, destroying the words and setting my hand alight with it: blue, then a flash of yellow. I throw the flaming ball of paper into the caravan, stepping back while flapping the flames out on my hand, the skin smarting in the cold air. The caravan ignites in an almighty white flash. The heat is incredible, everything around me is as bright as day. I begin to run through the site, out towards the main gate, onto Haven Road and down to the bridge, gulping the air into my lungs, running on adrenalin alone.

I gasp for more air, unable to suck in as much of it as I need. I have to stop near a wall to a house, the yacht club down in the distance to my right. I look back, the road is empty, I can't really see anything. When I catch my breath I begin to run again; this time I make it all the way to the bridge before I have to stop. I fall to my knees, it feels like I'm going to be sick, but I'm okay. I drag myself back up with my stick and look back over in the direction of Uncle Rey's caravan. I can see a red glow immediately, lighting up the night like a beacon sending a signal. I run across the bridge, puffing and panting, up onto Benfleet Station. From the stairs over the tracks, positioning myself halfway across I can see the burning caravan in the distance. I stare at it, transfixed, as it burns.

After a couple of minutes something incredible happens: I notice another flash to my left, up ahead over towards Hadleigh, up near the castle, I think. Another beacon has been lit, something else is burning just as brightly, receiving my own signal. Then, a few moments later, across the island, over the black water of the estuary, up in the hills of Kent another flash disrupts the night, another beacon, then another up ahead, along the line in the direction of London, beacons all around me, the signal reaching the next, passing through the blackness of night: things have come to an end, there is no past, no future, just now, endless now. They appear like new stars. I feel like I know them already. New suns; new light. It feels, somehow, like a victory, a small victory, my own victory. I take out my phone and begin to record; the light floods into its tiny lens, as I overlay each beacon of light, capturing it in perfect pixels, digitising it. I take about two minutes of footage, it feels enough. I look back up at the beacons burning in the distance before feeling the urge to watch what I've just recorded, holding out my phone over the real image all around me, still standing on the bridge over the tracks, pressing play as the beacons continue to burn behind the recorded image. It drifts in and out of focus after about thirty seconds, then at one minute or so the pixels begin to enlarge, revealing themselves before disappearing again. Then something truly incredible happens: the two images merge: the recorded image and the real image behind it. I want to keep it like this. It's the most beautiful thing I have ever seen.

some grand prologue

I walk back down to my platform. The message has been sent: I'm making my way home to her, each beacon joining up our absence. My train back to London is due in four minutes' time. I wait patiently on a bench. The evening creeps up all around me, everything seems lit up with beacons of hope. I take out the envelope from my rucksack: my next destination. Everything, everything that has happened to me, comes together in this moment, it feels real, like I've achieved something, like I've listened to everything all at once and an answer has been spoken.

Now all I have is this: all of this has happened as if I haven't been here, like I'm some form of electronic node, something technological sent to record and transmit the action back to myself; some kind of conduit relaying each ordinary fragment of the whole, caught in my own absence, like interference, the crackle behind a signal, as if everything that has happened to me is part of some grand prologue – the beginning of something else. Something bigger.

The train arrives. I step on board, the doors hissing shut behind me. The carriage is warm. The train is busy: teenagers listening to music on their phones, couples laughing, endless talking. The train begins to pull out of the station. I pause, hesitating a little, before falling into my seat. I sink back into it, ignoring my reflection in the window. I don't look back.

ACKNOWLEDGEMENTS

Certain sections of this work of fiction could not have been written without the initial research on Petrarch undertaken by Prof. Nicholas Mann in his work *Petrarch (Past Masters)* (Oxford University Press, 1984). Of particular interest is Mann's exploration of Virgil's own debt to Homer, et al.

Equally, Thomas G. Bergin's *Petrarch: Selected Sonnets, Odes and Letters* (Revised edition, Harlan Davidson, 2011) has left an indelible mark upon this work. Translations of Petrarch's *Rerum vulgarium fragmenta* have been reproduced with the kind permission of the publisher.

It goes without saying that this book could not have been written without W. F. Jackson Knight's wonderful translation of Virgil's *The Aeneid* (Penguin Books, 2000) and Robert Williams Buchanan's little known gem *Andromeda: an Idyll of the Great River* (Chatto & Windus, 1900).

I would like to thank Wilko Johnson (to whom this book is dedicated) for his music, wise words and inspiration. It's a pleasure to sit down with you and simply listen to your stories.

Special thanks to Olly Rowse, a truly great editor and scholar, and all at Fourth Estate, a truly great publisher. And to Mark Richards, who believed in my work from the beginning. Without your initial input this work of fiction might never have seen the light of day – I owe you.

Thanks, of course, to Deborah Levy, Stuart Evers, Tom McCarthy and Eimear McBride for their kind words (especially to Stuart Evers who read an early draft and gave me invaluable advice). I'm truly honoured.

And to Gavin James Bower, James Miller, Nikesh Shukla, Niven Govinden, and Suzanne Azzopardi – for the banter along the way. Zöe Howe for Dr Feelgood advice. My agent Donald Winchester. And especially to Will Wiles (for your knowledge and our wonderful conversations about container ships).

To Anne Rourke, Damon Rourke, and my father Brian Rourke for your continued support. To my in-laws Pat and Marion Ahern, who first took me to Canvey Island, revealing to me its charm, secrets and strange ways – something I just couldn't ignore. Your sense of adventure, vim, and thirst for life is truly remarkable.

Finally, I would like to thank my wife, Holly Ahern, for being my inspiration and true love and our daughter, Theola (Thea) Elodie Rose, for bringing new joy to my heart – my love for you both is without end. These words will never be enough.